D1198779

TEMPTING
Tristan

HARBORSIDE NIGHTS

New York Times Bestselling Author
MELISSA FOSTER

ISBN-13: 978-1-941480-51-9

TEMPTING TRISTAN

Cover Design: Elizabeth Mackey
Cover Photography: Michael Stokes

WORLD LITERARY PRESS
PRINTED IN THE UNITED STATES OF AMERICA

A NOTE TO READERS

I am thrilled to bring you Tristan and Alex, two sexy, big-hearted alpha heroes. When I met Alex and realized how his tragic past consumed him, I knew he needed a love like only Tristan could provide. And Alex has just as much to offer his man. If this is your first M/M romance, rest assured that it is written with the full range and depth of emotions as all of my M/F romance novels, and it's one of my favorite stories to date. I hope you enjoy Tristan and Alex's sizzling love story as much as I do.

Sign up for my newsletter to keep up to date with new releases and to receive a free short story.
www.melissafoster.com/NL

More Harborside Nights Books
Catching Cassidy
Discovering Delilah

Harborside Nights is just one of the series in the Love in Bloom big-family romance collection. Characters from each series make appearances in future books, so you never miss an engagement, wedding, or birth.

See more Love in Bloom books here:
www.melissafoster.com/love-bloom-series

Download FREE first-in series-ebooks here:
www.melissafoster.com/free-ebooks

CHAPTER ONE

Tristan

LIVI BURSTS THROUGH the door from the outdoor dining area of the Taproom, the restaurant and bar where we work. She slaps a drink order on the bar and scowls at me and Charley, the other bartender. "There's a storm brewing outside, but it's nothing compared to how much I hate you both right now."

We were in for heavy rains, but hopefully they'd hold off until after closing time. I glance at the order. "Because of two rum and Cokes?"

She rolls her pretty green eyes. "No, Tristan. Because the hottest man on the planet just parked his motorcycle and he's heading in here. All of my female customers are drooling, and I'm sure you'll see a flock of them coming in any minute now. Meanwhile, I'm stuck outside and soon I'll have a pier full of empty tables." She grabs a handful of napkins and waves them at me with a smirk. "Drool rags."

"Dibs," Charley says as she whips up a cocktail.

I laugh and hold my hands up. "I'm on a hiatus from all things male, so be my guest." My ex, Ian, is a self-absorbed ass, and I was an idiot for letting him treat me like shit. Which is why I'm taking a break from men—even if it kills me. It's been weeks since we broke up and I moved into my buddy Wyatt's house. Wyatt and his twin sister, Delilah, own the Taproom. They inherited it when their parents were killed in a car accident a little more than a year ago.

"I'm sure he's straight anyway," Livi says. "The guy swaggers like a stud."

"Hey, gay guys can swagger like studs," I tease.

"I know that." Livi peers out the pass-through window to the outside seating area and tosses her blond hair over her shoulder. "You'll see what I mean. He's a total badass."

I tend to my customers as the girls discuss the *badass hot guy*, and when the front door opens, I can't help but let my eyes drift over. Livi and Charley fall silent, ogling what truly might be the hottest guy on the planet. Linebacker shoulders fill the doorframe. The godlike creature is carrying a shiny black motorcycle helmet in one very large hand. His white T-shirt is stretched so tight across his chest I can see every ripple of his shredded abs, and his deliciously defined biceps are seriously struggling to be set free from his short sleeves. *Tear, baby, tear.*

He steps inside and runs a hand through his dirty-blond hair. Deep-set, brooding eyes slide over the customers sitting at the bar, sweep over Charley and Livi, and finally land on me. Charley whimpers, and Livi makes a sound in the back of her throat, both mimicking what I'm feeling, though my mouth is too dry to make a sound.

He swaggers, full of hard-core attitude, to the vacant stool at the end of the bar, giving me a clear view of his perfect ass—and catching the attention of nearly every woman, and several of the men, in the place. My cock twitches, reminding me it's been way too long since I've gotten laid.

The pretty brunette seated next to Hot Guy leans in close,

says something, and he flashes a crooked smile, which softens his hard edges but doesn't take anything away from his rough vibe. His hand cruises through his hair again, and he slaps a sketchbook on the bar. Pulling his massive arms up onto the bar, he nearly knocks into the pretty brunette. He apologizes and pushes his stool farther way.

Livi groans and shoves another order pad in the back pocket of her jeans as I finish making her order. "I swear I'm going to go to bartender school."

"Hands off. I have dibs. Besides, you have that pen pal from overseas," Charley reminds her.

"Jason is my best friend, not my pen pal. And you don't sleep with best friends, especially when they're a million miles away." Livi lost her mother to cancer when she was fourteen, and although she doesn't talk about that time of her life much, I know Jason has been there for her ever since. She takes her drinks and heads out to serve her customers.

Rusty, one of the waiters, sidles up to the bar, shaking his head. "The new guy has my female customers' panties in a bunch. Table four wants to send him a drink with the message"—he speaks in a high-pitched tone—"'We'd like to take *you* for a ride.'" He scoffs. "Lucky bastard."

"Oh, no, they are *not*." Charley turns her back to the bar and pushes her boobs up so they practically tumble out of her tight black V-neck shirt. She's usually a Levi's girl, but tonight she's wearing skinny jeans. I wonder what's up with that. "I'm on *him*." Charley waggles her dark brows. "I mean, I'm on *it*."

"What is with you tonight?" I have to ask. This pushiness is new. She's usually the girl who assumes hot guys are all hung up on themselves and barely gives them the time of day.

Charley sets her eyes on the guy who's got *my* briefs in a

bunch. "Just feeling competitive."

I serve a few customers, keeping an eye on Charley's flirting. Harborside is a close-knit beach town, but it's also a college town, which makes it a party town. We get aggressive and handsy transients from time to time, and more than once Wyatt and I have had to step in.

Charley's pulling out all the stops, leaning over the bar, touching Hot Guy's hand. She's beautiful, funny, and smart, studying marine biology and working two part-time jobs. She has a nose for bullshit, and her patience for stupidity hangs by a very thin thread. Given the amount of time she chats the guy up, I assume he's got more than looks going for him.

She turns to fix him a drink as I tend to a group of scantily clad women waving me over. I toss my bar rag over my shoulder and flash my own pearly whites. "What can I get you ladies?"

"Your phone number?" the redhead says with a giggle.

Tips are tips and flirting's the name of the game. "Barking up the wrong tree, sweetheart. But if I were straight…" I say coyly and take their order, ignoring their offers to *turn me straight*. If I had a buck for each time I'd received that ridiculous offer, I'd be rich.

Charley nudges me as she fills another drink order. "He's not giving anything up. All I found out was that he just got into town last week." She shrugs. "He's no dummy, though. The guy's got brains and brawn. A wicked combination. He seems nice, but very closed off. It's yet to be seen how rough he is. He might be lock-you-up-in-the-basement rough, or maybe he's just sexy-as-sin rough."

"You can tell that much from, 'Hey, wanna hook up?'"

"*Tsk.*" She places her hands on her hips, and with a snap of her chin she tosses her brown hair over her shoulder with an impressive amount of attitude. "You know me better than that. I *did not* ask him to hook up. I was just checking him out and staking claim. *In case* I'm interested. But he's so focused in that sketchpad, I can't get him to give me the time of day."

I steal a glance at the guy, who's watching us intently. "Seems like he's into you," I say, and before she can respond, a loud group of girls comes through the door and flocks to the bar. I assume they're the customers Livi mentioned. The fact that they're just now coming in means Livi took her sweet time taking care of their checks. Hopefully she has a slew of new customers to take care of. I know she needs the tips.

The rest of the night is a mad rush of keeping up with drink orders and overzealous girls vying to pick me up. I can't help but notice Hot Guy's occasional snicker at my dismissal of the girls' advances.

Livi whips in from the pier for *one more glance* a few times instead of using the pass-through window, and whispers with Charley. Charley touches base with the hot guy, giggling and flirting, as do several of the women who are standing around him. He smiles, comments here and there, then turns back to whatever's got his rapt attention in that notebook.

As we near closing time, customers clear out, and Hot Guy is still sitting at the end of the bar in deep concentration. A bearded guy who had parked himself at the bar for the last half hour is standing by the door, watching Charley.

"Char, what's up with that guy?" I nod to the guy by the door.

She traps her lower lip between her teeth and waves to the bearded guy. "Can you close out the notebook guy for me?"

"Sure," I say, reassessing the bearded guy. "I thought you hated beards. What's up?"

"Don't laugh." She leans in close, her hair tumbling forward, curtaining her face as she whispers, "Blind date."

We've worked together for a long time, and I know Charley has her pick of guys. "Why? And on a Tuesday night?"

"Why does the day of the week matter?"

I shrug.

"The kind of guys I'm meeting on my own haven't really been my type." She smiles at the guy by the door. "Brian has a master's in natural resources. I think I can overlook the beard for a guy I've got something in common with. He seems nice enough, right?"

"I guess, but if you had this blind date set up, why were you flirting with him?" I nod toward the guy at the other end of the bar.

She sighs. "If you must know, ever since my sister fell in love with Sam, I've been hoping to find the same kind of relationship. Sam Braden was a bit of a bad boy before he and Faith got together, so I thought maybe…"

She looks back at the guy by the door, who definitely has kinder eyes than the broody biker. "But I'm not sure bad boys are my type. I'm more of a nice, smart, no-skeletons type of girl. And Mr. Mysterious over there"—she nods to the guy with the notebook—"hasn't cracked under my flirtatious pressure, so I'm thinking his skeletons might be too big to keep contained. But I would never know that unless I tried, now, would I?"

She pats my chest and I set my hand on hers, holding her there while I eye Brian one more time. "Fine, but it's still a *blind* date. How'd you meet him?"

Charley presses her lips into a thin line.

"Please tell me you didn't meet him on Tinder."

"No! Geez, Tristan." Her cheeks flush. "He's one of

Brooke's friends."

Brooke Baker owns an Internet café on the boardwalk called Brooke's Bytes. I've been friends with her for years and I trust her judgment explicitly. "Okay, but keep your phone on and call me if you need me. In fact, text me when you're home for the night so I know you're not lying bloody in an alley somewhere."

She rolls her eyes. "Ian has no idea how badly he messed up by losing you. Not that he deserved you in the first place." She reaches up and hugs me. "I'm not leaving until we close, but I promise I'll text you. Even though I think you should spend less time worrying about your friends and more time finding some new guy to take that jerk's place. The right guy is going to be very lucky to have you."

My gut clenches at the mention of my ex. I should be over all the shit he did, but some hurts run too deep to be easily cast aside. Unfortunately, almost everything Ian did was hurtful, from ignoring me to making me feel like an imposition. Man, I sound like a pussy. My self-esteem definitely took a pounding, but I'll never put myself in that situation again. I shove those thoughts aside for the hundredth, and hopefully the last, time. Charley heads toward the bearded guy, and I make my way down the bar. The blond guy's still laboring over his notebook. His jaw is tight, and his eyes are narrowed in concentration.

I grab the empty bottle in front of him. "Last call. Can I grab you another beer?"

"Sure, thanks." He's too engrossed in whatever he's drawing to spare me a glance, but he's got one of those in-control voices that makes *me* want to thank *him*.

I bring him his beer, and he lifts intense admiral-blue eyes that connect with mine and momentarily steal my breath.

When he flashes that sexy crooked grin, heat flares between us, and I wonder if he's bisexual. Or maybe just curious. We get our fair share of those around here, too. Straight guys looking to experiment for a night. *Not my thing.*

"Thanks, man," he says, and reaches a hand across the bar. "Alex."

His handshake is firm and his hand is rough, like he does manual labor. My sex-deprived brain moves straight to how those strong, rough fingers would feel wrapped around my cock.

Wyatt comes through the door with his girlfriend, Cassidy, tucked beneath his arm and calls out my name, rescuing me from my ridiculous straight-guy fantasy.

"Be right there," I tell Wyatt.

Wyatt kisses Cassidy and heads into the stockroom.

Alex knocks back half his beer in one gulp and tears a piece of paper from the back of his notebook. He quickly scribbles on it, folds it in half, and passes it across the bar to me. "I've got to go. Would you—"

I snag the note. He's clearly not gay and looking only for a favor. "Sure, I'll give Charley your number."

There's no mistaking the seductive darkness staring back at me. My entire body electrifies.

"It's not for her," he says in that commanding voice that makes every part of me stand at attention. "It's for you, Tristan."

Did I tell him my name? He probably overheard it. Either way, it sounds hot rolling off his tongue.

He rises to his feet, our hands still touching. When he reaches for his helmet, our physical connection breaks, but the tantalizing heat remains.

"Call me." Alex takes a few steps away and looks over his

shoulder. That mind-numbing grin sends another blast of heat below my belt. "See ya around, T."

Wyatt comes back into the bar and sets a bottle of champagne on the counter. "What's up with Alex?"

I'm still trying to process that Alex isn't straight. The endearment he used, and the way he said it so confident and casually, as if we were old friends, makes my mind stumble again. *T?*

"You know him?"

"Wasn't that Arty's grandson, Alex Wells?" Wyatt asks. "I only met him once a few years ago, but I'm pretty sure it's him."

Arlene "Arty" Bindon was a local sculptor who lived in a bungalow down the beach. We'd met a few years ago when I was out running. Unfortunately, she passed away over the winter. She was a tiny woman, about five feet tall, with frizzy gray hair that always looked windblown. From the moment we met I was drawn to her sassy nature and creative outlook. She reminded me of my own grandmother, who passed away when I was just a kid. Arty and I became close, and I checked on her when we had storms, brought her groceries every so often, and sometimes I drove her to appointments in town. She talked often about her grandson, who was in the military. She used to say, *He's a good boy, like you.*

I glance down at Alex's number, seeing the brooding biker with new eyes. "I thought he was just passing through."

"Maybe he is." Wyatt drapes an arm over my shoulder as Brandon comes into the bar, guitar in hand, followed by Delilah and her girlfriend, Ashley, and two of our other friends, Jesse and Brent Steele. Brent's also carrying his guitar. "Are you done, or do you want to talk about Alex some more? Because I have huge news."

"Sorry," I say, shaking my head to clear it and noticing, for the first time tonight, Wyatt's big-ass grin. "Huge news? Cough it up already."

Wyatt laughs. "Finally! Cassidy and I got engaged. It's time to celebrate."

CHAPTER TWO

Tristan

LAST NIGHT'S STORM dredged up rocks, bits of driftwood, black skate egg cases, and stringy strands of seaweed, all of which I dodge as I run down the beach. Rough waves batter the shore, like thoughts of Alex have been crashing through my mind all night. I still can't shake the feeling that he acted like he knew me. Knowing Arty's propensity to chat, he probably does know *of* me. The question is, how much does he know? Dodging an inky mass of seaweed, I think about how Arty would have hunted through the stringy mess. Her frizzy hair would dance in the breeze like that of a rebellious child refusing to be tamed. She'd pull one of her thick cardigans across her frail shoulders, gaze down the beach as if it were her lover, and say, "Don't you love the beach after a storm, when the treasures of the ocean floor are unearthed and cast ashore?"

My mind returns to Alex, who it hasn't strayed far from. I've been racking my brain, trying to remember seeing him at Arty's funeral, but for the life of me I can't. I wonder if he's here to stay, or just to settle up her estate and move on. Knowing how much Arty adored him, it would sadden me if their relationship meant so little to him that he'd swoop in and sell her place, cash in on the equity, and move on.

As I near town, more people meander along the beach, bundled up in sweaters and clutching steaming mugs to ward off the September-morning chill. Squinting against the rising sun, I see a broad figure approaching. He's carrying a long piece of wood over his right shoulder. His sweatshirt hangs open, giving me an amazing view of his athletic physique. His face is downcast, searching the wet sand. The view of his bulging biceps straining against his sweatshirt sleeves stirs all the parts of my body I've been trying to ignore for the past few weeks. It's about time to stop this ridiculous break from human touch and get back in the saddle. I slow my pace to get a better look, and he lifts his face. *Alex.* Our eyes catch, and a wide smile spreads across his chiseled jaw.

I tell myself to calm the hell down, but the guy is even hotter in the light of day. He picks up his pace, closing the distance between us, and I realize he walks with a slight limp, favoring his left side.

My goddamn heart is running like a freight train. I stop walking as he nears, and he steps in so close, I think he's going to drop that piece of wood and grab me. *Hell, yes.*

"T," he says in that commanding tone that melts my insides.

His eyes are even deeper blue than I remember. They are riveting, soulful and guarded at once.

"I didn't know you were a runner." He flashes the crooked smile that did funny things to me last night, and yup, my stomach goes squirrely again.

I have to clear my throat to stop myself from staring at his deliciously plump lower lip. What is it about his slanted smile that I find incredibly sexy? I fantasized all night about his mouth and his rough, commanding voice. Needing to get a grip, I push my hand through my hair and drag my eyes over the water.

"I'm taking a break after a rough breakup, and a guy can only take so many cold showers. Running takes the edge off."

He laughs, and it rumbles into the air. "I hear ya."

His eyes rake down my body like a stroke of heat. I'm wearing only running shorts, and if he does it again, he'll get an eyeful of the effect he has on me. I remind myself to slow the hell down, because no matter how hot the guy is, there is a good reason I'm taking a break. And falling off the wagon for a guy who's only in town for a few days wouldn't be the smartest decision.

"You're in great shape," he says. "We should work out together sometime."

"Yeah, that'd be cool." My mind's stuck in the gutter, and despite my need for smarter decisions, I'm hoping he means something else by *work out*. The way he looks in his cargo pants and tight white shirt is doing nothing to help my condition.

I glance at the driftwood on his shoulder and meet his piercing stare. "Nice wood."

"The storm brought in a few nice surprises." He raises his brows, and his eyes slide down my chest again.

I swallow, breathing harder. "So, you're into wood?" Aw, man. My brain's gone. I can't even make normal conversation. Something about this guy's rough demeanor and penetrating eyes has me tied in knots like a kid with his first hard-on.

The sinful smile that creeps across his face is too much, and a laugh slips out. I scrub a hand over my mouth, and thankfully, he laughs, too.

"I'm sorry." I turn toward the water, trying to regain control of my inane laughter.

"Why? Because you're wondering about my affinity for wood?" He bumps me with his shoulder and it sends us both into another burst of laughter.

"Apparently taking a break equates to acting like a fool. Can we start over?"

He drapes his free hand over my shoulder like he's my best buddy and says, "I kind of like this foolish T. How about we keep him around for a while?"

Our eyes connect again, and along with searing heat I feel the stroke of friendship. I like his mix of rough and playful, and his crooked smile, and the way he's looking at me right now. *Especially* the way he's looking at me right now. As if he likes *me*, and not just the idea of hooking up. Although the seduction radiating off the man is enough to set the sea on fire.

Alex

THE STRENGTH OF the vibe between us catches me off guard. Tristan's even hotter than I imagined, but it wasn't his incredibly hot body or handsome face that had me giving him my number so quickly last night. It was the way he protected Charley. There are three things I hold in high regard: family, loyalty, and strength. Okay, four. Knowing when to use that strength is important, too. The restraint in his eyes last night told me how hard it was for him to keep from having a talk with the bearded guy before Charley went out with him. But he drew the line, allowing Charley to be the strong woman she obviously needed to be. After two tours in Afghanistan, I know a thing or two about when to let people fight their own battles and when to step in. Tristan seemed to respect that line, too, even with my grandmother, who could be as headstrong as me.

I drop my arm from Tristan's shoulder, adjust the driftwood I'm carrying, and try to figure out a way to spend more time with him.

"I wasn't going to call," he confesses.

So much for my hopes of spending more time together. Not knowing how to respond, I mumble, "No?"

He shakes his head. "No. Then Army said you were Arlene's grandson."

An icy shiver ripples through my chest at the word *army*, and I wonder if he's got the whole scoop on me. "Army?"

"Sorry. Wyatt Armstrong. That's his nickname. He doesn't use it much, but sometimes it still slips out. He said he knew you."

It was a chickenshit move last night to leave before Wyatt came out of the back room and roped me into a conversation, but I didn't want to talk about my grandmother. And around here that's where conversations seemed to lead. I've yet to meet a person who knew my grandmother and didn't share stories that nearly wrecked me. I'm pretty sure a guy with tears in his eyes wouldn't be a turn-on for a big guy like Tristan.

"Yeah. We met a while back when I was here on leave. Nice guy." I want to lead the conversation away from my grandmother, but I have a feeling there will be no deterring Tristan if that's where he's headed.

"He is. I've known him forever."

Lucky Wyatt.

"He got engaged last night. He was there to celebrate." Tristan gazes down the beach, and I remember he was out for a run. My mind spirals back to the years when I could run without pain, when carrying sixty-plus pounds of equipment and trekking for miles was all in a day's work. That was before the incident that nearly cost me my life—and kept me from my grandmother's funeral. Now I have a torso riddled with scars, painful memories so thickly encased in guilt nothing can touch them, and a mangled leg. *Aren't I a catch?*

"Hey, I don't want to hold you up," I lie. He's the only person I've actually wanted to talk to for months. My grandmother spoke of him often, and I'm curious to know if he saw her at the end, and if so, if she said anything that I should know about. But at the same time, I'm afraid of what I might hear.

He cracks a warm smile, and his gaze moves over me. I'm not even sure if he realizes he's checking me out because the look in his eyes is more like he's thinking than turned on. I'm not sure if that's good or bad, and shift my stance. The ridiculous idea that he can somehow see my injured leg through my pants sneaks into my mind, and my chest tightens again.

"Then you *are* Arty's grandson?"

Was. I grit my teeth. The sound of the waves crashing against the shore compete with my grandmother's voice from our last visit. *I hear Bruce in those waves. I think he's still here.* She spoke of my grandfather often. She'd turned to me with a spark of rebellion in her eyes and said, *Maybe neither of us will ever leave.* I sense her so strongly in the bungalow, I'm pretty sure she's still hanging around, making sure I came to Harborside as she'd encouraged me to. Or more likely, making sure I'm okay.

"Yes," I finally answer.

He runs his hand through his thick dark hair. It's been so long since I've touched another man, my hands itch with the desire to do the same. I can see he's packing some heat in those shorts, and he's shredded from neck to ankle. Gripping the wood tighter, I force myself to turn away before I start sporting wood.

"I've run enough for this morning," he says. "Mind if I hang with you for a while?"

Mind? I'd like him to hang out in my *bed*. "Not at all. That'd be cool."

"You can tell me about your need to show off your big wood," he teases. "Making up for a deficit?"

The comment stings, but I know he doesn't mean it the way I'm thinking.

"Hardly," I assure him.

We walk for a while, making small talk and picking up a few choice pieces of driftwood. Tristan takes them from me, freeing up my hand.

"Just like to have your hands on wood, then?"

Tristan arches a brow. "Look who's talking."

I laugh under my breath. "I'm good with my hands." *Want to see just how good?*

"Somehow I don't doubt that." He nudges me up the beach as a wave rolls in at our feet.

We both lean down to pick up a piece of wood at the same time, and the air between us sizzles and pops. We hesitate, as if the world is suddenly standing still, waiting for one of us to make a move. I wave my hand for him to pick it up. My mind's busy imagining how well our bodies would fit together. Knowing that's not going to happen anytime soon, I push those thoughts down deep and continue walking.

"I make furniture from driftwood, metal, glass."

"Do you have a workshop?" he asks.

I look up the beach at my grandmother's bungalow. Even

though I didn't grow up here, and I've visited only a few times while on leave from the army, it feels like home. Anywhere my grandparents lived feels like home. Lord knows my mother never settled down in any one place long enough to create a real home for us.

"I'm hoping to use my grandmother's studio at some point." *When I get the guts to clean it out.* My mother cleaned out the bedroom when she came for the funeral, but she left the contents of the kitchen and studio, assuming I'd want them. My heart aches every time I think about going into the room where my grandmother poured her soul into her artwork.

"So you're not just here to settle her estate and then move on?" There's a hopeful lilt to his voice.

"In a sense, coming here *is* my way of moving on."

"From?"

I shrug as a breeze sweeps off the ocean, and I quicken my pace, hoping to outrun the question.

"Skeletons?"

"Something like that," I admit.

"Your grandmother spoke very highly of you, so they can't be that bad."

I mull over my response, walking in silence toward the house.

"Sorry. I don't mean to pry," Tristan apologizes. "I really liked Arty, and I know you were important to her. If you want someone to talk to, I'm here."

"Thanks, T. I appreciate it." We walk up the rocky steps and lay the wood we're carrying in a pile in front of the house.

Tristan wipes his hands on his shorts and squints against the sun as he takes in the view. "I miss her, you know? She loved walking the beach after a storm."

"Yeah, she used to write to me about it."

"She's the only person I've ever met who actually *found* sea glass. People talk about it, but I'd never seen anyone lucky enough to find any. She found pieces often, and every time, she'd hold out her hand—" He holds out his hand and says, "You know how little her hands were."

"Yeah," I manage, remembering holding her hand as a boy, when her hand could contain mine, and our last visit, when I noticed how frail her hands had become. "Her hands should have been dry from all the sculpting she did, but they weren't. They were soft as butter."

"I think that was her hand lotion. Lovely Lilac. She used to get it delivered from a woman named Roxie Dalton in Sweetwater, New York. She bought it by the case."

"How do you know that?" It's a strange feeling to realize he knew things about my grandmother that I didn't.

He shrugs. "She had a hard time reaching Roxie, so I got online and ordered it for her. Sorry, I got off track. I wanted to tell you about the sea glass. She'd find these pieces, and she'd get this look of disbelief, and she'd say, 'In eighty-plus years, do you know I've only found nineteen pieces of sea glass? Until today. This is number twenty.' She told me that every time she found a piece, and the number changed with every telling. Sometimes it was eleven, other times it was twenty-four." He laughs, and it's as easy and comfortable as the rest of his demeanor.

For a beat we both gaze out over the water, the memory filling the silence. I want to hear more about my grandmother and their friendship. I want to thank Tristan for looking after her. But the ache of missing her is too raw, so I do what I do best and repress those thoughts.

He turns toward the house. "Do you have anything you've made here? I'd love to see them."

"Seriously? I mean, don't feel obligated."

"Obligated to see furniture? I'm nice, but not that nice."

"Why do I have a feeling that's not true?" I pull open the creaky wooden door of my grandmother's bungalow. Technically it's mine now, but I'll always think of it as hers. Tristan follows me in, his eyes moving swiftly over a string of mismatched lights hanging from the exposed-beam cathedral ceilings. Sunlight shimmers through the windows onto the painted concrete floor. I know he's been inside before, but I wonder what he thinks of the cold stone bleeding through the painted concrete walls and the mismatched furniture. My grandmother bought the place back in '83 and refused to let me paint it. She said she liked that it looked as though it had been battered by the sea.

I wave toward the wooden table by the windows and at the glass-top coffee table. "I made both of those."

I wonder if he feels my grandmother's presence as I do. If he does, he keeps it to himself as he crouches by the coffee table and touches the driftwood standing on end beneath the glass.

"There are twenty-two pieces of wood," I explain. "My grandmother and I collected them together one summer. I wanted to give the impression—"

"Of fluidity?" he asks, rising to his feet.

"Yeah. Not many people see that."

He glances around the room and walks over to the shelves I made for her when I was on leave two years ago. Two thick branches form a V. I cut holes in three slabs of driftwood, slid them over the branches, and secured them in place with twine, giving the shelves a rustic feel to match her bungalow.

He raises his brows. "This yours?"

I nod and cross my arms over my chest. "Hers, but yeah. I made it."

"These are really cool." He moves to the windows and picks up a picture frame I made when I was twenty, a few months before I joined the army. My grandparents moved here six months after my grandfather retired. He was a stubborn old man, and he never cared for doctors. His cancer had gone undetected for too long, and he passed away four months later.

Anger and sadness well in the pit of my stomach.

Tristan waves the frame in my direction. "Yours?"

I nod, and he sets it back down.

"She has this mirror in the bathroom. The frame is—"

"Made from thick pieces of driftwood and shells. Also mine. For years I made furniture and accessories and stuck them in storage. I've got a lot of my equipment stored, too. I'm opening a retail store as soon as I can find the right space."

"Wow, you really are planning to stick around."

"I hope to. This is home now." It feels good to say *home* and know that if I ever leave, it'll be my decision, not the army's or my nomad mother's.

"There are some vacant properties right in town. A lot of retailers can't make ends meet over the winter, so they take seasonal leases."

"I know it's tough to keep a business going in a resort town, but furniture isn't seasonal. I've got friends on Cape Cod and in Maryland who have bought a few of my pieces, and once the store is up and running, they're going to help me spread the word. I'm pretty confident that once I get my shit together, I can make it work."

"That's great. I know the area like the back of my hand. If

you want someone who doesn't have a financial stake in your finding a place to go with you when you look at properties, I'd be happy to give you the inside scoop on locations."

Like I'd turn down spending more time with him? "Really, T? That'd be great. I don't know the area well enough to decipher a great location from a mediocre one. I'm actually meeting a real estate agent at noon if you're free."

"Sure. I don't work until six tonight." Tristan points to my grandmother's studio and takes a step toward it. "There's some unfinished furniture in there."

I grab his arm and shake my head. "I know," I say too sternly. "I'll get to it."

He eyes the door. "You don't like people seeing your unfinished work?"

If only it were that simple. I point to the archway leading to the kitchen across the room. "My current work is in there." I put a hand on his back, feeling his muscles tense beneath my touch. "Come on, I'll show you."

"You don't have to—"

"I want to." I'm enjoying his appreciation of my work, despite the awkwardness of avoiding my grandmother's studio.

The kitchen table is pushed against the wall, stacks of wood, scraps of metal, glass, shells, pieces of netting, and other items I've collected lay in piles on the floor. I still have a lot of my equipment in storage, but the lathe and table saw sit where the table used to be. Pieces of a chair I'm building cover the top of one of two wooden workbenches.

I feel Tristan's eyes on me as I touch the toe of my shoe to a stack of driftwood. "These are for a free-form chair."

I walk to the pile in front of the stove. "The last time I was here, my grandmother and I drove to her friend's house out near Falmouth after a storm and collected a number of these pieces that had washed up on shore. I'm making a chandelier from them."

He holds my steady gaze as he steps confidently across the floor. I try not to stare at the way his chest lifts as he breathes, or the ripple of his abs as he nears, and fail epically. Just like that, I get hard.

"I was going to give it to my grandmother this Christmas," I say, trying to distract myself from the lust in his eyes and the sculpted bronze shoulders before me. But the heady sound of desire in my own voice is too thick to disguise.

"You miss her." His dark eyes never leave mine.

In the months since my grandmother's passing, many people have told me they were sorry for my loss, and they've shared stories and told me they missed her, but not one of them has removed themselves from the equation long enough to see my pain.

I nod.

"You're not ready to face her studio." There's no judgment in his tone. He touches my arm, and though his words emote friendship, the darkness in his eyes offers much more.

"Not yet." My voice is croaky, and our eyes hold for so many beats the air between us shifts and simmers again as it had on the beach.

His chest rises as his hand slides down my arm to my fingers, lingering there. I'm tempted to curl mine around his and pull him against me. As my fingers begin to move, his slip away, and he takes a reluctant step back.

I step closer, unwilling to allow a disruption in the energy buzzing between us. I want more of what we just felt. "It's been a long time since I've wanted to touch a man." I have no idea where the confession comes from, but there's something about Tristan that makes me trust him and want to keep him close. *Very close.*

He doesn't say anything, but he doesn't step away. The desire in his eyes is raw. I drop my gaze to his formidable erection straining against his shorts and step closer, pushing the limits because that's who I am. That's how I handle things. Only I've forgotten that until this very moment. I've repressed taking what I wanted for so many years, the unfamiliar urges roaring through me feel primal.

Tristan holds his ground, lifts his chin. His jaw tightens, and his eyes go impossibly darker. He's so fucking hot I want to take him against the wall.

"I can't." His voice is strained with unmistakable hunger, heightening my ache for him.

"Can't or *won't?*"

His jaw clenches repeatedly. "Both, I guess."

I shift my hips forward, brushing against his cock, hoping to tempt him into tasting what I'm certain will be unfuckingbelievable. "Because...?"

There's a war going on behind his eyes. He doesn't know me and I don't know him, but we're both caught up in the inferno.

"Damn it," he growls, and grabs my head.

Our mouths crash together, and my first taste of him unravels me. I back him up against the wall, our bodies grinding together. Taking the kiss deeper, rougher, he groans, and heat streaks down my chest, throbs between my legs, and I *need* to touch him. I palm him through his shorts, and his head tips back. He's every fantasy rolled into one delectable man, and I'm like a rabid dog, unwilling to deny myself his pleasures.

"Fuck," he grinds out.

He's hung like a fucking horse, and as I claim him in another scorching kiss, all I can think about is his cock in my mouth. He grabs my head, angling my face, and intensifies the kiss, wrestling for dominance. I widen my stance, pinning him against the wall with my hips, and grab his hands, imprisoning them beside his head.

"Fuck, T. You're so fucking hot."

He grinds against me. "I can't do this, Alex. Not yet."

In the space of a breath I try to process the way his body is contradicting his words. Then his mouth is on me again, taking me in another turbulent kiss. We're both moaning, clawing for more, and I lose myself in the kiss, the heat of our bodies. He takes advantage of my momentary weakness. Shifting his weight, he pins *me* against the unforgiving concrete wall. His eyes are fierce, he's hard as steel, and he's got a harsh scowl on his perfect, fuckable mouth.

"There's nothing I'd rather do," he pants out, "than push you to your knees and have you suck my cock until I come."

Holy hell. "Done." I slide down the wall, and he lifts a knee between my legs, stopping me.

"Then what?" he challenges.

"Whatever you want." I top, but my mind is gone. I'm fantasizing about what it would feel like to bottom for him. I freeze with the thought. There's no way in hell I'm going to let him see my leg, which means I need to get a fucking grip. Dropping my pants to my knees is one thing, but taking them off?

As if he sees my inner conflict, his mouth comes coaxingly down over mine in a sensual, deep kiss, calming the erratic storm inside me.

"What I want," he says as our lips part, "and what I'll do are two different things. I want *this*."

He strokes my cock through my pants, and I grind my teeth against the incredible feeling of his strong hand driving me out of my mind.

"But I've made enough mistakes," he says with a pained look. "I need to do things right this time."

I lean forward and steal another kiss. His hand moves to mine, and he laces our fingers together, holding them beside my head as I'd done to him, only his grip is lighter. He *knows* I want this.

"What is it about you?" he asks against my mouth. "You make me forget to be careful."

"I blame you." I narrow my eyes but can't stop the grin tugging at my lips. "I haven't *wanted*, I haven't *taken*, in so long, I'd almost forgotten how."

I feel his strength ease and I shift us again, bringing him against the wall. He's smiling, though I know his back has to be scratched from the rough concrete.

"I'd almost forgotten how, but then I see *you*," I admit accusatorily. "You open that hot mouth of yours, and every word that comes out of it, every look you cast my way, claws at me."

I cup his cheeks and press my lips to his in one final kiss.

"You're going to walk out that door, go home, and take an ice-cold shower." Sending him away is the last thing I want to do, but I respect what he's told me. "But you won't be able to get me off your mind, the same way I won't be able to think of anything other than you when I walk my ass into my own icy shower."

The liquid heat in his eyes is now tempered with amusement. "I won't?"

"Yes, T. You won't. Where can we meet for our date?"

His eyes fill with confusion at my change of subject. "Date?"

I kiss him softly. "You want to be careful, do things right. I haven't done this in…well, *ever*. But a date seems like the right first step, and since you offered to go with me to meet Dinah, the real estate agent, why don't we meet for coffee first and make it into an afternoon date."

"A date? Yeah, I'd like that. Brooke's Bytes, the Internet café on the boardwalk. Does eleven work? And do you mean Dinah Crickenton?"

"Eleven's perfect, and yeah, I think that's her last name."

Tristan cringes. "She's not the best agent around."

"See why I need you?" I step away and eye his erection straining against his shorts. "You might want to wait for that to go down before taking off."

"Like that's going to happen?" He utters a curse, walks over to the refrigerator, and throws it, and the freezer, open, standing in front of the cold air.

I grab one of my clean T-shirts from the laundry room off the kitchen and toss it to him. He catches it with one hand.

"Come on, stud. I'll give you a lift on my motorcycle."

He closes the doors and puts on the shirt, which hangs over his shorts.

"Does this mean we're going *steady*?"

"You wish. We'll see how the date goes." I grab my keys off the counter and head outside. As he slips a helmet on, I climb on my bike and pat the seat behind me.

He straddles the bike and wraps his arms around me. "Oh yeah, like this is going to help my situation?"

"Probably not, but I'll sure enjoy it."

CHAPTER THREE

Tristan

ALEX IS WAITING for me outside of Brooke's Bytes at eleven. *Alpha* doesn't begin to describe the gorgeous tight-jawed creature watching people walk by with his arms crossed and an intense look in his eyes. It's easy to imagine him standing guard in his military uniform, taking in everything around him. It's no wonder Livi thought he was straight; the hard-bodied man is all rough edges. When his eyes find mine, his crooked smile softens those chiseled features. *All for me.*

He steps forward and possessively places a hand at my waist. His smoldering eyes stoke the fire that has been burning since this morning, and he kisses my cheek.

"Hi, T. I'm glad you made it."

I'm too busy soaking in the feel of his hand and his clean, musky scent to form a response, so I go with a smile.

The bell above the door rings as he pulls it open, and we follow the aroma of fresh-brewed coffee inside. The jukebox, which only plays eighties music, is playing "Kiss on My Lips" by Hall and Oates. Three guys are sitting on red vinyl stools at the counter, drinking coffee and gazing at their laptops, and almost every table is taken by people equally as enamored with their tablets, laptops, or cell phones, with the exception of one by the window.

Brooke looks up from behind the counter. "Hi, Tristan. Grab a seat. I'll be right with you."

She fills her customer's coffee mug as we claim the vacant table. Alex takes the seat beside me. I secretly love this, because while it's common for heterosexual couples to sit side by side, the guys I've been with have always preferred to have their own space. Coupled with his warm greeting, I'm feeling pretty damn good.

Alex reaches for my hand, oblivious to how much these little things mean to me. He must notice the surprise in my eyes because he starts to pull his hand away.

"Too much?" he asks.

I tighten my grip. "I'm not sure there is such a thing."

The relief on his face is palpable. "It just feels good to be away from a military base. If I cross a line, kick me in the ass or something."

I'd like to do a few things to his fine ass, but kicking it isn't one of them.

Brooke serves the table beside us, then hurries over with two coffee mugs and a coffeepot in hand. "Sorry, guys. It's been crazy in here this morning." She has a curious look in her eyes as she sets the mugs down and fills mine.

"Brooke, this is Alex Wells. Alex, Brooke Baker."

"Nice to meet you," Alex says warmly. "You've got a nice place here."

She looks around and sighs happily. "Thank you. Some days I want to pull my hair out, but most of the time I love it. Would you like some coffee?"

"Please." Alex holds up the mug, and as she fills it, he

thanks her.

The bell above the door rings, and Brooke calls out to the young couple that walks in. "Grab a seat and I'll be right with you." She returns her attention to us and pulls a pen from where it was tucked behind her ear and a pad from her back pocket. "Are you guys here for breakfast or just caffeine?"

"Just coffee," I answer. "Go help the others. I'll leave cash on the table when we're done."

"You're a doll." She slips the pen above her ear again and squeezes my shoulder. "Nice to meet you, Alex. Sorry I don't have time to chat."

"No worries." He shifts a heated gaze to me and says, "I'm sure we'll be seeing each other again."

After she moves on to tend to her other customers, I lean closer to Alex and lower my voice. "You'd better stop looking at me like that, or I won't be able to walk out of here."

He laughs and squeezes my hand. "While I make a mental note to give you *more* of those looks, why don't you tell me something about you that I don't know. What are your hobbies? Favorite things? Most hated things?"

"Am I being interviewed?"

"No, but you've already learned a lot about me, and I don't know much about you."

I sigh as if it's a great imposition, but the truth is I'm delighted that he's asking. Most guys never ask more than if I'm a top or a bottom, something he hasn't even asked yet.

"I'm afraid I'm not very interesting. I read and surf, like everyone else in Harborside."

"I can't surf worth beans, but I love to read. Who's your favorite author?"

"Stephen King. I collect his books, signed when I can find

them."

"Awesome. Maybe we can hit a few bookstores on one of our *dates*. What else?"

I'm still stuck on the idea of going on a date to a bookstore. That's one of my favorite things to do, but I usually have to go alone.

"There is one other thing I like." I turn away, slightly embarrassed.

"Based on your expression, I'm guessing it's an odd sexual fetish?"

I laugh. "You might wish it was after I tell you. It's gardening." I wait for him to laugh, but curiosity, not humor, shimmers in his eyes. "My mother makes these elaborate rock gardens. Ever since I was little she'd create them. Then every year she'd change them in some way, expand them, plant different flowers, make bigger hills. I love watching the plants grow over rocks and wood and whatever else she includes. Shells, statues. They've been as much a constant in my life as the turning of the seasons, and when I finally get a place of my own, I hope to have my own gardens."

"Rock gardens?" he asks with a serious face.

"I told you it wasn't interesting."

His eyes brighten. "You're talking to a guy who grew up not knowing where I was going to lay my head down from one month to the next. I think it's fascinating. I can only imagine how incredible it must have been to have that to look forward to and count on from year to year. What else?"

"You're going to think I'm a walking cliché." I sip my coffee, watching him watch me and thinking about the nomad details he's revealed. Everything about him is intense. The way he looks, the way he speaks, the look in his eyes right this very second, as if he doesn't want to miss a word I say.

"A bartender who enjoys reading, surfing, and gardening is far from cliché."

"Thanks, I appreciate that. But I also have a thing for organizing events and interior design. *Total* cliché, I know, but not only from a decorative standpoint. I like the process of reconfiguring space. The second year I worked for Wyatt's father, he renovated the Taproom. I helped him redesign the interior layout in a way that worked best for customers. After the renovations were done, I organized an event for the opening, lined up local press, helped figure out some marketing strategies to expand the customer base."

He sits back and crosses his arms with a skeptical look in his eyes. "Do you want to become an event planner?"

"No. I enjoy bartending, and planning events full-time would drive me crazy. But planning a few events a year like Mr. Armstrong used to do? That was cool. I do miss that."

"Can't you still do it?"

"We do two events a year." I take another drink of my coffee. "I wouldn't mind doing a few more."

"I'm beginning to think we were meant to meet, because I am *not* good at organizing, and while I can make kick-ass furniture, my interior design skills leave a lot to be desired." He drinks his coffee, and a coy smile appears. "Think I can convince you to help me out with those things, too?"

Oh yeah, and a lot more.

After we finish our coffee, Alex insists on paying, and surprises me again by taking my hand as we leave the café.

"Our first date," he offers in explanation.

He won't hear any complaints from me.

Scents of fried foods, popcorn, and carefree days hang in the air as we make our way toward the parking lot. The crowds, the smells, the noise, and people playing on the beach are the hallmarks of summer. There are fewer now that it's September, and in a few weeks, when most of the boardwalk shops close for the season, it'll be almost deserted. But the last time I was here with a man I was seeing was the night I broke up with Ian. I'm glad to replace that awful memory with this happier one.

Alex bristles as a group of burly looking guys brush past us, eyeing our joined hands.

"You okay?"

"Yeah," he says tightly. "Just getting used to not hiding."

"I can't imagine what it was like, but if you notice that we get any more looks, just ignore them."

His eyes move over the people walking in the other direction. "I've spent years ignoring assholes. Kind of makes me want to set them straight."

"I get that, but around here, more people accept than don't. Sometimes it's worth a fight, but when you really think about it, ignorant is as ignorant does. We don't have to lower ourselves to their level."

He grins again and stops short, tugging me against him. "My voice of reason, huh?"

The urge to kiss him is strong, but I have a feeling if the wrong person sneers or makes a comment, regardless of how *out* he wants to be, Alex is too tightly wound to keep from flying off the handle. So I bite back the urge. *For now.*

"I've fought that fight before," I explain. "We won't change their minds, so it's a futile effort."

"Your confidence makes you pretty damn sexy, T."

The compliment and the way he says *T* gets me. Despite my concerns, I lean forward and give him a chaste kiss. "What about your parents? Does it bother them that you're gay?" I ask to distract myself from how much I want to keep kissing him. I can't even begin to understand how I've gone weeks without coming close to breaking my no-male rule and then in just a few hours I'm ready to bend over the railing for this guy.

"My father's never been in the picture, and my mother's totally cool with it. She's okay with pretty much everything. She's not exactly someone who lives by any rules."

"Drugs?" I ask, preparing for the worst.

He laughs softly and shakes his head. "Not even close. My mother does what makes her happy, every minute of the day." He tilts his head toward me with amusement in his eyes. "Made for a fun, and confusing, childhood."

"How so?" I ask as we leave the boardwalk and cross the parking lot, hoping he'll shed some light on his comment.

Alex pulls his keys from his pocket and stops by a blue Ram truck. "Every way you can imagine other than booze or drugs. She wasn't neglectful or anything like that. She just did her own thing. She'd put up Christmas trees in June, or wake me at three in the morning to watch a movie and eat popcorn with her— when I was *seven*. She once took me out of school for two weeks because she thought it would be a better learning experience to go camping in the mountains and learn about the stars. Only she didn't know anything about astronomy, so we basically fished and camped and had a mini vacation. I didn't mind, but the school wasn't pleased. Needless to say, we moved a lot. Apartments, group houses, slept in the car a few times when she'd get the urge to drive down to the shore for a weekend."

He unlocks my door and pulls it open, then circles the truck and settles into the drivers' seat.

"Somewhere along the way, being guarded became easier

than trying to fit in with new kids at school because I knew my mother would get bored and we'd be moving on. For obvious reasons, my grandparents insisted that I stay with them as often as she'd let me. School breaks, summers. She sounds crazy, but she's not. She's just restless."

I hear love and amusement in his voice, but also a hint of something darker. Disappointment, maybe? "Do you see her now?"

"Here and there." He starts the truck and drives away from the center of town. "She's been married twice; neither lasted longer than six months. Not currently married, or at least not that I know of. She's off on one of her adventures right now, staying in a yurt in Montana."

"I guess there's something to be said about living life to the fullest." That earns me another sexy smile. "I was trying to remember seeing you at Arty's funeral, but for the life of me, I can't. Arty made it sound like you two were close. Did I misread that?"

"No, you didn't misread it." Alex grinds his teeth. "I wasn't able to go."

"Were you overseas?"

"Something like that," he says in a low voice.

"Doesn't the military give you leave for stuff like that?"

He's silent for so long, I wonder if he's going to answer at all, and when he does, it's with a grave face.

"Not when you're lying in a hospital bed."

IT'S EASY TO see why my grandmother was so enamored with

Tristan. It's as if he instinctively knows I need time to process what I've just confessed and doesn't push me for details on my hospital stay. It's also easy to see why assholes could take advantage of him. As tough as Tristan is—and he's all man for sure—he's got what my grandmother used to call a *tender heart*. It makes me want to protect him from people like the bastards walking by and eyeing us up with disgust on their faces. There aren't many of them, but the few I've seen deserve to be fucked up for their ignorant attitudes. One look at Tristan, though, and respecting his wishes wins out. I err on the side of the passive.

Tristan tells me about Harborside while we head off to meet the Realtor. He describes local businesses, tells me to be careful of seedier areas, and mentions the strong community bonds between families that have lived here forever. It's clear by his tone how much he loves his hometown. I heard the same excitement in my grandmother's voice when she'd tell me about the area—*and* when she talked about Tristan. As he speculates about the cause of small-business closures, I reflect on how lucky I am that he and my grandmother connected. My grandmother believed in fate. I have never been a big believer in destiny. I've seen too much unnecessary death to believe in such a thing, but now I wonder...

By the time we arrive to meet Dinah, I have a solid grasp of Harborside, and Tristan is already making a list of potential locations for my store.

"This is a seedy area," he says as I park in front of a row of shops that's pretty far off the main drag. "Two streets behind this is where druggies hang out."

"Why would she suggest this place?" I take in the torn awning over the window on the corner and the broken window on the vacant property beside it. The grass out front is dead, and there are two empty shopping carts that must have come from the grocery store several blocks away pushed up against the far end of the building.

"My guess would be cheap rent."

"*Great.* She said she has four places to show me, but if this is her idea of an acceptable location, then chances are they'll all be a waste of time, and I'm not interested in wasting one second of our time together. What do you suggest?" *That we blow her off and go back to my place?*

I can see by his devilish grin he's thinking along the same lines as I am, but he's made it clear he needs to move slowly. "I think we should figure out the areas you feel comfortable looking in, and then you should get a new Realtor. Dinah isn't known for her solid decision-making skills. You should call Dave Jacobson with Harborside Realty. He's the best agent around."

We step out of the truck, and I eye the buxom blond real estate agent wearing too-high heels and a too-short skirt, and ogling Tristan like he's what's for lunch. I make a mental note to track down Dave Jacobson and take Tristan's hand. I want to claim him even from a female. *Go figure.*

I lean close enough to get a scintillating whiff of his spicy, citrusy cologne and say, "Let me get us out of this. Then I want you to show me those gardens you're so fond of."

After I get us out of the next three appointments, Tristan gives me directions to his parents' house.

"You don't have to pretend to be interested," he says as I drive. "Gardening isn't exactly something most guys are into, and you've already impressed me with your listening skills and big cock."

"Jesus, T." I laugh. "I'm not out to impress you. I want to see the things that mean something to you. Although I am glad my big cock impresses you. I'm equally impressed with that sword you're wielding."

The drive across town is paved with dirty jokes and lots of laughter. We climb out of the truck in front of a cedar-sided saltbox-style home with a yard that looks like it slipped off the pages of *New England Garden* magazine. Raised rock gardens snake alongside lush verdant plants and colorful flowers. Tall grasses shoot up between leafy low plants, interspersed with shrubs and taller trees of varying sizes. Another rock garden trails along the right side of the yard, cascading down the gentle slope like a waterfall.

"Wow, T. This is where you grew up?" I follow him around the side of the house and take in the breathtaking view of a quiet cove and more magnificent gardens. Clusters of knockout roses and decorative trees rise above flowerbeds and rocky ledges surrounding a wide expanse of manicured lawn.

"Yup." He stands at the top of the yard, looking hot as sin with the sun shining down on his chiseled face and a smile on his very kissable lips. "My childhood was pretty much the opposite of yours. Stable and predictable, which was just fine with me. I like knowing what tomorrow will bring."

"It sounds like what I've always longed for."

Tristan gives me an empathetic look, and I know he gets it. But as he did with the comment about my hospital stay, he doesn't linger on the subject.

"My older brother, Brody, and I were pretty wild. We used to play catch, wrestle, and basically tear up the lawn."

"Bet your mom hated it when you hit a ball into the gardens."

"Nah, she's not like that." He walks along a path that weaves through the gardens to the grass. "My parents were concerned with grades and how we treated others more than they cared about us messing up a garden. But that didn't stop me from feeling guilty when we did. I hated messing up her hard work, but I was a kid." He shrugs. "Shit happens."

As we walk around the yard, Tristan explains how the gardens have changed over the years, and he tells me about the summer when his mother broke her hand and he maintained the gardens for her. It's easy to imagine him as a boy tending to the gardens alongside his mother, pouring his heart into creating the perfect beds for each plant.

"That was when I realized how much work went into them and how much I wanted one of my own."

He leads me through a thick patch of spiky green bushes to the far corner of the yard, where the gardens fade and long dune grass takes root on a small dune leading to the sandy beach. We look out over the water, and I imagine what it might have been like to wake up to this view every day, year after year.

"Brody always wondered what it would be like to get on a boat and sail away, but I've never had that curiosity. I know it seems silly, but all I've ever wanted was to be here in Harborside. To have the kind of life my parents have." He turns a serious gaze my way. "How about you?"

"Brody and my mother would get along great." I reach for his hand. "I want rock gardens."

CHAPTER FOUR

Tristan

THE NEXT DAY can't move fast enough. Alex is picking me up for our second date at eight o'clock, after my shift at the Taproom, and every time the door opens my heart accelerates. A couple comes into the bar and makes their way to a booth in the back. Disappointment coasts through me. I feel like I've stepped into an alternate dating universe. The men I know don't date. They hook up, get together with friends, and talk about bullshit. In fact, it's usually all about the sex. I have to admit that Alex came across as that type of guy at first glance, all attitude and badass swagger. He's nothing like I expected him to be. He's surprising me at every turn with a softer, family-oriented side that rivals his unstable upbringing. But a loving parent is a loving parent, no matter how many times they uproot you.

"Dude, you're like a nervous chick." Wyatt hands me a shot of tequila.

I stare at it. It's seven forty-five. "I'm still on the clock."

"I'm your boss, and I'm officially ending your shift. You're done for the night." He shoves the shot glass toward my mouth as I hear the door open again.

I'm facing away from the door, but the hair on the back of my neck prickles, and heat doesn't consume me. It *slams* into me. The women sitting at the bar begin to whisper, looking at the man who's got me hard with nothing more than a memory. I glance at Wyatt, who's smirking, and I down the tequila.

He takes the empty glass from my hand and winks. "Never seen you like this."

Tell me about it.

As I turn, Alex moves between two women seated at the bar, and those sinful baby blues blaze a path straight through me. He hasn't shaved, and his scruff has grown in thicker, making him staggeringly hotter.

"Excuse me, ladies." He leans on the bar, and I notice a few scars on the underside of his left forearm I hadn't noticed yesterday. The women visually devour him as he eats up every inch of me.

"Hey, T." He winks, and I'm as nervous as a frigging teenager about to get his first hand job. "Wyatt, how's it going? I hear congratulations are in order." He reaches a hand across the bar to shake. I want to pounce on him, scale the bar and wrap myself around all his hotness.

Wyatt shakes his hand. "Thanks, man. I haven't seen you in forever. How're things? Is your tour over?"

Alex's eyes skip to me again. "Yeah."

"Signing up for another?" Wyatt asks.

"No, man." He rakes a hand through his hair, his eyes suddenly shuttered. "I'm done with that, and here to stay."

"It'll be good to have you around." Wyatt slaps me on the back. "Go on, buddy. Have fun."

"Thanks, Army." I hold a finger up to Alex. "I just need to clock out."

Alex pushes away from the bar and matches my stride as I walk to the bar pass, meeting me as I come through it.

His hand slides to my waist, and he leans in and says in a rough whisper, "I thought about you all day," then kisses my cheek.

I'm so used to jerks like Ian wanting to appear available that the kiss surprises me, even though it shouldn't after how openly affectionate he was yesterday. It takes me a few seconds too long to move. In those startled seconds, Alex's eyes fill with concern. He pulls away, and a gust of cool air drifts between us.

"Be right back," I say nervously, and push through the doors into the back room. In the privacy of the back room, I press my palms to the wall and bang my forehead on it.

"Dude. Need me to go kick some ass?" Dutch, the cook, asks from behind the stainless-steel counter. He's a big guy with thick curly hair, and reminds me of Seth Rogan. He's funny, blunt, and a little awkward.

"No. I need to kick *my own* ass."

He shrugs and flips a burger. "I'd be happy to do that for you if you need it."

"I'm good, thanks. I just did an asshole thing and I need to go apologize." I clock out and head back into the bar.

Alex is leaning against the wall beside the door with his arms crossed. He snaps upright when I come through the door.

"Sorry." I'm not sure what to say, and I don't want to get into my issues here in the crowded bar. "Ready?"

He nods, and as we walk out the door, the silence turns oppressive.

"Look—" he says at the same time I say, "Alex."

We both laugh, and his smile cuts right through me.

"Go ahead," I say.

The door to the bar swings open, and Alex puts a hand on my arm and guides me farther down the pier, away from the bar. When we're out of earshot, we stop. Frustration rolls off of him as loudly as the waves crashing against the pilings below.

"I'm new at this," he says. "I'm sorry if I was out of line in there, but I'm not on a military base anymore. I'm not about to hide who I am. I've done that for long enough, and—"

"What?" I snap. "You weren't out of line, Alex. I was the one who acted like a prick. I'm so used to guys wanting space, wanting to look available, that I've come to expect it. You shocked the hell out of me. I was an ass, and I'm sorry."

We step forward at the same time, and he presses his rough hand to my cheek. "I don't know what kind of pussies you went out with before, but I wanted to fucking *claim* you in there."

He slides a hand around my waist, tugging our bodies together. I feel every hard inch of him, and he's got me so hot I'm sure we're going to combust.

"I've spent almost nine years hiding who I am, and I'm not willing to do it anymore," he says through clenched teeth. "Not here, where I came to start over. Where I came to live on *my* terms without the goddamn military hanging over my head."

"I have no interest in hiding," I assure him.

"You're sure? Because I really want to kiss you right now, and I don't care who sees us."

I respond by pulling his mouth to mine, my break from men long forgotten. We stumble backward, crashing into the railing, fighting for dominance as we did yesterday morning. The passion between us has a life of its own. My hands claw over his ass, up his back. I want to strip him down and take all of him. I want to discover why he's so rough and learn about those shadows that are lurking behind his gorgeous eyes. Instead

I *take*, and *give*, and take *more* of the angry kisses. When we finally tear our mouths apart, my body's still reeling, and we both curse under our breaths.

"Okay?" he pants out.

I nod, knowing if I open my mouth, *I want to fuck you*, is going to come out.

As if we've made a silent agreement, we walk down the pier toward the parking lot. His limp is more pronounced, and I'm sure it's because he's as rock hard as I am.

"I thought the military was more accepting now," I say to break the silence.

"There's a world of space between *allowing* gays in the military and *acceptance* of gay men among the troops."

I try to imagine what it would be like not to be able to own your sexuality as a grown man, and my mind spins back to Delilah. Her parents unknowingly did such a guilt trip on her, she'd never even experimented with women until after her parents' tragic accident. Even then she had a hell of a time trying to move past the guilt.

I glance at the man beside me, thinking about what he said about the military. The world can be a pretty fucked-up place, and I count myself lucky for not having to deal with what he and Delilah have.

We walk off the pier and down the beach toward the boardwalk. I have no idea where we're going, and I don't care. It's nice to be with a man who isn't hung up on himself to the point of hardly noticing I'm here.

Alex stirs something visceral in me that I haven't experienced before, and it should scare me, but it doesn't. Maybe it's because I know how much Arty adored him, or maybe it's the honesty in everything he says and does. I trust him, and I don't even try to resist the urge to link my fingers into his and squeeze his hand.

"You're in the right place now," I reassure him. "People around here are pretty accepting."

Relief and gratitude reflect in his eyes, along with something deeper I can't read, but I can feel—all the way to my bones. He leans over and kisses me, cracking that crooked smile I already know by heart.

Alex

AFTER YEARS OF hiding my private life, it feels good to be openly holding Tristan's hand despite the few annoying looks we received yesterday. We pass Brooke's Bytes, and I think about what he said yesterday about the work he used to do.

"Tell me about the Taproom. You said you work for Wyatt's parents?"

"I used to. Wyatt and Delilah's parents were killed by a drunk driver a little over a year ago, and they inherited the Taproom. I worked for their parents for three years before the accident. Their father was like a second father to me. He taught me a lot about what it takes to keep a business afloat, marketing, operations..."

"That must have been a horrible loss for all of you."

"Yeah, it was tough," Tristan says solemnly. "Wyatt, Delilah, and a handful of our friends have known each other since we were little kids. They'd come into town with their families for the summers, and after the first few, we became like one big, extended family. We helped each other pull through. Wyatt and Delilah are doing really well. Their beach house has become a catchall for our tight-knit group. I'm staying with them for a while, and our buddy Brandon Owens lives there, too."

"You're lucky to have such close friends. You seem to enjoy working for them, and from what I saw the other night, you enjoy your job, too."

"I do. My friends push me to do more with my life. Maybe one day I'll want to do something different, but for now I'm perfectly happy."

We stop and watch a group of teenagers playing with a lighted Frisbee on the beach.

"I guess you don't mind listening to sob stories?"

Tristan laughs. "For every sob story, there's an equally happy or interesting one. Besides, those sad people? They need someone to talk to who won't judge them or try to fix their issues. Sometimes all it takes to go from sad to okay again is a willing ear."

The moonlight shines down on his handsome face. His eyes are bright and clear, not shadowed by having seen an inescapable amount of death and devastation. His scruff is perfectly manicured, which is something I never found appealing until now. I'm used to the military, where we're forced to conform, from clean-shaven cheeks to short-cropped hair, and our bodies are the result of knowing every move might cost you or your buddies their lives. We're hard, inside and out, and covered with scars—not just the physical kind. The deep-seated type that lie beneath the surface. The kind I see in the mirror every day.

I force those thoughts away, counting my lucky stars to be alive.

"Based on what I know of you, you could do any number of things, but it sounds like you're right where you're supposed to be. At least for now." *And I'm glad you're here with me.*

"For now," he says. "Unfortunately, winters are slow at the Taproom, and now that we've hired Livi, Charley, and Rusty, we're overstaffed and we'll have to cut back in a few weeks."

"That can't be an easy decision to make."

"No, it's not. They need the money to get through school. I volunteered to take the hit and work someplace else part-time."

"Really? You'd do that? Give up the place where you just said you loved working, for them? College kids can find work anywhere, can't they?"

"It's hard to find work in a resort town over the winter." Tristan shrugs. "They're more than college kids. They're friends. We've worked together a long time now. Besides, I've got plenty of money saved to make it through the winter. I'd rather be careful and find other work than have them worried about how they're going to make ends meet while trying to keep up with their schoolwork."

"In the military we hear a lot about war heroes, but I think it's all twisted up and wrong. Soldiers fight because it's our job. It's what we signed up for, and we know the risks going into it. What you're doing? That makes you an everyday hero."

Tristan shakes his head and laughs. "Nah, it's just me being me. Some people would say it's a flaw. I always lead with my heart, and hearts are not nearly as smart as heads."

"Well, all I can say to that is that I think it takes a lot of guts to give up something you love for others. Any way you cut it, it's an admirable quality."

"Thanks." His expression is one of wonder or disbelief, as if he isn't used to compliments.

"Are you hungry? I thought we'd head over to Shab Row for dinner at the Spot, but if you'd rather, we can grab a few slices of pizza or something."

"The Spot, huh?" he says flirtatiously. "That sounds perfect."

We cut through an alley between two shops and head down the dimly lit streets to Shab Row. I chose the Spot because it's off the beaten path, and I wasn't sure how *out* Tristan was. Obviously he's comfortable in his own skin, and that makes it easier to be comfortable in mine.

We make our way down the brick-paved sidewalks, passing beneath old-fashioned streetlights that make me feel like I'm in a 1940s movie and should be donning a trench coat.

"Listen, T." The endearment that comes so easily earns me that sexy grin again. "It's not easy for me to open up about certain things."

"Really? I hadn't noticed."

The tease in his eyes drives me to pull him closer. Everything he does makes me want to be closer to him. He joins me willingly, and his free hand moves to my hip.

"Thanks for not pushing me for answers. I know it's not fair to throw the hospital comment out there and then clam up. I'll share it with you. I want to share it with you."

"I know you will." He says it like it's a fact.

"How?"

"Arty once said you were a born leader, like your grandfather, and all strong leaders keep their cards close to their chest."

"She said that? That I was like my grandfather?"

He nods, and I tuck away that compliment with the other meaningful ones I've saved over the years.

"Can I ask you something? You don't have to answer."

Tristan shrugs. "Have at it."

"Why were you taking a break? I get that your ex was a

prick, but is there more to it?"

He looks down the street, across the street, and then his hand cruises through his hair as it has so often that I've already come to expect it when he's nervous.

"Ian was a prick, but the rest is going to make me sound like a pussy," he admits.

"I've only known you a day, and I already know nothing can make you sound like a pussy."

He meets my gaze, and his jaw tightens. He lifts his chin and I recognize the struggle between feeling proud and worrying about looking weak. I fight that battle on a daily basis.

"I give away my heart too easily, and I end up getting hurt."

His eyes never leave mine, and that trust, that confidence, is the sexiest thing I've ever seen.

"I was right. Nothing can make you sound like a pussy." I slide my hand to the hard ridge of his jaw and lean in closer. "I've never given my heart away. That makes you braver than me."

CHAPTER FIVE

Tristan

THE SPOT IS one of my favorite restaurants. The room is lit only with candles at each table, and it's divided into sections by walls that are painted red and black with chalkboard paint. Customers are given colored chalk to write on the walls. People write poems, riddles, declarations, drawings, all sorts of things, and they are wiped clean at the end of each week. We're sitting at a quiet table near the back of the restaurant. We share entrées and keep the conversation light, and still there's a constant hum of electricity between us.

When the waiter arrives with the bill, I reach for my wallet.

"Please don't," Alex says. "What kind of guy makes his date pay for dinner?" He hands a wad of cash to the waiter and says, "Keep the change," but his eyes remain on me, just as they've been all night.

"Thank you. Next time it's on me." When we first arrived, Alex requested this table in the back, and when the waiter took our order, Alex asked what I wanted before giving his order. I don't even have to ask if he's a top or a bottom. I can't imagine anyone *topping* Alex, but that doesn't stop my mind from toying with the idea of being the first.

"Ready to get out of here?" he asks, rising to his feet.

The women at a nearby table have been eyeing us all night, and when he stands, their eyes rake down his body. Jealousy spikes through me, and as ridiculous as it is, I have to bite down hard, because it's not rolling off my back as it should. Even though Ian was gay, he would have eaten up that attention and milked it for everything it was worth, flirting with the women and making me feel like nothing more than arm candy. Alex doesn't even seem to notice them checking him out.

He grabs a stick of chalk, and his eyes fill with mischief. "You care what I write?"

I stand and shake my head. "Not even a little."

He scrawls ALPHA horizontally and TANGO vertically, connected at the *A*. He points to his chest and mouths, *Alpha*, then points to me and mouths, *Tango*, and my heart does a silly little happy dance. He sets the chalk down, slides a hand to my jaw—a possessive move I'm totally digging—and kisses me hard.

He grins and slides that hand over my shoulder, clearly staking claim to me as we pass the leering women on the way out. It's a move I've waited for my whole life, and it's such a fucking turn-on, the minute we're out of the restaurant, I slam him against the brick wall beside the door and crash my mouth over his, taking the kiss I've been dying for. He surrenders to me at first, kissing me back hungrily, letting me lead. Then his hands fist in my hair, and his entire body flexes. He deepens the kiss, taking complete control.

When he tears his mouth away, his eyes are volcanic, and I want to feel the lava coursing through him more than I want my next breath.

"Who *are* you?" I growl.

He kisses me again, there beside the entrance to the restaurant, as a couple comes up the stairs and brushes by us. He never breaks our connection, never flinches at the intrusion. His fisted hands relax, caressing my head as his tongue caresses my mouth, and I'm so gone, so hard, so lost in him, I can barely think. When we finally part, I don't want to move away from this moment. I want to pull him back and kiss him again.

"I'm the guy you deserve," he says, and as if he's read my mind, he takes me in a torturously slow, sensual kiss.

I hear girls giggling and we part again, but our eyes don't seek the gigglers. They remain locked on each other. There's a storm brewing between us, and I'm not sure I know how to—or want to—slow it down. Every kiss, every touch, every time he feasts on me with those gorgeous eyes, he stokes the fire inside me. Everything with Alex feels amplified, like all the men before him were practice, gearing me up for the man who would challenge my every move. Preparing me for *him*.

"Walk?" he says, thick with lust.

"Yeah."

We walk shoulder to shoulder down the steps and shove our hands in our pockets, as if he's struggling with the inability to control himself, too. We're quiet as we wind through the streets. Neither is leading; neither is following. We're two men stuck in a bolt of lightning, ready to detonate. I hear him breathing and want to hear it from behind as he pounds into me. I feel his body brush against mine and want to see his broad shoulders moving from above as he sucks me off.

This is not slowing down.

This is Trouble with a capital *T*.

Or maybe I've got it all wrong, and Alex Wells is exactly what I need.

Alex

I CAN'T TAKE the lust coursing through me for another second. My every breath chases Tristan. His kiss, his touch, his fucking smile. What the hell is *that*? I'm like a chick. His smile…?

When we come to the alley leading up to the boardwalk, the buildings block the light of the moon. Tristan and I glance around at the same time, and that sexy smile of his wrecks me. I fist my hands in his shirt and back him up against the building. We're both shaking, but there's no fear.

"Slow," I remind him—and myself—but it comes out like a threat.

"Yeah," he says halfheartedly.

Unlike me, Tristan's laid his heart on the line. He's trusted me with knowledge he thought would make him look like a pussy—and here I am holding my truth back. Who's the real pussy?

"Good," I say, having no idea if I'll be able to go as slow as either of us needs. "Because it's been way too long since I've been with a man, and once I'm inside you, I won't last long. Not the first time. It'll be desperate and rough." I have no idea where this verbal flood is coming from, but I'm powerless to stop it. "But then. *Then*, T, it'll be worth every second. I promise you that. If you're still around, that is."

I touch my lips lightly to his. It's hell not ravaging him, but these soft, teasing kisses pack the power of a bullet train, and in seconds we're grinding and groaning, but neither of us takes the kiss deeper.

"We suck at slow," I say with a laugh.

He bites my lower lip. "No shit."

A silent *We're so screwed* passes between us.

"Walk," we both say at once, and head for the boardwalk.

We cross through the crowd and jump off the boardwalk onto the beach without a word. We walk in the opposite direction of the pier. When my pulse calms, I reach for his hand, and he slides those rich chocolate eyes my way.

"Thank you for looking after my grandmother."

"I enjoyed spending time with her. I still think of her often."

"Really? Or do you just want to get laid?" I'm teasing. I know he gets that, but I catch a moment of hurt in his eyes, and it slays me. "I'm kidding, T. I'm sorry. I was on tour too long. Sometimes I speak before thinking."

"It's cool." He smiles again. "But if you do that shit again, I'll have to take you down."

"And you think that'll shut me up? You just gave me a very good reason to be an asshole." I wrap my arm around his shoulder and pull him against me. "I really am grateful for your kindness. My grandmother mentioned you in several of her letters."

"She did?"

I nod. "Nothing too revealing, just stuff about how you cared for your friends, or took her to the market. Fixed a broken shutter after a storm. Shoveled her walk last winter. You were good to her. You did the things I wish I could have. I envy the time you had with her, and I appreciate you looking after her."

"Stop it already. I liked doing it."

"I can't believe I'm going to tell you this, but she said you were the kind of guy I needed. That's why I sought you out at the Taproom. I thought, if nothing else, you were a connection to her. I've been trying to get up the courage to meet you since I got into town."

"The courage?" He looks me up and down, and I know what he sees. A rough exterior. A soldier through and through. The thing is, I also have no doubt in my mind that Tristan isn't that simple-minded. He's being kind, because that's who *he* is. He knows I've got demons, but he's too respectful to call me on them.

"Do I look like a bullshitter?" I ask cockily.

He arches a brow, and I laugh.

"How can you doubt that it takes courage? When I walked into that bar, half the women were eye-fucking you and the other half were practically throwing themselves across the bar. Forget the number of guys sizing you up. I thought maybe my grandmother had read you wrong and you were really straight."

"Oh, there was no reading to be done. Arty was pretty forthright. She looked me in the eye, screwed up her face like this"—he squints and cranes his chin forward, scrutinizing me—"and she said, 'Are you into men?'"

"Christ," I grumble. "Can you imagine if you were straight and she'd said that? She was something." I laugh at the thought of my tiny grandmother eyeing up tall, dark, and strappingly virile Tristan and questioning his sexuality.

"When I told her I was into men, do you know what she did?"

"I'm afraid to ask." A wave crashes into the shore, bleeding up the sand to within inches of our shoes, and we move up the beach.

"She asked if I was, and I quote, 'one of those switch hitters.'"

A laugh escapes before I can stop it.

"I'm glad you find it so funny. I felt gut punched. I mean, she was a *grandmother*. A sweet old lady."

Tristan is easy to talk to, and I don't need to reach far to find the courage to ask what had been impossible to think about last night. "Did you see her the week…at the end?"

"No," he says solemnly. "It's one of my biggest regrets. I went to see her that afternoon. I didn't know." He swallows hard. "Are you sure you want to hear this?"

"No," I admit. "But I need to."

"Okay. You probably know she sculpted right up until the end. I don't remember a day when I saw her and she didn't have a spot of clay on her chin, or cheek, or clothes. She made these tiny people and animals, and once a month a driver picked her up and took her to Harborside Hospital, where she gave them to children in the pediatric wing. I went with her a few times, but not that morning."

He clears his throat, and I tighten my hand on his shoulder. I know it's probably as hard for him to relive it as it is for me to hear it. He feels good against my side. He feels solid and right. We're nearing my house, and I slow our pace. We've only just regained control, and I know that once we're alone, we'll be all over each other again. I want that. *Man, do I ever want that.* But I don't want anything to distract us from this important conversation.

"I came by about the time she should have been arriving home. I wanted to make sure she got home okay, and she liked to talk about the kids after her visits." He lifts pained eyes to me. "They'd just taken her away. The driver had gotten worried when she didn't answer the door and called the police. They said she went in her sleep, which you probably already know."

His voice cracks, and I gather him in my arms, offering

strength and borrowing his in equal measure.

He pushes free and says, "Sorry."

I pull him back in. "Get over here and be a pussy with me."

He laughs, and we embrace for a long moment. Then we stumble up the beach toward my house.

"Tell me what you want, T. What are you looking for in a relationship?"

"That's a pretty deep question."

"Not any deeper than what we were talking about, and it's important."

He stops at the bottom of the steps leading up to the house. "I'll make you a deal," he says as my hand returns to its new home around his waist. "Grab us a few drinks, and I'll answer your question, but in return, you need to share something with me."

As I head inside, grinding my teeth against the idea of telling him about my leg, the incident that caused it, or the guilt that haunts me about my grandmother, I realize my reaction is force of habit. Even if he doesn't answer my question, I want to try to let him in.

CHAPTER SIX

Tristan

ALEX AND I are camped on the clearing beside the boulders behind Arty's bungalow, where spiky dune grass grows in tufts between patches of sand. It's a gorgeous spot overlooking the ocean and is where Arty drank her coffee in the mornings. I've always thought it was the perfect spot for a rock garden. Alex and I are drinking beer and dancing around touchy subjects. Part of me is terrified to admit what I want in a relationship. Not only because it would make it easier for him to pretend to be the type of man I'm looking for, but also because it's doing exactly what I told myself I wouldn't: opening myself up to being hurt, giving fuel to a fire that could easily trounce on my heart. I'm only just recovering from the last time I was used as a doormat.

Alex reaches for my hand, and a small smile appears on his face. He's too sexy in all the ways that are dangerous to me. Beyond being insanely hot, he says things that stop me in my tracks. *I'm the guy you deserve.* It takes a lot of balls to say that to a guy he's only known for a day. And somehow, when he said it, I felt like it was true—which is what scares me the most. Lord knows there is *nothing* in my dating history to show that I'm a good judge of character.

"Thanks for going out with me tonight."

His comment takes me completely off guard, just as he did when he asked me out—or rather, *told me* he would pick me up for our date. Hell if I don't like that about him, too. He's not like any of the guys I've dated in the past, and for now I take that as a very good sign.

"I should thank you," I say. "You paid."

"No, I mean it. I pushed my way into your evening, and this has been one of the most enjoyable nights I've had in years."

I agree, and work up the nerve to answer his earlier question. "You asked me what I'm looking for in a relationship, and the truth is, I'm not looking."

"I know you said you were taking a break. I'm not asking you to marry me, so don't freak out. But, T, I've only spent a short time with you, and I can't imagine how some guy hasn't snatched you up already. Are you looking for someone unattainable, or do you have really lousy taste in men?"

As laughter falls from my lips, I realize I've laughed more tonight than I have in weeks. "My buddy Brandon, who's bisexual and will most likely try to fuck you at some point, tells me I should have been a lesbian."

He takes a long pull of his beer. "I think I need fuel for this conversation."

"He says I'm like a chick," I explain. "Guys are always looking for the next best thing. To bring another guy into the mix or to conquer their next prey. I've never been wired that way. According to Brandon's vast experience, lesbians have two awesome dates and they're setting up house. That's why he says I should have been a lesbian."

"Because you want monogamy?"

I shrug. "You make it sound so *normal*. It sure doesn't feel normal based on the guys I've been with. What are you looking for? You said it's been a long time for you, too."

"My long time and your long time are a world apart," he says seriously.

"As wide of a world apart as allowance and acceptance?"

He nods. "You're a good listener."

"So I'm told." I finish my beer and set the bottle beside me.

"I've never *looked*," he says quietly.

"Never looked?"

"For a relationship. For a guy. For a hookup." He stares out at the water. "I went to college and guys found me. But hooking up wasn't my goal. I was there to get my degree, and sure, to get laid. But you know, that wasn't the end-all for me. I grew up with a mother whose idea of stability was staying in the same location for longer than a month. I didn't want that to be my future, and I knew I couldn't do much with a degree in fine arts. I figured the military was about the only way I could make ends meet, build a career."

"Why didn't you give your woodwork a try? You're so talented."

"Thanks, but it was complicated. Starting a business takes time and money. I knew I wanted a family of my own one day, which meant being the man of the house. Earning the lion's share of the income. I was a kid with no business knowledge, no experience in anything other than meaningless part-time jobs, school, and instability. I knew the military would give me a stable foundation and a hope for some kind of future. I figured I'd find time to work with my art at some point. And I know you're wondering, so I'll just put this out there. Yes, I knew it would be hard to be a gay man in the military. My grandfather was a vet, and he told me how difficult it would be. I knew it was going to be an uphill battle, but I wanted to make my family proud and I hoped that one day I'd be the type of man my partner could be proud of. I figured I'd save money, one day open my business, and in the meantime, do something meaningful."

"How long were you in?"

"Just under eight years. My grandfather's warning could have been ten times harsher and it wouldn't have come close to being accurate. I made the mistake of telling the guys on my team, who seemed pretty accepting. It quickly became apparent that they weren't. They made jokes and that kind of shit. In the army, your team becomes your family. They're the ones you're with no matter what. They're with you when you join a squad, a platoon, a company, or a battalion. The number of people in each of those groups multiplies exponentially—and so do attitudes and opinions. *Lock down, shut up, and act straight*— whatever the hell that means—became my silent mantra."

"I've never run into anything on that large of a scale. I can't imagine how difficult that must have been. Why did you stay in so long?"

"Because those guys were my family. My stability. They'd give their lives for me, as I would for them. Sex is sex. But that camaraderie? That brotherhood? Regardless of what they thought of my sexual orientation, our bond was tight. It was everything I'd missed growing up."

"But what did you do for sex?"

"I took care of it when I was on leave. It's not like I had time to think about sex. We were in the field a lot, and I couldn't afford to have my mind anywhere but in the fight.

When we were on base, I was working out, designing furniture, catching up with my family, and trying to fit in. I hooked up with a few guys, but it was like a covert mission every damn time." He releases my hand and runs both of his through his hair. When he meets my gaze, his eyes are dead serious.

"I'm clean. I was tested every two years. I've never had unprotected sex, and in case you're wondering, I top. It's been more than a year and a half since I've been with a man. And I spent several of the last nine months in the hospital and going through rehab, both of which gave me a chance to think about what the hell I wanted out of life."

"I'm clean, too," I reassure him. My eyes roll down his body. "What happened?"

He shifts his eyes away, but not before I see darkness shrouding them. The muscles in his jaw bunch, and his hands curl into fists. "A particularly bad day at the office. One I'm not ready to relive."

He turns to me again, and the pain in his eyes makes me want to take him in my arms and make him feel so good he forgets whatever it is that's haunting him. But somehow I know that's what I would need, not what he needs. He needs walls. That doesn't bode well for me and my poor choices in men, but there's so much about Alex that I'm attracted to, I don't want to pull back or close myself off. I want to know *more* about him, and if he's really here to stay, we have nothing but time.

"And during all that time of introspection? What'd you come up with?" I ask, letting him know he's off the hook about whatever happened that landed him in the hospital.

"Tristan, I'm almost thirty years old. I'm not a kid looking to get my rocks off, no matter how badly I might need it at the moment. What I want hasn't changed since before the military.

I want to start my business, have stability, and be with a guy who respects the same things I do. Family. Loyalty. Honesty. I want to finally live life on my terms. A life I can be proud of. I'm proud of my career in the military, but I spent those years lying for everyone else's benefit. Hell, I was lying for myself, too."

I search his face, trying to figure out if I'm being played. Everything he said seems too tailored to what I crave, and need, in my life. But my heart tells me I can trust him.

"I've got baggage, T. A lot of it. I'm angry for having to lie about who I was, and at the same time, I'm proud of what I've done for our country. But it cost me in so many ways. I carry a lot of guilt and anger about it. I might never be an open book, but I'm not an asshole, either."

I don't know how to do anything other than be who I am, and I'm realizing that Alex has never had that chance. As he takes my hand, I don't want to turn him away, but I don't want to be a fool, either.

"Alex, I *know* who I am, and I've been down this road too many times before with guys who are just starting to figure themselves out," I finally manage. "It never ends well for me."

Alex

I'VE JUST REVEALED so much of myself, I feel like I'm standing naked before Tristan, but there's not an ounce of judgment in his eyes. There's no room for it with the desire and hesitation warring for residence. I can't resist the urge to move closer, hoping to end his fence sitting.

"I can count on one hand the number of times I've known

exactly what I wanted. Working with my hands and creating things as I feel them and joining the military. I knew I wanted both. I knew they were the right things for me at the time. Coming to Harborside was hard as hell, and facing my demons will be even harder. But I want to be here, and not just because my grandmother wanted it for me, but because in all her letters, and every time we talked on the phone, I heard a calling. And now. *This*. You and me, T. I want this. For the first time in my life, I went *looking*, and I found *you*."

His fingers close around mine. His hand is strong, his palm is hot, and as a gust of wind blasts up the rocks, my body sizzles against its chill.

"I can't imagine not kissing you again," I tell him, because honesty is what we both need. "And I'm not willing to walk away because you're scared. I've spent the better part of the last decade facing death. My fears were about ending up six feet under—yours are about *feeling like* you're six feet under because you're wading through the aftermath of guys like your exes."

I have to touch him. Have to let him know he can count on my strength, rely on my word. My hand moves to his jaw, as it has done so many times over the course of the evening. It feels like it belongs there.

"You have no reason to believe me, but I'm not going to screw you over, Tristan. That's not who I am."

His head turns slightly, pressing his scruff into my palm, and I know he wants this, too.

"And in a week?" he asks. "After we've fucked like rabbits, and you're ready for the next best thing? This is the first time since you joined the military you've been able to openly explore your sexuality. And Harborside is a great place to do it."

"I can't promise you forever. I know better than anyone our

lives can change in the blink of an eye, but I can promise you that I'm not made of cheating cloth. I'm as loyal as the ocean is deep. And sure, you might decide I'm too broken for you or that my demons run too deep. Or I might decide you're too…" I shake my head, because I can't think of a damn thing that could turn me off to this sexy, honest man.

"Aw, hell, T. I could decide you're too good for me. As screwed up or corny as it sounds, I was jealous of the people in the Taproom before we even spoke. Now that I know you? Now that I've listened to you lay out your fears and know what it cost you to do so?" I pull him closer. "Now that I've tasted you? The thought of any other man's mouth on yours makes me want to beat someone to a pulp. I've never felt that before."

The sounds of our heavy breaths drown out the waves crashing against the shore.

"*You're* the next best thing, Tristan. How can you not know that about yourself?"

"Fuck," he growls, and captures my mouth, kissing me like he's been starved for me.

I take control, kissing him harder, because I *am* starved for him. Our bodies collide as we fall to the sand. My thigh traps him below me. My hands play over every inch of him—his muscular chest, his abs, and the hard heat pulsing between us. He rocks against my hand, and I want to taste him so desperately, I claw his shirt up, reluctantly breaking our kiss to pull it over his head. He's so fucking gorgeous I can't stop a greedy moan from escaping my lungs.

"Fuck, T. I don't know where to start."

Before he responds, I kiss him again, my hands cupping his strong jaw, feeling the need in his powerful kiss, in every stroke of his tongue. I bite his lower lip, kiss the hard line of his jaw, and sink my teeth into his neck so hard his nails dig into the backs of my arms.

"Christ," he swears.

He grabs my head, keeping me against his salty, hot skin.

I grab his hands and force them down to the sand beside his head. "It's not enough."

I don't give him a chance to deny me, and move down his body, kissing and nipping as my hands squeeze and rub, memorizing every hard plane. I suck his nipple into my mouth and groan as it pebbles against my tongue. His hips piston off the ground, and the moan it elicits is nothing short of erotic. I rock my cock against him and follow the divot between his abs to the button on his jeans. As I grip it between my teeth, a voice in my head whispers, *He needs slow. I need slow.* I lift my eyes, and the lethal look in his is all the green light I need to tug that button free and crank his jeans down his thighs, freeing his formidable erection. I'm like a kid in a candy store, wanting to taste every part of him at once and wanting to give him so much pleasure, he'll forget Ian altogether. As I reach for his cock, cool air rolls over my hands, and I remember we're still outside. We're on a dune and the lights are off. I'm fairly certain no one can see us, but my mind races to Tristan. He needs to trust me. He needs to know I care.

"T," I pant out. "Should we take this inside?"

He looks around and says, "Fuck no. Not yet."

I press a kiss beside his cock as I take him in my hand and give one tight stroke. He moans and his hands fist beside him. I slick my tongue along his hard length and his hips buck, but I'm not going there yet. No, this is half the fun. I want to see this beautiful man begging for my mouth. I run my hands down his muscular thighs as I lick his sac, feeling it tighten with need.

I seal my lips over his inner thigh, pressing my fingers into his rigid muscles. My teeth graze along his sensitive skin, until I get so close to his balls I know he feels my breath on the wetness I've left there. He curses under his breath, and I lavish the other thigh with the same sensual attention. His cock bobs when I drag my tongue up his inner thigh.

"Alex—" he pleads. "Suck me."

I spent so many years taking commands, it's second nature to follow his demand. I wrap my fingers around his shaft, lower my mouth to the broad head, and pause. I'm not in the military anymore. I swirl my tongue over his most sensitive glans, and as I slide my tongue over the glistening bead at the tip, I get my first taste of his essence.

"Damn, you're sweet, T."

I lick under the ridge of the crown and make my way south, along the thick vein down the center, around the sides. His cock pulses against my tongue, and when I wrap my hand around him, he jerks through my fist. I'm so hard I can barely stand it, and grind against his legs. The heat of his gaze bores into me like a laser, and when I lift my eyes, the look in his is raw and wicked, spurring me on. I lower my mouth over his thick shaft, and his eyes flutter closed. He strains to keep them open as I work him with my hand and mouth. He pushes himself upright, flexing all those glorious muscles as he grabs my head, guiding me to the speed he needs. I want to strip off my jeans and fist my cock as I suck him—or even better, I want him to do it, but it's too complicated of a position for where we are. And seeing his eyes turn coal black, watching his abs flex, and feeling his strong hands on my jaw is too fucking hot to miss for even a second. I cup his balls and tug gently, and his whole body goes rigid. His hands have been tight on my head, guiding, driving, taking whatever I'll give, *demanding* it, but now they slide gently to the contours of my jaw.

"Alex, I can't last. Fuck, you're good at this."

Heat rushes through me at the desperation in his voice. His hands trace over my jaw as I quicken my pace. His fingers ghost over the corners of my mouth, and I feel his cock grow impossibly thicker. I hollow out my cheeks, then take him deeper, anticipating his release, craving it. His hands cup my jaw tightly, his thumbs stroke over my cheeks in the same rhythmic pulse of my mouth taking him in, and I'm *gone*. Lost again in the pleasures of Tristan. His touch is mesmerizing. His erotic, greedy sounds slip into the night, and when the first hot jet hits the back of my throat, I take him deeper, to near choking. Despite his thick shaft clogging my throat, despite his release pulsing inside me, for the first time in forever, I feel like I can breathe.

CHAPTER SEVEN

Tristan

I LEAN DOWN and kiss Alex, not bothering to tuck myself back into my pants. I *need* to be closer to him. As our mouths come together, he scales my body like a mountain, pushing me down to the hard earth again. The scratches on my back from earlier in the day when he crashed me against the concrete kitchen wall sting, and his shirt is rough against my chest. I tug it up, and he slows the kiss to suck-the-brain-cells-out-of-my-head speed. My hands splay on his back, dipping and sliding over grooves in his skin. I don't mean to, but my hands still as I try to assemble the pieces of what I'm touching in my mind.

Alex shoves my hand away and rears up to his knees. I rise to a seated position before he can exhale and grab his arm.

"Don't," I warn against the angry gleam in his eyes. "I get that you've gone through something traumatic, but if you think for a second you can blow me and then storm off because of whatever it was, then you're proving just how bad my judgment is."

"Tristan," he says through clenched teeth.

"What, Alex? You think a few scars are going to make me think any less of you? You think I'll treat you differently?"

He looks away, his jaw working overtime. "It's more than a few scars."

"Obviously." I pull myself up to my knees in front of him, but he refuses to look at me. Pain billows off of him, and I can tell it's not the kind of pain that I can take away with a few carefully chosen words, maybe not even with hours of assurances.

"You may not be ready for a guy like me after all," I say honestly. "I see you're in pain, and I want to help you through it. That's who I am, and that's not going to change. But I'm not going to force you to let me in. I've gone that route and—"

"It never ends well. Yeah, I got it," he says coldly. He scrubs a hand down his face and curses.

When he slides a hand to my jaw, my instinct is to lean into the touch I've already grown accustomed to, but I fight it, tightening against it, resisting even as he pulls me closer. He has no choice but to come to me. His forehead touches mine and he breathes deeply.

"My turn to ask," he says roughly. "Who *are* you?"

I can't help the soft laugh that escapes as I say, "I'm the guy *you* deserve."

"Tristan." His hand tightens around the back of my neck. "Goddamn it, Tristan."

"How bad?" I ask, knowing I'm skating a line he doesn't want to cross.

"Bad." He draws back and sits on his heels, watching me hike up my pants and fasten them.

I sit on my heels, mimicking his posture. A little unsure of how to respond, I try for humor. "I'm not a taker. I didn't want to leave you blue balled after that earth-shattering blow job you gave me." That earns a crooked smile, a fissure in his armor.

"Earth-shattering, huh?"

"You're seriously talented, and I'm a lucky bastard."

We both laugh, but the seriousness of what I've just discovered hangs heavily between us.

"The way I see it, we've got a few choices. I can leave now, and you can show up next Tuesday night at Wyatt's place for a get-together we're having and we can try to figure out where to go from there. Or we can grab a beer and talk it out."

His brows furrow. "What about the more obvious option?"

"I'm not following…" Although I am, very closely.

"You can end things with the fucked-up war vet."

"Obviously that's not an option, or I would have suggested it."

A shy look washes over him, conflicting with his powerful presence.

"Tristan," he says, and shakes his head.

"Maybe I have a thing for your talented mouth," I tease. "I told you I'm a horrible judge of character, and the men I've fallen for have proven that to be true over and over again. But in the *friends* department I actually kick ass."

"So, you want to put me in the friend zone?"

"Oh, hell no." I can't stifle my grin. "With a mouth like yours, I'm definitely keeping you in the fuckable zone. But right now you need a friend more than you need a lover, so get your sorry ass up, grab us a few beers, and let's hammer some of this out."

He stands and reaches for my hand, tugging me up to my feet, and I pull on my shirt.

"Hey," he says solemnly. "Thanks for not wigging out on me."

"So far you've been nothing but honest with me. That's more than I can say for most of the guys I've been with."

Alex

"I'M NOT A vain person, or at least I've never thought of myself as being vain," I explain to Tristan as we nurse our beers on the couch. "It's not the scars that I care about. It's what they stand for, the memories they evoke. What they stole from me."

"I assume it happened when you were overseas?"

I know if I don't respond or if I change the subject he's not going to push me to elaborate, and that makes me want to let him in even more. He was right about not being able to change. With Tristan, what you see is what you get—unlike with me and most of the soldiers who have spent years as chameleons, our lives hinging on our stealth abilities. It's such a contrast to what I'm used to that I want to strive to be more like him in that way. He deserves that—hell, *I* deserve that.

I nod and set my beer on the coffee table, pressing my hands to my thighs, staving off the urge to evade the question.

"You know when you wake up from a nightmare, and it takes you a minute to realize you're out of it? That it wasn't real?" I don't wait for him to respond. "On a combat operation, there's no escaping the nightmare. As a soldier, you stand and you sleep ready to deploy, engage, and destroy the enemy. There's only hoping it stays at bay for longer spans of time. When you close your eyes, you replay the locations of your enemies, the strategies you've worked out in case of attack. You're on edge twenty-four seven, because you have to be ready to fight for your life and the lives of the other men. We were under attack by what they estimate was two-hundred-plus enemy fighters occupying high ground just before dawn. We were surrounded on all four sides of our post." I dig my fingers into my thigh muscles, remembering the roar of adrenaline, the fleeting panic that quickly turned to rage.

"Antiaircraft machine guns, mortars, rocket-propelled grenades—you name it, they had them. I held the forward battle position, running through a gauntlet of enemy fire to resupply ammunition and defend our position." My chest constricts, and I pause, swallowing the bile rising in my throat. Tristan places his hand over mine, giving me the strength to continue.

"There was no break in the fire, no pause button, no time to think or plan or pray. All I had was my rifle. I took aim and did my part to beat them back, protecting our position. We fought for hours, battling unrelenting enemy fire. Whenever I saw one of our guys go down, I ran out and carried him to safety. I don't remember breathing, I don't remember being shot, and I sure as hell don't remember the impact that nearly left me dead. They tell me I ran through rocket-propelled grenades and machine-gun fire several times, recovered our squad's radio, enabling someone to coordinate our evacuation. I remember a soldier pinned down and exposed to the enemy, and I remember going after him. I have a vague memory of going down and thinking no fucking way would the guy I was carrying die because I couldn't get up. They tell me I carried him seventy meters through enemy fire and fought to return to my post."

Memories fire off in my head. My instinct is to pace it off, but I don't. I can't. As if guided by something stronger than myself, I turn my hand over and link my fingers with Tristan's.

"I woke up a couple days later in the hospital. The next day I learned that my grandmother had passed away hours before I'd woken up. And what's really effed up is that I saw her. I know it couldn't have been real, but I swear to you, T, before I woke up in that hospital, I saw her. She took my hand just like this."

I lift our joined hands and place my other hand over the top of his.

"She said it was time to come home." I've been thinking about that moment for months, replaying it in my mind, trying to figure out if it was real or if I'd somehow dreamed it up. I never told my mother when she came to visit me. I never mentioned it to a soul until now. I let out a long breath, feeling like a weight has lifted from my shoulders.

"And she meant here?" Tristan asks.

I nod. "She'd been asking me to settle in Harborside after my tour was up. The last letter I received from her included a list of the galleries and stores carrying her sculptures. She suggested that they might be interested in carrying my furniture when I'm ready. She told me who to contact about buying a truck, which I did when I first arrived so I could move my stuff from storage when I'm ready. And of course she'd been telling me about you for months."

"That's why you missed the funeral."

"Yeah. I would have done anything to be there, but I was really messed up."

"Thank you for trusting me enough to share that with me." Tristan stretches an arm over my shoulder and takes my other hand in his.

He doesn't ask any more questions, though I'm sure he's wondering about the extent of my injuries, and he doesn't make a big deal about the lives I saved. I'm most grateful for that, because I have never understood how one soldier is considered more heroic than the next. We were all fighting the same war, all giving everything we had and *more* to keep each other alive.

I don't know how long we sit there with the sounds of the sea and my admission swirling around us, but by the time I take

Tristan home the bond between us is stronger and the foundation of trust now goes both ways. I owe him more of an explanation, but tonight I opened a door that I never saw myself opening, and it's all I can do to make it back to my own bed.

For the first time in months, when my head hits the pillow I no longer feel like I'm standing alone in the middle of a battlefield.

CHAPTER EIGHT

Tristan

FRIDAY AFTERNOONS ARE always the busiest at the Taproom. College kids flash fake IDs like library cards, and tourists come in droves. Livi and Charley want all the details on Alex. They're used to me sharing information about the guys I date, but I find myself hesitating. I tell them we went to the Spot and about how smoothly he handled Ditzy Dinah, but I don't share any of the details about Alex's past. I know how hard it was for him to share them with me, and I feel protective of him because of that.

I'm clocking out when Wyatt comes through the back door. "Tristan, I'm glad I caught you." He pulls me into Cassidy's office. In addition to working part-time with Brooke, Cassidy handles the books for the Taproom. She looks up when we walk in.

"Hey, guys." Her eyes move curiously between us as Wyatt closes the door.

"Hey, babe. Sorry to barge in," Wyatt says. "I wanted to talk to Tristan in private."

"Want me to leave?" Cassidy stands, and Wyatt shakes his head.

"No. I just didn't want everyone else to hear." He turns to me. "Are you sure you want to volunteer to work part-time this winter?" Wyatt asks. "I haven't mentioned it to anyone, but you're my priority. You've worked here for years, and my father wouldn't want you leaving. *We* don't want you to leave."

"I appreciate your asking, but I'm cool with it. It's only for a few months." I dig my keys from my pocket to keep him from seeing my face. The Taproom has been such a big part of my life for so long, I know it'll be hard when I'm not here full-time. I'll miss everyone, but it's the right thing to do.

"All right. Then let me be a real asshole and ask you what I've been stressing over ever since you offered to take the hit." Wyatt puts his hands on his hips, and it's a stance I remember his father doing anytime he was uncomfortable with a conversation.

"Wy," Cassidy warns, and shakes her head.

"I know it makes me a prick," he says to Cassidy.

"But you'll do it anyway." She sighs and turns her attention back to her computer.

Totally lost, I ask, "What makes you a prick?"

"That I don't want you to find something part-time that leads to full-time and we lose you altogether."

I can't suppress my smile, because while Wyatt's been working hard to fill his father's very large shoes and handle the business in a professional manner, his heart is every bit as big as mine.

I pat him on the shoulder and reassure him as much as myself. "It would take an act of God to keep me from coming back."

He lets out a long breath.

"Told you!" Cassidy comes around the desk and takes Wyatt's hand. "He's been stressing over this so much. I told him you wouldn't leave for good." Then she takes my hand and adds, "But I also told him that if or when you do, that's your prerogative, and he needs to man up and realize that one day you might find something different that holds your interest."

"I love my job, Cass. I love working for Wyatt and Dee, and with everyone here. I'm not going anywhere."

"But one day you might want to do something more, and Wyatt needs to accept that. That's part of being a friend *and* an employer."

"The sucky part," Wyatt says as we walk out of Cassidy's office.

"I'm not going anywhere. Full-time or part-time, you're stuck with me."

On the way home I mull over my decision. If Jesse and Brent's restaurant were open, helping them get off the ground would be a no-brainer, but it's nowhere near completion, and none of the others in the area are appealing to me. I don't just love what I do for a living. I like knowing I'm helping Wyatt and Delilah keep their family's business afloat. Nothing about this change is easy, but nothing worth doing ever is.

After showering, I find Brandon leaning against the kitchen counter scrolling through his phone. His straight black hair hangs in his eyes. I've been suggesting he get it cut now that he's working out and looks less like a starving artist, but so far he has no interest.

"How was your date with alpha boy?" he asks without looking up.

"Wyatt told you?" I grab my keys from the table and lean on the counter across from him. I told Alex I'd swing by after work, and I'm anxious to see him.

He lifts his eyes. "I saw you two sucking face on Shab Row. It was *hot*."

"Eyes and hands off," I warn him. "Why didn't you say something?"

He shakes his head, and his hair dances around his eyes. He pushes from the counter and stretches his arms over his head, then shoves his hands in his pockets and leans against the counter again. Brandon's a night owl, and chances are he's just woken up. He works as a graphic artist, taking on just enough work to keep money in his pocket, and he plays in a band with Brent Steele and a few other guys. I got in at two in the morning after my date with Alex, and Brandon was sitting out on the deck playing his guitar with some chick I'd never met. When I got up for my run at six thirty, he and the girl were heading into his bedroom, which is across from mine on the first floor.

"I was with Delilah and Ash, walking into the Sandbar to meet friends for a drink, and I know you've been hard up lately, so I wasn't about to cock block you. Especially not with that fine piece of ass." Brandon grins. "So, how was he?"

Brandon's filter is set to skirt every line there is, but he's a good guy, so I tend to give him shit right back or ignore the comments I don't like. He's had a rough time with his family, and the brash exterior is full-on rebellion, just like his head-to-toe black attire. I choose to ignore his question.

"Who was the girl you were with this morning? Is she still here?"

"Tawny, and no way. She got me off and I sent her on her way." His phone buzzes, and he picks it up off the counter and reads the text. "You bringing your man candy Tuesday?" Brandon's band is playing at the house, and we've invited a few friends over.

"His name is Alex," I clarify. "I am, and he's a good guy, Brandon. Don't pull any shit."

"I take it your self-imposed break is officially over?"

"Looks like it."

As I turn to leave, he grabs my arm, and his tone turns serious. "Tristan, you sure he's a good guy?"

"Am I sure?" I know my track record for being a good judge of character when it comes to boyfriends sucks, and the truth is a hard pill to swallow, but today seems to be the day for dealing with hard shit. "Yes, papa bear, I'm fairly certain he's a good guy. In my gut I feel like he is, and that's all I've got to go on."

He nods curtly. "Fair enough." I catch a glimpse of mischief in his eyes. "We both know you've been through hell. If all you need is release, you know I'm here for you." He does a pelvic thrust.

"There's the no-boundaries Brandon I know and love." I shake my arm from his grasp. "Not happening. *Ever*."

He laughs. "Probably a good thing. You can't handle a guy like me anyway." He drapes an arm over my shoulder and walks with me toward the door, fidgeting with my shirt and smoothing my pants like a doting aunt.

"Be safe, little one," he teases in a high-pitched voice. "Remember, honey, you shouldn't kiss boys on the second date, but if you decide to get down and dirty, use a condom."

"Idiot," I say as I pull the door open.

"That's 'sexy idiot' to you," he calls after me.

Ten minutes later I drive down the road leading to Alex's house. The nearest neighbors are pretty far down the beach, which was one of the reasons I visited Arty so often. She was adamant about retaining her independence, and I worried that if she fell or became ill no one would find her for days. I'm glad I was wrong about that. I push away the sadness that follows the thought and park behind Alex's motorcycle and truck.

I follow the sound of music around to the open kitchen door on the side of the house. Alex is inside leaning over a workbench. He's shirtless, pushing his right hand along the length of the wood he found yesterday on the beach. The scratchy *swish* of sandpaper is barely audible over the music. My eyes are drawn to the scars and dimpled skin marring the contours of his thickly muscled torso, trailing down his left flank and disappearing beneath the waist of his low-slung jeans.

I take a step back, feeling the impact of the pain he must have experienced and remembering how upset he was when I'd touched his scars last night. I freeze in a moment of indecision, desperately wanting to walk through the door and let him know the scars don't affect me in the way I'm sure he worries they will and equally as anxious to duck out of sight and give him a heads-up to my arrival. I know he would prefer to reveal his scars when he's ready, and I back off the patio, promptly stumbling over a bush.

Alex spins around, and his mouth curves up in a way that tells me he's missed me as much as I've missed him, and just as quickly that happiness fades and he reaches for his shirt.

"Please don't," I say as I find my footing and walk inside. I gently take the shirt from his hand.

"T, please." His eyes plead stronger than his words, and it just about kills me to toss his shirt aside, but I need him to know this isn't something that should stand between us.

I tug off my shirt, holding his gaze. "Level playing field," I say with a smile, and as I'd hoped, his crooked smile slides across his unshaven cheeks. The reserved expression I saw last night comes down like a mask, and I pretend I don't notice. I'm determined to keep his internal grief at bay.

"I missed you today." I put one hand around his waist and kiss his neck.

"T." It's still a plea, but with a different cadence.

I sense that he doesn't want to be alone in his anguish, and I know he's too manly to say so. I step closer, holding our bodies together. Feeling uncertainty in his rigid stance, I tighten my grip around him. Somewhere in my mind I acknowledge that this is where I belong. This is where I'm at my best. Opening my heart, helping others through their anguish. That's always been where I shine, and in relationships, that's always led to me being taken for granted. I wait for the impact of the feeling of weakness that usually comes on the heels of this acknowledgment, and for the first time in my life, it doesn't come.

He closes his eyes and breathes deeply, letting me in instead of pushing me away. I know this is at least as tumultuous for him as telling me about how he got the scars was last night, and I'm determined to distract him enough that he has no choice but to accept that these scars don't have to own him.

He opens dark and troubled eyes. I can practically see the movie of his past playing in his head. I'm with him on the battlefield, surrounded by rapid fire, taking each hit as he does. I know he wants to push me away, and I'm up for the challenge.

"My badass alpha has a tender spot for me, and I want to own it."

"Tristan, it's not that easy."

"Nothing in life is easy." I touch his cheek, and he leans into my hand. "I know you need to bridge this gap to move forward, and I'm well aware that we're new. That I could be left in the dust—"

"That's not it."

"Let me finish. I'm not stupid, Alex. I know what I'm risking, that I'm putting myself right back where I swore I never would. But this is a risk I'm willing to take. You've made it clear, no promises. And I wouldn't ask for any. Promises are usually broken. But this is the only way I know how to be. If we have a chance together, we need to get through this."

He softens his tone. "You could get a guy who isn't quite so broken."

"You're not broken. You're scarred. You carry your scars on your body. I carry mine on the inside. We're no different, Alex. Can't you see that?" There's only one way to distract him to the point of allowing us to move forward. I press my lips to his warm pecs, run my hand down his bare chest, and feel him go hard against me.

"As I recall, I owe you a blow job."

I reach for the button on his jeans, and he grabs my wrist. I twist from his grip and push his hand to the side.

"We can do this one of two ways," I say sternly, knowing exactly what he needs. "You can give in to me, or I can make you."

When he doesn't respond, I turn his rigid body to face the workbench, and he reluctantly follows my lead.

"I only care about your scars because they make you the man you are." I kick the inside of his right foot, spreading his legs, and pin him with my hips against his ass. He's breathing hard, but I can feel the difference between anger and fear. The adrenaline pumping through him has nothing to do with anger toward me, of that I'm certain. I curl his hands around the far side of the workbench, and he glares at me over his shoulder with a mix of heat and threat.

"Tristan."

I press my hand between his shoulder blades, holding him against his efforts to rise. "By the time I'm done with you, you're going to be begging, not warning."

I touch my lips to the top of his spine. His muscles bunch against the imprisonment, but as I kiss my way down each of his vertebra, I feel his body reluctantly surrendering.

"Relax, Alex. I see *you*." White lines stretch like gnarled fingers from his sides toward his spine, leading to thicker, jagged scars along his left side. I trace them with my tongue and his body stiffens again.

"You're perfect," I say, moving my hands down his sides. "Take a deep breath, Alex."

He follows my command, and his head drops between his shoulders. I kiss my way over the jumping muscles near his waist on his right side. He breathes hard, struggling to accept my touch. I wrap my arms around him and press a kiss to his back, feeling his heart thundering wildly.

"Relax, Alex. I've got you."

"T." A quieter warning.

"Shh. Be with me. I can tell you hate not being in control, but you've been in control your whole life, and you need this."

His hand comes off the workbench, and I know he can overpower me. I widen my stance, strengthen my position, and his hand grips mine.

"That's it, baby," I coax. "Trust me."

My free hand plays over his abs, along his scarred ribs, to his peaked nipples, lingering there, letting him know he's still every bit as attractive as when he's in control. His hand tightens around mine, and he presses back against my cock. I've never wanted to be the one in control, but I know he needs this, and I want to be what Alex needs. Our movements are intense and tentative at once. I withdraw from his grasp and run my hands along his neck, over his cheeks, to his luscious lips. He opens his mouth and sucks my fingers, inciting a greedy moan from me. My other hand moves south, and I palm his rigid cock through his jeans.

"Mine," I say, squeezing enough to feel the full girth of his heat, and bite down on his shoulder. His body jerks beneath me, and I continue stroking him, kissing my way down his body. I have never been the one to claim. I've always been claimed. I've changed over these past few weeks, but I know that's not what's causing my internal switch to be flipped. Yes, I've gotten stronger, but here I am, putting my heart at risk *and* doing things I haven't done before. I have no doubt this surge of confidence, this change in me, is caused by Alex. Or more specifically, by the gravity between us.

His back is exquisite, despite the scars, and as I kiss and stroke, the scars fade away, and all I see is the man slowly giving in to the pleasure. I tug open his jeans, and he tries again to rise. I force him back down with my body.

"You will not win, Alex. I'm not going to fuck you, but I'm going to get your cock in my mouth one way or another, and you know you want me to." I slick my tongue around the shell of his ear, then delve inside. "Did you jerk off thinking of me last night?"

He makes a sound deep in his throat, and I push my hand inside his jeans, fisting his cock. "How about this morning? Did you think about me while you came? Was it my cock in your mouth or in your ass?"

"It was *my* cock in *your* ass," he growls.

"Even better," I say, and slide my thumb over the slickness

at the tip of his erection. I push my other hand into the back of his jeans, massaging his firm cheek.

"Fuck," he mutters, rocking from fist to palm.

I'm thankful his jeans are loose, as they give to the force of my hand moving between his cheeks to his hole. It clenches against the invasion.

"Mine," I say again roughly, enjoying the empowerment of taking control.

"I top," he says just as harshly, and as I force my finger into his ass, he curses.

"We'll see about that." I tease and stroke, and when I withdraw from his ass and his cock at the same time, he lets out a hiss.

I grab the waist of his jeans and tug them down his hips. He spins with the force of a tornado, grabbing my wrists so tight I have no doubt he can break them. His face is flushed. His eyes are dark and hotter than sin, and his jeans are stuck around his thighs.

My eyes drop to the tattoo on his chest, to the gnarled and puckered skin on his hip, and finally, to his mammoth cock bobbing between us, and I lick my lips in anticipation. The warning in his eyes is clear: I'm stepping close to the fire. But I want his fire. I want his rain. I want whatever he has to give.

"Let me touch you," I whisper, and press my lips to his, kissing him tenderly. As I reach for him, he tightens his grip on my wrists.

"You can touch me." His tone is angry, but I know it's vulnerability I hear, not anger at me for wanting him. "Do *not* lower my pants, got it?"

"I promise," I assure him. "Now let go of my arms, or I'm going to make you."

Despite his frustration, the beginnings of a smile curve the edges of his luscious lips.

"Now," I demand.

His grip loosens, and I guide them to the edge of the workbench, curling his fingers under. "Hold tight, baby, because if you even try to move my hands again, I swear I'll turn you around and fuck you so hard you won't be able to sit for a week."

Alex

"I DON'T BOTTOM." I scoff at Tristan's threat, but my cock twitches at how enticing it is.

He strokes his hand over my cheek and roughly clutches my face, his eyes darkening seductively. "I don't usually top, but mark my words. I'm going to."

I grit my teeth, unwilling to fight a battle I'm not sure I want to win. He kisses me again, so softly it's surprising, given the atomic vibes thrumming through the room. He bites down on my lower lip and gives it a tug, sending a bolt of heat through my core. His hands move over my scars, but his eyes never leave mine. I clench my teeth, preparing for the questions I know he must have, for the pity I'm sure he feels. But his eyes are dark pools of desire, and as his hand glides down my side to my mangled hip, he presses his palm flat against my scars.

"I see *you*, Alex," he says, void of pity or uncertainty. "I feel *you*."

His hand slides to the front of my thigh, and I widen my stance, trapping my jeans midthigh. His brows slant, and as understanding dawns, he brings his other hand to the back of my neck and pulls my lips to within an inch of his.

"It's so easy to get lost in you," he says. "I already forgot."

This time he kisses me hard. His hand moves to my throbbing cock, and my thoughts unravel with every stroke, every plundering thrust of his tongue. The primal sounds spilling from his lungs make me want to slam him against the bench and fuck him until he comes so hard he can't breathe.

"Love your mouth," he says, then slicks his tongue over my upper lip, sending rivers of heat straight to my balls.

He steps back and pulls a chair over, then shoves me into it. I land with a *thud*. He unzips his pants and holds his hand in front of my face.

"Lick," he commands, and like a dog to his master, I wet his palm.

He fists his cock with a dirty-as-sin grin, and drops to his knees between mine. Watching Tristan stroke himself as he takes me in his hand and swirls his tongue over the head of my cock nearly makes me come. I *did* jerk off to the image of him sucking me off last night, and again this morning, but this is a thousand times hotter. As he lowers his mouth and takes me to the back of his throat, I can't control the hungry sound that escapes my lungs, or keep my hips from bucking off the chair. I grip the sides of the seat, watching as his cheeks hollow out, fill with me, over and over again.

"Tris, *fuuuck*." I fist my hands in his thick hair, not guiding—he's perfect just the way he's moving, but I want to touch him. I want to feel him trembling as he takes us both up, up, *up* to the verge of release.

"It's been too long," I say, my hips rising off the chair, wanting to bury myself to the root. I feel his throat relax, and he swallows me deeper. Holy fuck, I'm going to explode.

"I can't hold back," I warn, giving him time to release me if he doesn't want to swallow, but he strokes me faster with his hand and works me into a blithering frenzy.

Lightning sears down my spine, through my balls, and I lose it, coming so hard a stream of indiscernible noises flies from my lungs. Somewhere in my head I know I'm pulling his hair too hard, but my eyes are slammed shut and the pleasure is too intense to break free. I come until I feel drained to my very soul, and he takes every last drop. When the last shudder rolls through my sated body, he rises to his feet, bringing his cock within an inch of my chest. I'm fucking salivating as his hot, sticky come drenches my chest and he grunts out my name.

My senses fill with the scent of his arousal. He leans down and ravages my mouth. I can't think, can't see. I'm consumed with Tristan. I taste myself on him, and when he straddles my lap, deepening the kiss, our chests a sticky, slippery mess, I have no memory of him stripping off his pants. All I know, all I care about, is that he's here, holding me, kissing me, making me feel like I didn't lose a piece of myself in that war—instead, I found a door leading to him.

CHAPTER NINE

Tristan

I FEEL LIKE I've been wrung dry as I reluctantly rise from Alex's lap and reach for his hand. We're both moving slow, in that drunken, post-orgasmic place, trying to pull the pieces of our brains back together. He grabs his jeans as he rises to his feet and secures them around his waist.

I glance at our sticky chests and lean in for another kiss. "You're a little addicting, so if you're going to be a prick, can you do it soon?"

He laughs.

"I'm only half kidding," I say more seriously. "It'll hurt less now than later."

He frames my face with his hands and kisses me. "I'm not Ian, so stop waiting for me to turn into a prick." His jaw clenches, and he adds, "Besides, you're testing me at every turn, so you're getting a pretty good dose of my attitude."

"If that's all you've got, I can deal with it. Come on, let's shower." I take his hand and step toward the living room, but he doesn't budge. I look over my shoulder, and his face is a mask of darkness.

"No, T."

"No…?"

"I'm not showering with you." He releases my hand, and both of his curl into fists, but his gaze softens. "I'm sorry. Not yet."

I step toward him, kicking myself for forgetting it's not just the scars on his hips and back he's worried about. I wonder what's going on below his knees, but I don't push it.

"I'm sorry. I wasn't thinking clearly. I just wanted to be with you." I try to lighten the mood and lead him toward the bathroom. "Come on. You can watch me shower, and I'll come back out here and fantasize about you in all your naked glory until you're ready for more."

We laugh and joke while I shower, and afterward, I give him the privacy he needs and step outside the bathroom. A few minutes later, when I can wrangle my thoughts away from the fact that he's naked one room away, I take a brief walk outside to clear my head. When I return to the living room, I push open the door to Arty's studio, looking over the unfinished furniture I remember from my visits and her unfinished sculptures on her worktables. Alex's arms circle my waist from behind, and I smile.

He presses his lips to my cheek and says, "I'm sorry about those scratches on your back. They're from the kitchen wall, aren't they?"

He must have seen them when I was in the shower. "Yeah, no biggie."

He whispers "sorry" again, then bites my earlobe.

"Hey." I turn in his arms. "What was that for?"

He looks hot in a pair of fatigues, a black shirt, and boots, and he smells as fresh as the breeze whisking in through the open windows.

"Because you opened the studio door when I told you I'm not ready to face it."

I search his face and see he's not nearly as uptight as he was when I suggested we shower together. "I know," I say softly. "I'm sorry."

"T, if you want to see me be a prick, then keep pushing."

Despite his warning, I take a step away from the open studio door, giving him a clear view inside. "I don't want to piss you off, but I knew her, Alex, and she adored you. I don't think she'd want to stand between you and your ability to move forward." When he doesn't respond, I add, "You said you saw her before you came to at the hospital. Don't you think that means something?"

"More than you know." His eyes never leave mine.

"Then shouldn't you honor whatever it is? You can talk to me, Alex. You don't have to deal with this alone." I reach for his hand, and he takes it willingly.

"She told me it was time to come home. Here I am, Tristan. Right where she wanted me. What more do you want from me?"

"I only want you to find peace in all of this. You're struggling with so much, and I want to help you through it. I can't help with the bigger things, but this is something I can be here to help you through. I know what it's like to have to move past a loved one's death. When Wyatt's parents were killed, we all pulled together to help him and Delilah figure out how to move on."

When his hand tightens around mine, my instinct is to pull him closer, but I've opened the door, and I give him space to find his footing and decide where we go from here.

"I think she died to save me," he says quietly.

His confession guts me, and I move in front of him, forming a protective barrier between the studio and the man I want to heal, not hurt.

"The world doesn't work like that." I say this hoping to make him feel better, but what do I know about these things? One look at him and I know he doesn't need to hear what might make him feel better. He needs me to tell him the truth, even if it's as confused as he is. "I do believe in some kind of connection to those we've lost, but I don't buy that your grandmother would have the power to..." *Make herself die?* "Do that."

"Maybe not," he says absently. "But what if when I got injured, it was too much for her, and then..." He shrugs.

"Alex, Arty lived a long, happy life. I don't think what you're describing is what happened, but if it were? Then that's the ultimate sacrifice for love, isn't it?"

He lifts a conflicted gaze. "She could have lived longer. I could have come home and taken care of her."

"And the minute she *needed* you to take care of her, she would have been miserable. She was the most independent woman I've ever known. She was eighty-nine, Alex, and I can't tell you how many times she told me that when I noticed signs of her cognitive abilities failing I should send her out to sea on a raft—and not a sturdy one. She was quite specific."

He smiles a little. "She told you that, too?"

"Often," I say with relief. "But even if you believe all of what you've said, you can't possibly think she'd want you to feel guilty for the rest of your life. She didn't have a spiteful bone in her body."

His gaze moves over my shoulder toward the studio. "Do you feel her presence?"

"Sure. This was her house."

Relief washes over his face again. "You do? So it's not just me?"

"Listen, you've got yourself wrapped up in what it all means. You were injured in the line of duty, and that couldn't have been easy news for her to hear, but this isn't a movie. People's hearts don't just give out at the sound of bad news. She survived her *husband*. If there was a time to go, it would have been then. According to Arty, she thought the world of him. It was probably just her time, and out there in the spiritual world, you crossed paths and she told you to come home. Be thankful you saw her one last time. Don't try to put guilt where it doesn't belong."

I gaze into his eyes and give him the only thing I have left to offer. "Even virile soldiers are allowed to grieve. If you're afraid of falling apart when you walk in there, don't be. I'll go in with you, and chances are, I'll fall apart, too."

Alex

"YOU'RE NOT EMBARRASSED to admit that, are you?" I have no doubt that the sole reason my grandmother tried so hard in all her letters to get me to come here is standing before me, pushing me, helping me, making me feel better in too many ways to count.

"Why would I be? I loved her like she was my own grandmother. I cried the day I came to see her and found out we'd lost her. I cried at her funeral. I'm not ashamed of those things. Wouldn't it be more shameful to feel nothing?"

The truth doesn't come swiftly. It comes bumpy and painfully, like it's been dragged up a craggy rock face. "I don't know what I'll feel when I walk in there. I might cry, or I might get angry. Or, Tristan, I could just…"

"Not be able to breathe?" he asks. He reaches for my hand. "Then it's a good thing I'm with you. Let's go in, and if you can't take it, we'll turn around and walk out. We can try again another day."

"I'm not used to all this touchy-feely comfort you're giving me." I squeeze his hand.

"You're used to doing things the army way. Suck it up and push through it without bitching?"

"Yeah. How'd you know?"

"I didn't. You just told me."

I don't understand any of this. I don't know why he's willing to push me when he's been hurt so many times in the past, or how he knows I need it. But I'm thankful, because I do want to get past all of my baggage.

"I'm a suck-it-up-and-push-through-it guy," I admit. "I always have been. Why am I having such a hard time now?"

"I have no idea," he answers. "Maybe because you're finally with someone who is telling you it's okay not to be that way."

"It is harder to shut myself off when I'm with you. You make me want to talk about, and deal with, my shit instead of dodging it and finding a way to live around it."

"I'm pretty awesome like that," he teases. "Ready to face the music?"

"Not really, but I will. Hey, my music…?"

"I turned it off on my way outside when you were in the shower. I had to do something to keep my mind busy so I didn't barge in on you."

I laugh, though I know he's not kidding. Tristan waves

toward the studio, and when I take my first step, he slaps my ass. I spin around with a scowl, and he holds his hands up.

"Just trying to ease the tension."

"Every time you touch me, tension rises." I snag his hand again and drag him into the studio with me.

The room feels chilly, and I notice the casement windows on the far side of the room are open. The earthy scent of clay hangs in the air. Like the rest of the house, the studio has concrete floors and walls. My grandmother's sculpting tools and unfinished artwork litter the tabletops along the walls. Her kiln sits in the far corner near the door that leads out to a patio on the side of the house, and several pieces of my unfinished furniture are stored against the wall to our right.

"You okay?" Tristan asks.

I squeeze his hand in response. I'm glad he's with me. We walk around the room, as if we're visiting a museum, taking in the unfinished pieces of my grandmother's life. There are vases and plates and figures with no faces. Rough wooden shelves hang above the tables, displaying more of her artwork. We stop before one of the tables, admiring a sculpture of a naked woman lying on her side, curled around a baby.

"She was so talented."

"Incredibly so." Tristan points to another table and a sculpture of a rowboat, complete with fissures in the wooden planks. "I asked her to teach me how to sculpt last summer. She said I'm a talker, not a creator."

I laugh. "Wow. She didn't hold anything back, did she?"

"Not usually, but she was right. I suck at drawing, so I'm sure I'd suck at sculpting."

"Maybe you and I will have to find out one day." I think about Tristan's strong hands and his tender touch. I've felt the magic his hands have to offer, and I think my grandmother might have been wrong for once.

"Alex," Tristan says softly, and nods toward a table by the patio door.

My throat thickens at the sight of a statue of a broad-shouldered soldier standing beside a flag. He's shirtless, every muscle defined. His pants are wrinkled and baggy, with boots peeking out from beneath the hem. My eyes settle on the tattoo on his sculpted chest, and my hand moves over my heart.

"Alpha Bravo Charlie, like yours," Tristan says. "I saw your tattoo earlier."

I nod, unable to look away from the strong figure my grandmother has created. It's strange to see myself without scars.

"*Alpha*, Arlene. *Bravo*, Bruce, my grandfather. *Charlie*, Caroline, my mother," I say absently. "I've never seen that piece."

He looks from the sculpture to me. "She nailed you. Look how gorgeous you are." He tugs me closer and says, "I'm *so* going to nail you."

"Christ," I mumble, and laugh. He's done it again, pulled me from my self-inflicted torture back into the world of the living.

He takes me by the shoulders and turns me back toward the rest of the room. "This was your grandmother's domain. Now it's yours. How do you feel?"

"Like it's a lot to process." I walk over to her kiln and Tristan follows. I pull it open, and dozens of little people and animals stare back at us. Silence presses in on me. We both know they're the presents she was never able to deliver to the children at the hospital.

I close the kiln, and the weight of her death comes crashing down around me. My chin drops to my chest, and I exhale a breath I feel like I've been holding for months. One more loose end to tie up.

Tristan touches my shoulder. "I'll go with you when you're ready."

How does he know exactly what I'm thinking?

I nod, acknowledging more than the fact that I believe he'd help me with anything. It's a nod of acceptance. I needed to take this step. My grandmother would want me to carry on, and she left me this house to enable me to finally create the life I've always wanted.

Tristan doesn't rush me as we begin clearing out my grandmother's things. He and I walk through the house together, choosing places to display the sculptures I want to keep. I set aside a number of pieces to give to the retailers and gallery owners who supported her over the years, and some of her larger pieces to display in my store when it finally opens.

By the time we call it quits for the day, the room is broom clean. I'm still trying to figure out how he got me to go into my grandmother's studio, let alone clean it out. He's stealthy *and* direct. If he were the enemy, he'd be my worst nightmare, but as a man, as *my* man, I respect the hell out of him.

I still have a lot of work to do to turn it into a workshop, but the ghosts are gone. And the only thing I feel when I walk into the studio is a renewed sense of determination to build the life I've always dreamed of.

"Thank you," I say to Tristan, but it's not nearly enough. I don't think anything could ever be enough to show him how much I appreciate all the ways he's pushed me—and all the ways I'm sure he'll continue to.

CHAPTER TEN

Tristan

THE NEXT EVENING, after my shift, I find Alex in his kitchen, leaning over the sink and staring out the window. His jeans hang low on his hips. The scent of freshly cut wood hangs in the air. Sawdust lies in forgotten piles beside various lengths of shelving and metal brackets. He's been busy.

I step around the mess on the floor and join him. My fingers trail over his back, and I press a kiss to his shoulder. His skin is warm and musky, and I imagine him toiling with his woodworking all afternoon. I lean my hip against the counter and take in his serious expression. When our eyes meet, his crooked smile slides into place.

He puts his hand on the back of my neck and kisses me. "I missed you, T."

"Good. I'll worry when you stop."

He moves in front of me, caging me in with his legs and arms. "Not going to happen."

"We'll see." We've come together so quickly and on so many levels that it's still a little scary. I don't like when my insecurities come out, but I've never been good at hiding them. And Alex never fails to surprise me the way he reassures me without getting angry that my ex-boyfriends have left me so untrusting. As my eyes roll over the beautiful imperfections mapping his strong body, I know if anyone understands insecurities, it's him.

He leans down and kisses my neck, holding me against the counter with his thick thighs.

"We *will* see. One day you'll spin around and six months will have passed. Then you'll spin around again, and two years will have passed. Then you'll be old and gray, and I'll still be right there by your side, proving to you that you can trust me."

He pushes away and washes his hands in the sink. "I need to finish moving my stuff into the studio tonight," he says as he dries his hands.

"Great. Let's get started, but why the sudden urgency?"

"My mother called today. She's in Vegas now," he says, as if that explains everything. He plants his hands on his hips and scans the kitchen floor, the machinery, workbench, and counters, which are all littered with bits of wood and glass, tools, and other woodworking paraphernalia.

"My whole life I've wanted to put down roots and create a meaningful, stable life, and here I am"—he waves his hand around the room—"making the one place that feels like home into a shithole. I don't want to live in chaos. I don't want your friends coming over and wondering if I'm renovating or getting ready to move out."

He begins gathering his tools. "I need to be working in the studio, and when that becomes too confining, I'll rent warehouse space somewhere or buy an old barn to work out of, but I don't want to put it off for another day. I've got new shelving ready to go up." He points to the shelving on the floor.

"I can't move my machinery or the tables without help. I

know it's a lot to ask after you've worked all day, but would you mind helping me?" He looks at me with a purposeful gaze, and everything about him—that look, his resilience, his ability to take control *and* ask for help—makes me fall even harder for him.

We spend the next several hours bringing Alex's workshop to life. We hang shelves, bring his machinery in from the storage unit across town, and we load his grandmother's worktables into the back of the truck for Alex to drop off at Goodwill tomorrow. As we organize his tools on the new shelves and clean up the mess in the kitchen, he relays stories about visiting his grandparents in Boston when he was a boy. He tells me about his grandfather teaching him to fish, to hunt, and how to use the tools he now crafts furniture with. It's obvious how close they were, and how much he misses both of his grandparents.

When he opens up about how badly he wants to make them proud, I know he already has.

Alex

AFTER TWO DAYS of tooling in my workshop, the chandelier I was building is almost finished. The room smells like cut and charred wood and heated metals, and my creativity has taken off again. I owe it all to my new handsome muse, the man who is on my mind every minute of the day and night.

Tristan.

In the week we've spent together we've become closer than the guys I spent years fighting alongside. He's really taken an interest in helping me find the right space for the retail store as well. He's got a sharp business mind, and I hope he'll want to continue helping me even after I find space, because I really enjoy working with him. We mapped out potential locations and made a list of marketing ideas. We have an appointment with Dave Jacobson this afternoon to see what I hope are viable locations. I'm excited to get the store under way.

Tristan gives me the lowdown on the different parts of town as we drop off my grandmother's artwork with retailers and gallery owners. I wasn't sure what to expect, and was pleasantly surprised when the people I met didn't dwell on the sadness of her passing and instead shared snippets of funny, heartwarming memories. Everyone in town knows Tristan and greets him like he's a long-lost relative. I knew resort towns could be close-knit, but it's different seeing it firsthand and seeing the man who's turning me inside out at the center of it. Of course, that means every stop takes forty-five minutes, but it's worth every second.

I'm glad he's with me, not only to help ease my nerves but also because he's much better with people than I am. I watch him talking with Mr. Hinkley, the owner of one of the last galleries on our list. Mr. Hinkley is a short, stout man with beady eyes that never seem to meet ours. If Tristan weren't here, I'd take his lack of eye contact personally. I'm guarded on so many levels it's not something I can hide, while Tristan has a welcoming demeanor that he extends to everyone. Watching Tristan magnifies the difference between being groomed by years of always being the new kid and growing up in a stable home and being part of a community.

"Alex, can you show Mr. Hinkley the pictures of your work?" Tristan reaches for my hand. He has unexpectedly taken every opportunity throughout the afternoon to pimp out my work. He's so smooth and unassuming it doesn't come across like a sales pitch, which impresses the hell out of me.

"Sure." I scroll through the images on my phone and hand it to Mr. Hinkley, who studies them intently.

"You're mighty talented," he says without looking up from the phone. "I'd be happy to stock a few pieces on consignment. If they move quickly, we can discuss a more permanent situation, like I had with your grandmother."

I squeeze Tristan's hand to keep from hugging the man. "That would be fantastic. Thank you." It is the third offer I've received like this today and I feel like I'm going to burst. It's hard to wrap my head around the fact that my dream might actually come true, and I know damn well I owe a large part of that to Tristan.

We talk for a few more minutes, and as we step out of the gallery and into the sunny afternoon, I take Tristan's hand again.

"Do you mind if we walk to our appointment with Dave? It's only a few blocks."

"Not at all."

"Thank you for coming with me today, and for hooking me up with Mr. Hinkley and the others."

"I didn't 'hook you up' with them. All I did was suggest they check out your work."

"You finessed them, which is something I couldn't have done. You're really good with people, T," I say as we walk past a pizza parlor that smells like heaven.

He shrugs. "I'm just myself."

"Well, *yourself* is pretty awesome. Have you started looking for something to fill the hours you'll lose over the winter? We can stop in at a few places while we're out."

"I haven't started looking yet. I have plenty of money, and

I'm not very excited about working in someone else's bar. I've helped Wyatt and Delilah keep the Taproom afloat. It sort of feels like cheating on a boyfriend."

I laugh and pull him closer. "That big heart of yours is sliding down your arm again."

When we reach the location of the available retail space, Dave Jacobson, the real estate agent, is waiting for us. I've only spoken to him on the phone, and he looks about ten years older than the picture on his website.

"Dave?" I offer a hand, and he shakes it overeagerly. "I'm Alex, and this is my boyfriend, Tristan." *Boyfriend* flies easily from my tongue, and I wonder how a military uniform can make the wonderful emotions coursing through me feel rough and wrong. Even thinking about the military makes my body go rigid.

"Nice to meet you both." He shakes Tristan's hand and turns to unlock the door. "Let's go inside and take a look around. I did a search of the area and I've got five other spaces I can show you if you have time."

We follow him inside, and the first thing I notice is how closed off the space feels.

As Dave rattles off information about square footage, utilities, and neighboring businesses, Tristan and I peruse the space.

"Does it feel like a coffin to you?" I ask quietly.

"There aren't many windows." Tristan crosses his arms and eyes the space from the back of the room. "I think you could make any space work. It's what's inside that matters. Think about the first gallery we went into today. It only had windows out front, and the space didn't feel closed in. You can set up each area like a different room, so the customer has a unique experience as they walk through."

He points to the front of the store. "If you make it interesting, people will want to walk through. You could create a nook up front with two chairs, a coffee table in between, the ladder shelves you built over there with maybe a chandelier and a table. That would allow the customer to envision the whole setup in their house."

Tristan and I discuss every inch of the space, and his vision makes me see things differently.

"Not that I'm pushing you out of your career, but, T, you really do have a knack for this kind of thing."

"Thanks. I learned a lot from Wyatt's father, which reminds me, you should get started on a website and the marketing materials you outlined in your marketing plan. Two of the people we saw today asked for brochures."

"Like I said, you've got a gift."

We spend the rest of the afternoon looking at properties with Dave. Tristan and I talk about everything from location to setup of the interior, to pros and cons of space.

At four o'clock I drive him home to get ready for work, and then I go back to meet Dave at the last property, which is located on the corner of the street where Jesse and Brent Steele's restaurant is under renovation. Windows span half of the side and the entire front of the space. The minute I walk inside, I hear Tristan's voice in my head suggesting the layout. The afternoon sunlight spills all the way to the back wall, and I feel him here with me, admiring the open, airy feel.

"Each of the properties on this block offers an outside area out back," Dave says as he unlocks the back door. "The restaurant down the street is building a patio area for outdoor dining." He opens the door, revealing a bare plot of land.

As I step outside, all I see is Tristan building a rock garden and filling it with all the ideas he's kept locked inside since he was a kid. And I know this is it.

This is the beginning of the next chapter of my life. *Our lives?*

CHAPTER ELEVEN

Alex

TUESDAY EVENING AS I drive over to Tristan's for the party, I think about my recent phone call with my mother. I told her about meeting Tristan but stopped short of giving her any details. I wasn't sure how to explain what I feel, and she always half listens anyway. Besides, I don't want her to be the first person to hear it when I figure it out. For most people it might be too much too fast. But after what I've been through, there's no such thing. She asked about the award ceremony, not that she'll remember to attend, but I realized I haven't mentioned it to Tristan, and I need to. I grind my teeth against the idea of it as I park my motorcycle behind the cars lining the road. Receiving the Silver Star is something most military men strive for, but for me it holds too many conflicting emotions to be elated over. I want to leave that day, and those years, behind me.

Wyatt's house sits on a dune overlooking the ocean. It's massive compared to my little bungalow, but it stirs no jealousy in me. I like my life to feel manageable, simple. After living in military quarters for so long, I'd feel lost in a house that big.

I follow two guys and the sounds of music to the back of the house, where clusters of people are dancing and talking on the beach. A couple is making out by the water, and a few feet away a group of people sit around a roaring bonfire. Colorful lights line the crowded deck, where the band is playing a song I don't recognize. Weaving my way through the crowd to the steps leading up to the deck, I scan the faces of the happy partygoers for Tristan. When I spot his thick dark hair and that wide, welcoming smile, my heart beats a little faster. I never knew I could miss a person over the course of just a few hours as much as I've missed him.

He and Charley, the flirtatious female bartender from the Taproom, are serving drinks from behind a long table at the opposite end of the deck from the band. I take a moment to watch Tristan while he's unaware of my presence. He laughs as he mixes drinks for eager friends and elbows Charley, who rolls her eyes. A dark-haired guy reaches over the table and kisses Tristan's cheek. Jealousy prickles my skin even though I can see Tristan isn't interested. It's obviously a friend, not a come-on. Two pretty blond girls approach the table. They're holding hands, and Tristan watches them with a thoughtful gaze. He clearly cares about them. His eyes move over the crowd, and my pulse ratchets up even more. Just as his eyes find mine, a heavy hand lands on my shoulder.

I turn and find Jesse Steele standing beside me and tug him into a manly embrace. I met Jesse and his twin brother, Brent, a few years ago, when I was here on leave visiting my grandmother. "Jesse."

"Alex? Holy shit." He searches my face. "Man, you look great. I didn't know you were in town. Are you here on leave?"

"I'm here to stay, actually. I inherited my grandmother's place."

"I'm sorry about your grandmother. Half the town showed up for her funeral. I reached out at the time and left you messages, but…"

"Sorry, man. I should have returned your calls, but I was messed up pretty badly, in the hospital for several weeks. Then I had rehab, and…Hell, Jesse, there's no excuse. I was just dealing with a lot."

"Don't sweat it. Are you okay now?"

"Yeah. Scarred, you know, but whatever." Brushing off my injuries is second nature.

"Glad to hear it."

"Actually, I just put a bid in for the corner property by your restaurant. Don't tell Tristan, though. If it comes through, I want to surprise him."

"Tristan?" Jesse looks over at Tristan. "Are you and Tristan…?"

"We are." I can't suppress the pride in my voice. "I had no idea you knew him."

"Yeah, I know him. I've known him since he was yay high." He puts a hand by his knees. "It's about time he found a good man." He looks at Tristan, who's smiling at us like a guy with a secret. "Let's get a drink and you can tell me about your plans."

Tristan watches me every step of the way, looking like he wants to tear my clothes off. I lean across the table and he meets me halfway. "Missed you, babe," I say.

"Do you know how many people are giving me the stink eye right now for this?"

"I think it's meant for me. I'm claiming the hottest guy here." I grab him by the collar and pull him into a blazing kiss.

"Geez, get a room you two." Jesse yanks me away with a laugh and drapes an arm over my shoulder. "You have no idea how glad I am you're with him." He levels me with a serious stare. "But if you hurt him, I *will* kill you."

Jesse's a formidable guy. He's my height, with dark hair that hangs past his collar. Tattoos snake down his arms to the leather band at his wrist. I know damn well he means what he says, and I wonder if he ever went to bat for Tristan against his asshole boyfriends. Knowing Tristan, though, he wouldn't have allowed it. Proprietorship courses through me. I want Jesse, and everyone, to know I'm not going to be like Tristan's exes.

"I can take you if it comes to that," I say in jest. "But it won't. That man's got me wrapped around his finger. He's already messed with my head so badly I called him 'babe.' 'Babe'? I mean, what is that? And it just came out, like I've said it every day of my damn life. I'm a *soldier*." I pound my fist against the center of my chest like a silverback gorilla. "I took bullets and nearly died. But that man up there? He turns me into melted butter, and if anyone wants to fuck with him, they'll have to go through me first."

I never could have admitted that to the men I shared trenches with. The men I fought to protect. There's something really messed up about that, and for the millionth time in the past few months, I'm glad I'm out of the military.

Tristan

IT'S AFTER ONE o'clock in the morning, and the party's gone from a crowd of fifty or sixty to a handful of my closest friends. As we often do after our parties, we're sitting around the bonfire raising our glasses to random toasts. Cassidy is circling the group with her camera, taking photos for one of her many albums. Brandon and Brent are strumming their guitars and flashing goofy grins. Cassidy lowers her camera.

"Do you have to act like fools in every picture?" she asks woefully.

Brent and Brandon shrug.

"Not every picture," Brent says, and lays his guitar across his lap. "Take one now. I'll behave."

Jesse coughs out a, "Yeah, right."

Cassidy lifts her camera again, her engagement ring glistening in the light of the moon, and Brandon puts up bunny ears behind Brent. It's a pretty typical night around here, except for the man sitting next to me, who is anything but typical. Alex's hand rests on my thigh, and he looks as relaxed as a horny man can. We've been exchanging hungry looks and heated kisses all night, but he's respectful of my friends' presence, and they've already taken to him like he's one of us. I've never experienced that before, but it's easy to like Alex, and I know what my friends see. He's been checking on me all night, never straying far, making sure I don't need anything. He's acting like a boyfriend, only it's obvious there's no acting involved. There's no pretense about the man.

Brooke holds up the beer she's sharing with Jesse and says, "To mine and Cassidy's newest clients, the Woodleys. We're catering their wedding in October." She and Cassidy work together to offer catering and photography through Brooke's Bytes. Their business has been going well, and several of Cassidy's photographs have ended up in local magazines and newspapers.

We all clink bottles and say, "Cheers."

"To the newly engaged," Jesse says as he holds up his drink.

Wyatt reaches up and pulls Cassidy into a loud, sloppy kiss.

Another round of "Cheers" follows.

"I cannot wait for your wedding," Delilah says from her seat beside Ashley. "And for a niece or nephew!"

Cassidy stumbles in the sand, her eyes wide. "What? Oh, no, Dee. We have tons of time before we even think about kids."

"She means tons of time to practice," Wyatt says with a wink.

"On that disturbing visual," Delilah says, "to Alex and Tristan."

"Now, there's a toast I can get into," I say, and touch my beer bottle to Alex's. He gives me one of his scorching-hot leers, and my body ignites.

"I'm glad you came over, Alex." Wyatt pulls Cassidy onto his lap. "Right, babe?"

She kisses him. "Definitely."

Wyatt and Delilah had such a hard time when they came to live in Harborside the summer after their parents died. I'm glad to see them both happy and settled.

Alex slides his hand up my thigh, and I want to drag his ass into my bedroom, but it's important that he has a chance to bond with my friends, so I'm trying to behave.

"Oh, good, you're still here," Charley says as she and Livi come around the side of the house. She sits beside Brandon, and he hands her his beer.

"What a night." Livi plops onto the sand beside Alex.

"I'm beat," Charley says, and takes a swig of Brandon's beer, *ahh*ing loudly. "And I'm sick of men." She points at Alex and says, "I owe you an apology. I had no idea you were gay. I never would have made a fool of myself by hitting on you."

Alex reluctantly shifts his eyes away from me and smiles at

Charley. "You didn't make a fool out of yourself."

"I have the worst luck," Charley says. "I need men to wear banners that say something like, 'Straight.' 'Smart.' 'Nice.' 'Not an Asshole.'"

"I like the 'Not an Asshole' banner," I concur.

We all laugh, and Livi nudges Charley. "What happened with Blind Date Brian?"

Charley rolls her eyes. "I don't want to talk about it."

She texted me after their date to say she'd arrived home safely, but she hadn't said a word about him since. Wyatt and I exchange a concerned glance.

Jesse leans forward. "Did he get out of line?"

"Not in a way I couldn't handle," she admits. "Why do guys *always* expect more than a kiss on the first date?"

"Because you're dating the wrong guys," Brooke offers.

"You don't want my opinion," Ash says, and kisses Delilah.

"If T and I are any indication," Alex adds, "maybe the right guy will come along when you're *not* looking for him."

Charley nods. "Maybe, but I've spent a lot of time not looking. I want someone like these guys. Someone who cares about more than just themselves and sex."

"Don't overestimate me," Brandon says with a wink.

Alex scoots close to me, and I swear we're throwing as many sparks as the fire. I need a little space to clear my lust-filled head before I throw him down and embarrass us both.

I push to my feet. "I'm going to start cleaning up."

"I'll help," Alex offers, rising beside me with a seductive glint in his eyes.

Perfect. We can slip into my bedroom.

Cassidy pulls Wyatt to his feet. "Come on, we all should help."

Before I can say they don't need to, everyone's heading for the deck. I hold on to Alex's waistband to keep him from following the crowd.

"I'm sorry this is dragging on so long," I say after the others are out of earshot.

"I like your friends, T. It's fine." He slides his hands to my lower back, holding me against him, and I can feel he's every bit as eager to get into the bedroom as I am.

"I'm glad, but I can't keep my hands to myself much longer."

"What about your 'going slow' rule?" He presses his hands harder against my lower back.

"You make me want to break *all* my rules." I pull his mouth to mine and kiss him with all the pent-up passion I've been holding back.

"Get a room," Jesse hollers over the deck railing, and the group descends on the beach.

Alex and I join the others in cleaning up, and half an hour later I'm standing at the sink washing glasses when Cassidy comes in and says, "That's the last of it."

Jesse puts a bottle of tequila in the cabinet, and Brooke pulls him outside again. "Come on," she says, smiling at me. "Ash and Dee are cuddling by the fire, and I need someone to lean on." I know she can tell I'm dying for time alone with Alex, who's talking on the deck with Wyatt.

Alone in the kitchen, Cassidy sidles up to me with a curious expression. She leans against the counter wearing one of Wyatt's hoodies, which covers her shorts completely, and asks me if I need any help cleaning up.

"No, thanks. I'm almost done."

"I really like Alex." She tucks a lock of her long brown hair behind her ear and asks tentatively, "Is he as good to you as he appears to be?"

I dry my hands on a towel and set it on the counter, meeting her hopeful gaze. She and Wyatt were best friends before they became a couple, and during the weeks when they were figuring things out, she and I became close. I know I can tell her anything.

"He is, Cass," I admit. "Why? Am I missing red flags?"

"No, and stop it," she says adamantly. "I know you don't trust your own judgment, but if there were red flags, you'd know. You knew with Ian; you just chose to ignore them." She glances at Alex again. "He's been nice to everyone, and he looks at you the way Wyatt looks at me."

"You noticed?" I'm sure everyone noticed.

She leans in closer as Alex and Wyatt come through the door and whispers, "I got a few pics of you guys. They're going to be hot."

I breathe a little harder as Alex's eyes find mine and he closes the distance between us.

Wyatt reaches for Cassidy and heads for the stairs. "I'll get the rest of the dishes tomorrow, Tristan. See you guys in the morning." We have a rule at our parties. No one from the group drives home after drinking. Jesse, Brent, and Brooke limit themselves to one drink so they can drive home since they have to be at work earlier than the rest of us.

When we're finally alone, Alex pushes his arms around my waist and kisses my neck. "Do all your boyfriends spend the night?"

"Not at the same time."

The tease earns me a jealous glare. Alex's hands tighten around me. I can feel every hard inch of him, and lust sears through my veins. The truth is, none of them have ever stayed over, because my friends disliked most of them.

"I want you beneath me, baby," he growls into my ear, and kisses my neck again, driving me out of my mind.

I grab his head and kiss him, slamming him against the counter. We both grunt at the force of the impact. I clutch his ass, and we stumble through the living room, kissing and groping, making our way down the dark hallway leading to my bedroom. He crashes me against the wall, stroking me through my jeans, and I swear I'm about to lose it.

I tear my mouth from his and reach for the doorknob. Alex pushes us through the door and kicks it shut behind him, turning the lock with a predatory look in his eyes that nearly brings me to my knees.

CHAPTER TWELVE

Alex

"YOU HAVE ABOUT ten seconds to tell me if you've changed your mind." The bedroom curtains are drawn, and the only light comes from the digital clock on the nightstand. It takes only a few seconds for my eyes to adjust. I know from how hard Tristan's breathing, and the raw passion in his eyes, he's not going to stop me. I'm trying to ignore the war going on in my head about how the hell I'm going to handle Tristan seeing my leg.

Tristan tugs his shirt over his head and tosses it to the floor. I drink in every hard muscle, every sexy inch of his broad chest and ripped abs as I pull off my shirt and close the gap between us. My hands move up his back, pressing his hot skin to mine as our mouths crash together and our cocks grind against the denim between us.

"You're sure, baby?" I ask between kisses.

He unbuttons my jeans in response, and I instinctively freeze, but I fight the urge to turn away, refusing to let my fucking leg ruin this for us. I grab his wrist and his eyes open.

"You're *mine* tonight." I devour his mouth as I unbutton his jeans and tug them down his thighs, setting his erection free. He leans back on the dresser as I pull off his shoes and help him strip off his pants.

Visually feasting on the man before me, I take my boots off. "Fuck, T. Look at you."

My hands move over his powerful thighs, up his chest, and down his flanks. I cup his balls and claim him in another demanding kiss as I stroke his eager cock. He groans, and I move us to the bed and push him down on his back. I follow him down, kissing and groping, and he reaches for my jeans again. I trap his wrist beside him.

"Alex, I want all of you," he demands.

"You'll get all of me, I promise." I unfasten my pants and push them down to my knees. I'm so fucked. I don't want to ruin this, but my gnarled leg is a definite buzzkill. And if I don't get inside Tristan soon, I'm going to lose it.

I move down his body and take his thick cock in my mouth, hoping he'll let the pants stay as they are. He grabs his head, his neck craning back as I suck him, teasing his balls until they tighten in my palm. I press my hands to the backs of his thighs, just above the crook of his knees, push his legs up to his chest, and bring my mouth to his rim.

"Oh, *fuuuck*, Alex."

He fists his hands in the sheets. I push his legs open wider and thrust my tongue beyond the tight ring of muscles. His ass clenches around my tongue, and the noises coming out of his mouth are so fucking sexy I can barely stand it. I slide my finger into his ass and lick his balls, stealing a glance at the sexy look on his face. His lips are slightly parted, glistening from our kisses, and his eyes are closed.

"Lube, baby," I say quickly. "Where is it?"

He looks at the bedside drawer. I move beside him and

open the drawer, pulling out the lube and a box of condoms. Tristan watches as I grab a few condoms and toss them beside us. I lube up my fingers and toss the tube to the other side of the bed. I kiss him as I work my fingers into his ass, and he thrusts his hips, silently begging for more. Taking the kiss deeper, I push a third finger into him. He hisses into my mouth, and I shift, moving between his legs, listening to him moan with pleasure as I continue stretching him with my fingers.

"You're so fucking sexy." I fist my cock and lean down to suck his dick as I fuck him with my fingers and stroke myself, doling out as much torturous pleasure for him as I am for myself.

"Holy shit you're talented." Tristan grabs my head, holding tight as I suck him off.

I'm in heaven, and it can only get better from here, but my need for him is too strong to deny for another second.

"I've got to have you." I grab a condom and tear it open with my teeth. He watches as I quickly sheath myself and lube up. I come down over him, pushing his legs back to his chest, my cock perched at his entrance. Our eyes meet, and I want to watch as I enter him, but I want to kiss him and feel what he feels at the same time.

"It's been a long time, T. It's going to be fast."

He laces his fingers with mine and holds them beside his head, surrendering to my will. "Take me, Alex. Make me yours."

All thoughts whoosh from my head as my mouth meets his at the same time my cock breaches his ass. I kiss him deeply and sensually, moaning at the intensity of feeling his body swallow every last inch of me, until my balls touch his flesh, and I swear

I've died and gone to heaven. I pull back and open my eyes, looking down at the most stunning creature I've ever seen. Tristan's eyes are trusting and eager and so full of emotion I feel mine stacking up inside me. I take him in another kiss and we begin to move. His tight heat draws all of me in—my emotions, my strength, my anger at my fucking leg. I press his hands deeper into the mattress like a tumbleweed gathering speed, pounding into him as I ravage his mouth, and as he tightens around me, my restraint shatters.

I tear my mouth away with the need to watch. I have to see his body taking me, see his eyes as I brand him from the inside out. He's clutching my hands, moaning and groaning with each hard thrust. I take in his incredible body, memorizing every inch as his muscles flex to the beat of our bodies joining repeatedly. His cock lifts from his stomach with our efforts. I want to give him so much, to pleasure him in every way. I pull one hand from his grasp and fist his cock, tightening with every upward stroke.

"You're exquisite, babe. Come with me," I coax.

His eyes open and I swear electric currents sear through my body at the emotions I see staring back at me. His fingernails dig into the back of my hand, and the pain cutting into my hand, the sounds of our flesh smacking together, and that insatiable look in his eyes bowl me over. His ass clenches tight, and I'm seconds from release.

"Come, T."

"Alex," he pleads, and arches off the bed.

With my next thrust, a magnificent force tears through me, as he comes in hot streaks across his chest, each of us grunting through our own intense release. When we've got no more to give, I come down over him, our chests sliding in the evidence of our lovemaking, and we kiss. The kiss is deep and raw. *Needy.* He lowers his legs to the mattress, and I push my arms beneath him, gathering him against me. We roll onto our sides. His gaze is sated and his body forms to mine.

"Tristan, baby, you own me."

I close my eyes and kiss him as I've never kissed another man, straight from my soul. I'm aware of everything: the feel of his tongue sliding sensually over mine, the strength of his fingers as he grips my back, the frantic beats of our hearts. Our bodies are slick with sweat and sticky with come, and I have no desire to move. I want to stay right there, holding him until we both fade into sleep.

"Alex," he whispers.

My name sounds like a thank-you, like I've found a piece of him that he's lost. My name sounds like I feel, and that's all he says.

As our breathing calms, his hands move down my side, and his lips press against mine. It's a glorious, luxurious feeling, to have a man I care for lying naked beside me without worrying about what anyone else thinks. In my head, I hear his name playing like a prayer. *Tristan. Tristan. Tristan.* And for the first time in my life, I know I'm exactly where I'm supposed to be.

I don't care that I'm free-falling over a cliff for him, or that I have no idea how to be a couple, or that I need to get my business under way. All I care about is the man whispering against my lips.

"Stay with me."

I am so into this man who's willing to walk through my convoluted battlefield without fear, I say, "Always."

His foot slides over my right calf. I want to feel that foot tomorrow, and the next day, and the next. It slides over my foot, up my calf again. I feel all of the stress and anger of the last year dissipating and relax against him, melting into his arms. His foot drops from my right leg to my left, and I'm hovering in a post-orgasmic daze, thinking about how good his legs feel against mine, how nice it is to be caressed by his foot, his hands, his breath as it whispers over my skin.

His foot glides down my mangled calf—and I freeze. My eyes fly open. I was so into us I forgot about my pants *and* my leg. I feel as though I've run headfirst into a brick wall.

I. Can't. Breathe.

Tristan's hands tighten around me, but I'm mentally trying to claw my way back from hell. I try to break free from his grip, but he presses his chest over mine, pinning me to the bed. I know I can overtake him, but the hurt and anger in his eyes stops me cold.

"Tris," I grind out, hating myself for being such a wimp about this, but the idea of him thinking I'm any less of a man, anything less than whole, kills me. The fact that those thoughts are also fucked up isn't lost on me.

"Shut up, Alex," he says sharply. "I won't look if you don't want me to, but I want to *feel* all of you. Unencumbered. I don't want to feel like I'm nothing but a cheap fuck, only worthy of your pants around your knees unless they fall off by *accident*."

My heart cracks wide open, and I'm powerless to restrain myself from pushing him onto his back. I have no idea when my pants came off, and it doesn't matter. *He* matters. "You are *not* a cheap fuck. Goddamn it. Here I am feeling all sorts of shit I never thought I'd feel, and now…"

I release him, ashamed at the bullshit weakness eating at my gut. With my heart in my throat, I push up to a sitting position on the edge of the bed. I take off the condom and tie it off, tossing it into the trash bin beside the bed.

Tristan rises behind me and runs his hands down my arms. I know he's making an effort by not moving to the edge of the bed, where he'd be able to see my leg. He's giving me the chance to tell him it's okay to look, and it makes me feel better and worse at the same time.

"I hate myself for making you feel like that," I say, knowing it won't fix this.

"I *don't* feel like that, but your pants came off for a reason, Alex. They came off because of *us*. If you storm out of here, it means you trust me enough to fuck me but not enough to let me in. That's cool. If that's where you are right now, just tell me. I can deal with that. But if you're debating storming out of here because you think something about you makes you a pariah, don't."

He grabs me by the chin and turns my face. I'm acutely aware of the fact that he hasn't tried to look at my leg. His eyes are full of empathy, not pity, and something much, much deeper.

"Nothing could make you a pariah. You fought for our country. You saved lives, Alex, and you *survived*. Don't put yourself in a mental prison you don't deserve because of it. Talk to me, because if you storm out without an explanation, I will not let you back in. Not tonight. Not tomorrow. Not in a month."

I know he's not fucking around, and that makes the crack in my heart deepen. He's been dicked over enough to stand up for himself, and I respect the hell out of him for it, but I still feel like I've swallowed a live grenade.

Tristan

ALEX IS SHAKING. I don't know if it's out of anger, embarrassment, guilt, or something else, but he's not in a good place right now. My gut tells me he needs to be pushed, but my heart is already too wrapped up in him to push too hard. Instead, I touch my forehead to his shoulder, listening to his fast breaths as he works this out.

"I see *you*, Alex. I want to see *all* of you." I move off the opposite side of the bed, giving him the privacy I sense he needs to deal with this. "I'm going to take a shower. If you're here when I come out, great. If you're not, it's okay."

I'm careful not to glance over as I cross the floor to the bathroom, stepping over our clothes. I hesitate in the doorway to the bathroom, wanting to hold him in my arms and feeling as though I'm turning my back on him, but I know I have to be strong. For both of us.

Forcing my feet to carry me through the door, I close it behind me, hoping he doesn't leave. I turn and press my hands to the door, fighting the urge to return to him. He's not an asshole. He's not a prick who ignores me or treats me like shit. He's a guy who's carrying so much guilt and heartache he can't see straight. Knowing that makes it even more difficult for me to be on this side of the door. I turn on the shower and step beneath the warm spray, remembering the feel of him moving inside me, the look in his eyes as our bodies joined together.

I turn my face up to the spray, washing away his touch, and I cover my face with my hands, wanting to sear it into my memory in case it's all we'll ever have.

"Fuck. Fuck, fuck, fuck."

The bathroom door opens, and as I turn in the direction of the noise, the shower slides open and I meet Alex's tortured gaze. My throat thickens as if we're being reunited after years apart. I reach for his hand, and he takes it with gratitude in his soulful eyes as he steps into the shower with me. Water trickles over his head, his chest, his back, sliding like tear streaks down his cheeks.

"This is me, T. All of me."

I don't look down at his leg. I don't drop my eyes at all. It could be scars that make him feel uncomfortable or an amputation from the knee down. The depth of his injury has no bearing on the magnitude of what he feels toward it. And after seeing how torn he was moments earlier, I'm overwhelmed by the courage it took for him to come in here and bare himself to me, no matter what his leg might look like.

Without a word, I take him in my arms, and he embraces me. His hands move up my back, cupping the base of my skull, and holding me as close as two people can get without being inside each other. His breathing evens as his body cocoons me, as if he wants to hold me against him forever.

When our embrace eases, our mouths come together. We don't speak. We don't need apologies or explanations. Not now. All we need is the safety of each other, the deep, unexplainable connection that makes him the wind to my embers, and as we kiss, all those shattered thoughts and hurt feelings fall away. He backs me up against the wall, and I go willingly, his rigid cock pressing against mine as he pins my hands to the tile wall and searches my eyes. I know what he sees, because he's torn my heart from my chest and I feel it beating on the surface of my skin, aching for him. I desperately want to heal him, to claim him as he's claimed me, but he needs this. I see it in his eyes. He needs to reclaim his spot as the alpha, and I willingly turn and face the wall, spreading my legs. His left hand clutches my shoulder, and I know what he's thinking. We have no condom. No lube. And I don't fucking care. I'm clean, he's clean, and I'm open to the pain.

I lift my hand and lace his right hand with mine. He presses against my back.

"No." He steps from the shower and I can't move. *What the fuck just happened?* As I try to wrap my head around how we went off track, he steps back into the shower behind me, and relief flares in my chest.

"I'm not going to hurt you, T. No matter how fucked up I am."

I hear the lube top flip open, and my heart swells. He interlaces the fingers of our left hands and caresses my ass with his right. His scruffy cheek touches mine, and I feel his cock press against my hole. When he pushes into me, I cry out at the sheer pleasure of having him inside me again. I feel *all* of him, his slick shaft, the ridge of his glans as it glides over the spot that makes my eyes roll back in my head.

"Fuck, T. Your ass is so hot, so tight. I've never done this bareback." He bites down on my shoulder and clutches my waist, holding me right where he wants me.

"Harder," I beg, wanting to feel everything he feels through our lovemaking—the passion, the hurt, the guilt, the trust, and finally, the release of it all.

He takes the invitation, driving into me over and over again. Then his hand drops to my cock, and he brings me right up to the edge with him.

"God, Alex. You feel incredible."

I spread my legs wider, planting them firmly so he can take

me harder. He releases my hand and grabs my hair, tugging my head back and craning my neck as he claims my mouth. Every slick of his tongue competes with the magnificent thrusts of his hard-as-steel shaft and the pump of his fist on my cock. In seconds I'm spiraling into oblivion, coming on his hand, the wall, my legs, and feeling him empty himself inside me. Then he's kissing my jaw, turning me in his arms, running his hands over every inch of my body, as if he's making sure he didn't hurt me. His eyes are glassy and serious as they search my face, and I have the feeling he's thinking about more than the electricity buzzing between us. I cup his cheeks.

"Alex, we're good, baby. We're good."

I don't know where his mind is, but I know he's wrestling demons. He blinks several times, as if a switch has flipped inside his head, and his eyes become clear as they focus on me. I don't need to know what those demons were, because I know we're moving past them.

He's breathing hard, taking me in his arms. "I'm so fucking sick of hiding. I don't want to hide from you, T."

His jaw tightens, and he drops his eyes to his leg and laces his hand with mine. As I lower my gaze, taking in his dimpled and scarred hip, I follow his leg south to the missing pieces of his calf.

"Compound fractures of my tibia and fibula. The bones broke through the skin. Muscle loss, vascular damage." His tone is solemn, his voice even, and when he squeezes my fingers, it's not hard and angry; it's warm and shaky.

My heart is beating so hard, not from the tragic details of his story, or his disfigured leg, but because I'm remembering what he said about carrying the injured man despite his injuries, and I realize just how brave this incredible man is.

"Half my calf was blown off. I was lucky. The other bullets hit soft tissue, perforated my colon. I had several rib fractures..."

He goes on, describing his hospital stay, weeks of IV antibiotics, rehabilitation, the guilt of missing his grandmother's funeral. He's pouring it all out, sharing every detail. I hear relief rather than anger, and touch my lips to his, but he continues spilling it all out between us.

"Alex." I have to say his name three times before he realizes I'm talking, and I press my lips to his again. He's shaking, and I gather him against me.

"I saved a bunch of guys. They want to give me the Silver Star for valor, but I don't want it, T," he says adamantly.

I draw back and search his eyes. I don't know much about military awards, but I don't have to. I know awards for valor are impressive, and I also know the way being in the military fucked with his head. I don't want to pressure him, but I'm curious about how he can just push it aside like that.

"I don't want it," he repeats.

I soap up my hands and begin washing him, trying to distract us both. "That's huge, isn't it? Why don't you want it?"

"It's a high honor from an institution that doesn't respect who I am as a person. *Beyond* being a soldier." His voice turns serious. "Can you do me a favor? Let it go for now, and please don't tell your friends about it. It's the last thing I want to talk about—my injuries, that day, or the award."

He must see my dismay at his asking me to keep this a secret, because he adds, "I'm sorry, T. Bad memories. I'm trying to move forward."

His shoulders drop, his eyes fall from mine, and I realize that the admission about the award is just as devastating to him as his injuries. I don't know what to do with this information, and since he's asked me not to mention it to anyone else, I tuck it away in a secret, troubled compartment to deal with another time.

We're silent as I lather up his chest and neck, the sounds of the water breaking up my thoughts. I wonder what he's thinking as he watches my hand move over his skin, and when I move to his back, his head tips forward. In relief? In surrender? I sense it's a little of both and something bigger as he lets me take care of him in a way I'm certain he's never been cared for before. I wash every scar, every rounded muscle and curve of his arms, neck, and back. I wash the swell of his ass, but I don't try to touch his legs, not yet. I want him to feel safe. With every touch of my hands, I feel tension leave his body, and I spend extra time around his shoulders and arms, the places tension seems to linger.

When I finally move away, allowing the warm water to wash the bubbles down his beautiful body, he exhales. He lifts his eyes, and the fine lines around them have smoothed. His jaw is no longer clenched.

"I'm going to wash your legs. Please don't get upset," I tell him, and kiss him firmly enough that he knows not to give me shit. We've come this far, and I know it's difficult, but he needs to know I've *got* him. I'm on his side.

He nods and closes his eyes as I lower mine. I run my hands down his thighs, trailing over a multitude of scars, and my chest constricts. His fingers ball into fists.

I wish I could have been in the helicopter when he was being taken out of the field, in the hospital when he woke up. I can't fathom the idea of him having gone through this without someone who loved him by his side. As my hands move over his

129

knees, I wish I could have been with him when he learned he'd lost his grandmother. Alex is all brawn, fierce and virile. He emits strength in everything he does, but even the strongest of men have a weakness, and I know Arty was his.

I move slowly, lovingly running one hand over each calf, feeling the difference in the two: One is whole and solid, the other a gap of reminders of all he's been through. A reminder, I realize as my hand travels over the puckers and scars lining the indentation where there should be a bulbous, muscular calf, of his grandmother telling him it was time to come home.

I take extra time loving this part of him, letting him know I'm not turned off by his injury. Letting him know I can touch all of him and it will only make us stronger. I press a kiss to his other calf, and I feel his muscles tense. When I do the same to his injured side, he lets out a ragged breath. My hands move gently over his feet. His left foot is riddled with scars.

"Shrapnel," he says gruffly.

We have different ways of showing affection, different reasons for craving it, but in the end, the emotions are the same. Deeply needed, desperately wanted, and scary as hell to accept.

I don't know how long we share this moment, how long he's held his breath, or how long it took to unfurl his fists. As I rise to my feet, his hands run softly down my arms, and I know we've begun bridging the gap between his past and his present and future. But as I take in his handsome face and his eyes come open, the fear of rejection still pools in them, and my heart aches for him.

This bridge is a long one, full of rocks and craters, but I know we can get over it. I want to help him heal, and I want to be the man waiting for him on the other side. This will take time.

Maybe even a lifetime.

"You're gorgeous, Alex," I say honestly. "I want you. *All* of you."

His mouth comes tenderly down over mine, and I know we've moved past the worst part of it. It's a kiss of gratitude and a kiss of desire. It's a kiss that holds the promise of something more.

He washes me with the same care I've washed him, and as we towel off, tension returns to his gaze, and he says, "T?"

He says it so sharply I wonder if he's having regrets for allowing me into this private part of his world. The part I know he sees as hell and I see as *him*.

"Yeah?"

"At the risk of sounding like a possessive dick..." His lips curve in a crooked smile, and it's like a gift after such a difficult time. "If any other man tries to fuck you, I might have to kill them."

There's strength in being wanted, strength in swearing off assholes and not allowing myself to be used or treated badly. Being with Alex has made me realize that shutting myself off wasn't the answer. I just needed to find my balls.

"If another man tries to touch me," I say, drawing my shoulders back and straightening my spine, "you won't have to."

CHAPTER THIRTEEN

Alex

"WHAT WORRIED YOU the most about me seeing your leg?" Tristan asks as we step out of the shower the next morning. He dries off and pulls on a pair of cargo shorts. The man has more clothes than anyone I've ever known.

He offered me a pair of his shorts earlier, but I'm nowhere near ready for that. It's hard enough getting used to the sight of my injured leg and the changes to my lifestyle. I can no longer run for miles or ride my motorcycle all day without experiencing a dull ache. I don't whine over it, but it's an adjustment. When I was in the hospital everyone told me I was lucky not to have lost the limb. They're right, and I fully appreciate that aspect, but it doesn't mean there isn't an adjustment period just the same.

"If you laugh I *will* kill you," I warn, reaching for my jeans.

He arches a brow. "A little confident, aren't you?"

"Shouldn't I be?" I step closer, unable to keep my hands off the man, and tug him against me. I never had a best friend when I was growing up, and I never went to slumber parties or had a sibling to bat shit around with. I've never known love that stems from friendship in the same depths that Tristan has with his friends. But waking up with Tristan in my arms, I feel like I'm blessed with the best of those things all rolled up into one incredible man. I cup his junk and give it a squeeze. He goes hard in my hand.

"You won't kill me," he says with a playful grin. "You love my cock too much."

I feign thinking about that and lift my eyes to the ceiling.

"Fair enough." I give him a chaste kiss and pull on my jeans. We made love again last night *and* this morning.

"So?" Undeterred by the deadpan stare I give him in response, he arches a brow.

His hair is still wet from the shower, and he runs his hand through it, pushing it away from his hard-on-inducing handsome face. I've spent years locked away in a fortress, and in no time at all he's scaled the gates, crept inside, and begun opening my blackout curtains.

"I don't feel whole," I say sharply. "And I hate you seeing me as less of a man."

He buttons my jeans for me, cups *my* balls, and says, "The way you fucked me last night? You are no longer allowed to use those words when speaking about yourself."

He tosses me one of his clean T-shirts and I shrug it on. It's tight across my chest and biceps. I lift my arm and flex, and the material strains. Tristan laughs.

"About that *less of a man* shit…" He grabs my hand, and we follow the aroma of coffee to the kitchen. Tristan grabs two mugs, fills them, and slides one to me. "Cream? Sugar?"

"You're the only cream I take, sugar."

He rolls his eyes. "Come on."

I follow him out to the deck, where Wyatt and Cassidy are standing at the railing looking out at the water. Wyatt's shirtless, and I can't help but notice he's built like he hits the gym a little too often. He's big and hard, bulbous in ways women go for. My eyes drift to Tristan and my cock twitches. *Oh yeah. Perfect.*

"Hey, boys," Cassidy greets us. She's wearing a short skirt and forest-green sweater that makes her eyes pop. "Sleep okay last night?"

"Sleep? I could hear them upst—"

Cassidy slaps Wyatt's arm, and he laughs.

Tristan and I exchange a slightly embarrassed, slightly proud look.

"Sorry about that," I say, lowering myself into a chair.

"No worries." Wyatt sits at the end of the table and pulls Cassidy down on his lap. "Paybacks are hell, though."

"Okay, can we stop the sex talk?" Tristan suggests.

I've noticed that while he dirty talks with me, he's not the kind of guy to flaunt it.

"Not a chance." Brandon's voice precedes his hand landing on my shoulder. "Man, when you get tired of pencil dick over there, stop into my room."

I push to my feet and grab Brandon by the collar. Wyatt and Tristan shoot to their feet.

"Dude? What the fuck? It was a joke," Brandon snaps.

I slide Tristan a questioning look.

"He's got no filter," he says, and nods, letting me know he's cool with this.

Well, I'm fucking not. I tighten my grip on Brandon's shirt. "Better watch that filter when it comes to my man, T. For a minute I mistook you for *Ian*." Ian's name comes out sounding foul. I release Brandon and smooth a hand down his shirt.

Cassidy laughs.

Brandon skulks to his chair. "Well played, asshole."

I walk over, put one hand on Tristan's shoulder and ruffle Brandon's hair. "Thanks, bi-boy, I try."

Wyatt and Tristan mouth, *Bi-boy*, and try to hide their chuckles. Brandon glowers at me, and I don't give a shit. I know he's Tristan's friend, and I'm sure they call each other names all the time, but he needs to know there's someone looking out for Tristan now.

Respect. Loyalty. Family. They go hand in hand in my book.

We drink our coffee, listening to Cassidy talk about the wedding arrangements she plans to make. Wyatt nods and gives us looks like he's going along with whatever she wants. After a while she looks at her phone and jumps off his lap.

"I have to go. I'm meeting Brooke and Delilah for breakfast." She kisses Wyatt, then leans down and gets in Brandon's face. "See you around, bi-boy."

Brandon sucks down the last of his coffee and leans forward, kissing her smack on the lips, which makes her laugh.

"What the hell?" Wyatt asks.

Brandon licks his lips, clearly enjoying poking the bear.

"Where's mine?" Wyatt teases, and dodges Brandon's lunge when he tries to kiss him. "Later, dudes," he says, laughing as he follows Cassidy inside.

"I need more caffeine for a morning like this." Brandon saunters casually into the kitchen.

"I'd say I'm sorry," I say to Tristan when we're alone, "but I'm not."

Tristan shrugs. "I thought it was hot. But he's really harmless."

"Got it."

"I've been thinking about what you said."

Tristan takes my hand, and I've already learned what that solemn look in his eyes means. He's going to push me about something. I bristle, but I know we need to talk.

"Alex, I am not minimizing what you've gone through, but I can't help wondering about a few things. You just spent years fighting for your country. You had a bigger purpose than half the population." He pauses, and I know he's letting that sink in.

And it does, like lead.

"And then you spent weeks in a hospital, you lost your grandmother, who somehow managed to pull you back to earth. Your body is different, and I completely understand how that can change a person. *All* of that. But, Alex, it doesn't make you less of a man."

"T—"

"Give me a second," he interrupts, and the sounds of the sea fill the brief silence. "I've only known you a short while, and already it's clear that you're a guy who needs a purpose. You protect. You take action. It's who you are. Maybe you're confusing what's making you feel less whole. You're looking for retail space, moving forward with your business, so I'm not sure what I mean by this, but maybe something else is holding you back from feeling like you are the same person you were before you got injured."

"Years of bartending made you into an armchair therapist?"

"Am I off base?"

I squeeze his hand, pulling him closer, and I have to smile, because he sees what I haven't wanted to face.

"I've never met anyone like you. You don't take what anyone says at face value. Not your friends and not me. So, no, Dr. T, you are not off base. There's validity in your observation, but getting through it is another story altogether."

"What's standing in your way?"

Push, push.

"A ghost." I swallow the urge to leave it at that. "I haven't been to the cemetery yet."

"You'll know when you're ready."

"I'm not sure I'll ever be ready. I still feel responsible." I lower my eyes, and he lifts my chin, forcing me to meet his gaze.

"I know you do, and that feeling may never go away. But maybe it doesn't have to. It's more important that you don't let that guilt keep you from saying goodbye to the woman who meant so much to you. You need closure, Alex. No matter how much it hurts."

LATER THAT AFTERNOON I hear from Dave that my offer was accepted on the property in town. I can't wait to tell Tristan, but there are a few hoops to jump through first. It's a lease-to-buy agreement, and there's paperwork to be signed and details to be worked out, so I decide to keep it to myself until everything's in order and surprise him when it's finalized.

I work on the chandelier, but my mind keeps returning to my conversation with Tristan. Regardless of how far I've come with the studio and moving forward with the business, the guilt surrounding my grandmother's death is mind-numbing. On one level I know it's ridiculous to blame myself, or even to feel guilty for not being at her funeral, but that does little to assuage my anxiety when I think about those things. I set down my tools and stalk through the house. My grandmother liked things open, as I do, which is why most of the furniture I build doesn't have doors and drawers. I like transparency, which I'm sure is one reason I'm falling so hard for Tristan. He lives his life the way I've always *wanted* to live mine.

The fucking military stole that from me.

It's time to move on.

Time to slay the enemy, only this one lives in my head.

I grab my keys from the counter and head out the door, knowing exactly what I need to do—and wondering how Tristan knew it before I did.

When I arrive at the cemetery, my determination wavers. Beyond the sea of headstones, a graveside service is taking place. Mourners stand in black attire, their eyes downcast. I turn away, fighting the guilt of not being there for my grandmother's service.

Like raindrops in my mind, the location of my grandfather's gravesite trickles in. I cross the grass in the opposite direction of the service, remembering the feel of my grandmother's hand in mine when we attended the service for my grandfather. She believed life on earth was a rehearsal for bigger and better things. As I approach her grave for the first time, I see her stone set beside my grandfather's, and I catch the scent of lilacs. A wave of comfort moves through me.

I drop to my knees and my throat thickens.

"I'm here, Gram, and I'm sorry it took me so long."

As I shed my first tears over her passing, I tell her about the fateful day that landed me in the hospital and about the days after I woke up and the weeks of recuperation and, finally, of the vision of her that brought me back. Words spill from my lungs unbidden, and when a *thank you* falls from my lips, I press my finger and thumb to my eyes, trying to ward off the flow of tears it brings.

I sit back on my heels, and when I regain control of my emotions, I tell her about the first time I saw Tristan and how it feels to be with him. I tell her about my plans for the store. As I pour out my heart to the ghost of the one person who was always there for me, stood up for me, and accepted me for who I was, goose bumps rise on my arms.

She's with me. She'll always be with me.

I wipe the tears from my eyes and clear my throat.

"You never blamed me, did you?" I shake my head at my stupidity. "I was so messed up about letting down my team by getting injured, and my leg, and losing you…" I push to my feet and scrub a hand down my face, feeling guilt turn to under-standing. "I need to be here, Gram. I need Tristan."

As I walk back to my motorcycle, the layers of guilt peel away, revealing more of the resilient, confident, and determined man I once was. The man I'm destined to become once again. The man Tristan deserves.

CHAPTER FOURTEEN

Tristan

"ALEX, COME LOOK at this list. See what you can add." I set my notebook on the table and put my coffee cup on it to keep the pages from lifting with the ocean breeze. It's Friday morning and we've been brainstorming marketing ideas for Alex's store while he works on his designs.

"Alex?"

"Hm?" He looks up vacantly, blinking his baby blues in confusion. It should probably annoy me when he disappears into his designs, but it doesn't. It's at these times that his creativity really runs wild, and it leads to amazing creations.

After a beat or two he shakes his head, sets his notebook aside, and looks at mine. "Sorry."

I laugh and shake my head. "What are you working on?"

He checks his watch. "Something for the store. Let's go over this one more time so we can get going."

"Going?" I'm off work for the next two days, but as far as I know, we don't have plans beyond trying to finalize marketing ideas for his store and meeting everyone for drinks at the Taproom later tonight.

"I have someplace I want to take you." He reads through my

list. "These are fantastic. Let's get out of here and we can talk more about it in the car."

"I found a few properties that are on the market. I thought we could drive by and see if they'd work."

He picks up our notebooks and reaches for the door. "No need to drive by. I trust your judgment. Come on. We've got to go."

"I thought you wanted to work on the marketing plans."

"I do, but this is more important."

Alex gives up nothing as we drive out of Harborside. Every question I ask is met with a Cheshire-cat grin. Forty minutes later he pulls off the highway and follows desolate roads lined by pitch-pine trees out to what feels like the ends of the earth. Alex pulls down a dirt driveway lined with a knee-high rock wall with statues, repurposed bottles, plates, buttons, and other paraphernalia embedded into it. Gorgeous plants spill over the sides of the wall, and bushes sprout up unevenly, their spiny branches pointing in all directions. He parks at the end of the driveway, which overlooks a small pond, and we climb from the truck.

Although I can't see a house, a metal arbor leads to a set of stone steps that disappears behind giant bushes.

"Where are we?" I ask, in awe of the eclectic setting.

"This is my grandmother's friend Metty Barrington's house. I've known her since I was a kid. She and my grandmother met at an artists' retreat when they were our age. My grandmother used to take me with her when she visited Metty for the weekend, and Metty would come to Boston and stay with my grandparents. She was the one who convinced them to look for property in Harborside. I thought you might enjoy meeting her and seeing her gardens, so I reached out to her. She emailed directions this morning and said she'd love to see us."

As we walk beneath the arbor and up the steps, I realize he's put aside the work we were doing for his store to take me here.

"Alex, that's..." *Thoughtful? Romantic? Too awesome for words?*

"What boyfriends do," he says, and nudges me up the steps.

The stairs wind through overgrown gardens bursting with colors, textures, and gorgeous plants of varying heights, the hallmarks of New England gardens. Massive boulders and small groupings of rocks appear throughout, along with sitting areas with moss creeping over jagged-edged rocks.

The stairs lead us to a mulched path with more leafy plants cascading over rocks and creeping along the edge of the path.

"Alex, I'm blown away." I stop walking and point to a bench made of driftwood, recognizing the intricate designs. "Yours?"

He nods. "I made it the first year I was in the army, when I was home on leave. Metty had taken care of my grandmother that winter when she had the flu, and it was a thank-you gift."

"Okay, let me rephrase. I'm blown away by the gardens *and* by you."

"Shut up," he scoffs.

At the end of the path is a tiny cedar and stone cottage that looks like it came directly out of a fairy tale. The shutters are a vibrant green with coral, yellow, and red flowers painted like vines snaking along the edges. The trim is painted bright purple, and potted plants line the perimeter of the house. Flower boxes are placed at varying heights along the walls, making the cottage itself look like a garden. Ivy climbs the corners of the building and snakes over the gutters, hanging down like thick bangs.

The front door opens and a willowy woman with thick gray

hair steps outside and throws her arms open. "Bruce Alexander Wells, get that fine ass over here."

Bruce Alexander? Fine ass? The woman looks to be at least in her mid-seventies, though she dresses like she's at Woodstock, with multicolored wide-legged pants and a gauzy blouse with sleeves that hug her biceps and widen at the cuff like trumpets. Her headband matches the mulberry, red, orange, and green design in her outfit, and she's got a ring on every finger.

"And you must be Tristan," she says, running an assessing gaze over me from head to toe. She lifts her finger and twirls it. "Spin. Let's see what you've got going on."

"Metty," Alex says with a laugh.

I hold my hands up like I'm being frisked and turn in a circle.

"Okay, you pass." She throws her arms around me and plants a loud kiss on my cheek. Then she squeezes my face and turns it from side to side. "Damn, boy. You are one fine specimen."

Alex pulls me away from her, laughing again. "Okay, that's enough." He turns to me and says, "I forgot to mention, Metty's as big a flirt as she is a gardener and artist."

She waves a dismissive hand. "You've only got so many years on this earth. Might as well enjoy them. Come on around to the patio. Let's chat."

We follow her around the house and down a hill, passing rock garden after rock garden, to a small stone patio overlooking the pond. She waves to the chairs and lifts a pitcher from the table.

"Tea?" she asks.

"Sure, thank you," Alex says.

She fills our cups and sits with a dramatic sigh that softens the fine lines in her sun-drenched skin. "Tell me how you're doing, Alex."

Alex fills her in on what he's planning for the business, and they talk for a few minutes about his grandmother. It's nice to see him with someone with whom he has history. He probably doesn't have many people like that in his life. Metty's eyes turn serious, and she leans forward and cups the back of his injured calf. Alex bristles. I hold my breath. Metty's eyes remain trained on him.

"Now," she says with the same firm tone my mother has used on me a million times. "Tell me how you're *really* doing."

Alex's eyes drift to me, and surprisingly, a crooked smile slides into place.

"Good," he finally answers, returning his attention to Metty. "It's an adjustment, getting used to not being able to carry eighty pounds of equipment and haul ass for miles, but I'm getting there."

Until now, I've been focused on Alex's issues with his leg stemming from the scars. As they talk about what it was like for him to go from carrying men out of battle to not being able to run for long distances without pain, I realize how shortsighted I've been. Now I understand what he meant when he said he didn't want me to think of him as any less of a man. The fact that he kept that to himself shows how much of a man he really is.

When Metty turns that welcoming smile on me, I know I'm in for the equivalent of a parental interrogation. Alex gives me an apologetic look, and I reach for his hand, letting him know I'm totally cool with this. I've dated guys for months and never met their family members. Metty seems as close to family as Alex has, other than his flighty mother. I feel honored that he's brought me into this special part of his life.

Alex is proving to be all the things I've ever dared hope for and never thought I'd find.

CHAPTER FIFTEEN

Tristan

OVER THE NEXT week, Alex and I fall into what Charley calls *happy, horny coupledom*. Alex works on his furniture while I'm at the Taproom, and he often stops in for lunch when I have the afternoon shift. Charley and Livi are constantly teasing me about the way Alex and I look at each other, and I can't deny that the man makes me hard with nothing more than a glance. Even when we're not together, all it takes is a thought about the things he says or does and I want him all over again. Most nights we don't make it to the bedroom until after we've devoured each other. Not only have our lives come together, but ever since the party, my friends have all gotten closer to Alex, too. Since we're not the quietest of lovers—which is also new to me; I'm totally digging not having to hold back—we spend nights together at Alex's house.

After a particularly grueling Friday-night shift, I come home and find Alex still in his workshop. He's sitting at his design table, hunkered down over a drawing, and he rises as I come into the room, reaching for my hand. I've never been with a man who's this attentive. It feels like we've been living together for months instead of dating for weeks.

"Hey, T." He embraces me and asks how my night was.

"Good. Busy. Normal Friday night. I'm glad to be home." *Home* comes out so easily it should probably jar us both, but it doesn't. "How about you?"

"I had a great day, but I realized we never cleaned out the kiln. The pieces my grandmother made for the kids are in there."

"I wanted to talk with you about those." Although he's gotten over me seeing his leg, whenever I bring up his award he brushes me off. So I came up with another way to bring some perspective to his military stint with the hopes that he'll change his mind about accepting the award.

"You've got your 'push Alex' face on."

I run my hand down his chest. I love his chest. I love the heated look he's giving me right now, like he's debating sidetracking me with sex. When I move my hand from his chest, he looks amused, and as eager as he is worried about what's going to come out of my mouth.

"I did some research, and it turns out there's a pediatric physical medicine and rehab clinic on the army base just a few miles from town."

He clenches his jaw.

"I thought it might be a good idea if we brought the pieces to the kids there. I called, and—"

"You called?" His brows draw into a conflicted slash.

"Yes. I called, and they have a support program on Tuesdays for the kids. I know it's not the same as what you've gone through, or what you're dealing with, but I thought it might be nice for you to go in and talk to the kids, and bring the things Arty made. I think it might help them." *And you.*

"They're kids, T. How's seeing me going to do anything for

them?"

"They're kids and you're a war hero. You can wear your uniform and bring the gifts from Arty, and—"

"I'm not a fucking hero." He paces, flexing his hands repeatedly.

"You are, even if you don't want to accept it. We should talk about your award at some point. When is the ceremony?"

He glowers at me. "Can we just get through one big thing at a time?"

"I think this is all part of *one big thing.*" I put my arms around him, ignoring his reluctance, and hold his angry stare. When I brush my lips over his, his lips part for me, and I feel the tension in his body ease. I know all it would take is a few strokes of his cock for him to give in to me, but I want him to meet me halfway on this, not give in to get laid.

"We're making headway, babe. But if you think it's hard to lose part of yourself, or to look different, how do you think children feel? You're a sinfully hot, virile man." That earns me a sexy smile. "You're strong enough to get through it, and clever enough to know how to camouflage it."

I pause, feeling tension rising in him again with the accusation. He needs to hear this. He is camouflaging his leg, and how long can he do that? And he deserves that award. I did some research on that, too, and found out that it's the third-highest military decoration for valor. I can't let him disregard something that he might regret when he's had some time and distance from the parts of the military he hates.

"These kids have got years of dealing with assholes ahead of them. Years of enduring hurtful stares and questions they might not be prepared to answer. They'll have to face the discomfort of being around kids who may shy away from them, for no other reason than because those children don't understand, or know how to deal with, a child who looks different."

I brush my hand over his jaw, marveling at his strength and his vulnerability. He already owns my heart, and it terrifies me to admit this to myself, but there's no denying the way I feel. Even if his body can't be as whole as it once was, I want him to feel as whole to himself as he does to me.

"It costs you nothing more than an hour of your time, Alex, and I'll be right there with you."

"It's not just about accepting my leg and my scars. You don't get it, Tristan."

"No, I guess I don't, but you have a chance to do something good here. If not for yourself, or for us, then for the kids."

"T," he says softly. "Why do you push me so hard?"

"Because even though I like you just the way you are, I can tell you're not there yet." I kiss him tenderly. "You still think part of you is missing. I think the part that you lost left you a stronger man, but until *you* feel that way, those ghosts you're wrestling with will never leave."

After a long moment, he turns back to the kiln, and I gaze out the window wondering how I can feel so fulfilled being with someone who has so far to go to find himself. The strangest part is, I don't see his leg or his angst with the military as obstacles we need to navigate around. I see them as issues we need to deal with together.

When Alex turns around, he's holding the statue of himself that his grandmother made. I hadn't realized he'd put it in there, and I wonder where he's going to put it. It's a gorgeous piece, and the resemblance to Alex is impeccably done.

He runs his fingers over the length of it with a thoughtful gaze, and then he holds it out to me. "I want you to have this."

My chest constricts, remembering the look on his face when he first saw it. "I can't, Alex. What if we don't—"

"T," he cuts me off. "I know we haven't been together for even a month yet, but it feels like much longer. You can doubt us until the cows come home if that's what keeps you sane, but I want you to have this. You never got to see me without my scars, and this is a damn good replica made by a woman we both loved. She loved you, and she's a part of us. She led me to you. It really would mean a lot to me if you would accept it."

I'm too overcome with emotion to speak.

He places the statue in my hands and pulls me against him. "I'm falling for you, T," he says in a rough voice, holding me so tight I can feel his heart beating against my chest. "You can worry all you want, but I'm not going anywhere."

I've waited my whole life to find someone who would treat me like Alex treats me. To find a man who is as loyal and emotional as I am. Here I am, in the moment I've dreamed about, and I feel like I'm standing at the end of a tunnel and the world is zooming around me. I hear Alex in the distance, beckoning me, repeating what he's just said over and over, and behind me, shrouded in darkness, are all the men who have hurt me in my past. Evil laughter spews from them as they beckon Alex over to the dark side. And there I stand, wanting to run full speed ahead into the arms of the man who has yet to lie to me, make me feel small, or unimportant, but I'm too damn scared to breathe.

CHAPTER SIXTEEN

Alex

TUESDAY MORNING I lay in bed watching the sun creeping slowly across the backs of Tristan's legs. He sleeps so soundly that as I turn on my side and run my fingers along his back and over the swell of his ass, he doesn't wake. I press my hand flat on the back of his thigh, remembering the first night we made love. Even now the thought of when we first came together brings a burst of heat to my chest. His hips are strong, his legs are muscular and well defined, and I wonder, not for the first time, what it would be like to have all that power, all his *emotions*, driving into me. He's beautiful inside and out. No matter how close we get, I want to be closer.

I trace the back of his thigh and ride the arch of his calf all the way to his ankle. I thought he deserved a man who was whole, a man who had no deficits, but Tristan makes me feel like I am whole. *He's* making me whole. Filling in all of the empty places inside me. He's stable and loyal. He's loving and smart, and I can't imagine how any man could have ever treated him like he was anything short of perfect. I've been lying here wondering why I let him talk me into going to the military pediatric pain clinic today, but in this quiet moment, I know there's nothing I wouldn't do for him.

I move over him, inching down between his legs, and caress his ass with light circular strokes. I touch my lips to his upper thigh and slick my tongue over his warm skin. He moans sleepily and hikes one knee up beside him, raising his ass a little higher. I kiss my way up his thigh, over his firm cheek, and slide my tongue along the crease, earning another sexy moan. I love when he moans. I love hearing what I do to him, seeing his muscles tense with desire. Goose bumps chase my touch up his skin. I continue my silent assault, kissing his other cheek, licking his succulent skin, until he's writhing against the sheet, his hips rocking as if I'm beneath him. I part his cheeks, loving him with my tongue where I loved him with my cock last night.

"Aw, baby," he says in a heated voice, and goes up on his knees, opening his legs wider and giving me better access to the places I crave.

Lust thrums through my body as I bring my mouth to his balls. His hips push back, and I circle his hole with my finger until he's rocking with need, trying to guide me where he wants me. Only then do I push my finger in deep, inciting another greedy moan. The man drives me crazy, his taste, his touch, his sexy noises. I flip him onto his back and claim him in a passionate kiss.

"T," I pant out. "God, T. I want to be inside you, but I want to watch you."

I roll onto my back and his eyes go nearly black. "Sit up," he says roughly.

I push myself up to a sitting position. "You're the only man I'd let *command* me to do anything." Seeing him take control is a whole new high. He straddles my hips and guides his cock into my mouth.

"That's it, baby. Suck me." He palms the back of my head, cupping my jaw with his other hand as I take him to the back of my throat. I love the feel of his hands on my face. They're strong but gentle, and the combination is nothing short of erotic.

I cup his balls and his chin falls to his chest with a curse. His eyes close, and his jaw clenches. His abs are tight and his thigh muscles are pure power as he pumps his hips and fucks my mouth.

"I need you, Alex." He withdraws from my mouth and reaches for the lube.

I grab it from his hands and get us both ready; then I lay down on my back and guide his hips as he sinks down onto my cock. The feeling is out of this world. He braces himself on my chest and rides me slowly at first. He's the epitome of male perfection, and for the first time in my life, I know what it feels like to have my breath swept away by something other than force. I'm ridiculously caught up in him, and I have no desire to fight it.

When he reaches behind him and fingers my hole, my hips buck hard.

I utter a curse and a grin splits his lips.

"My new favorite game," he says with a sinful look in his eyes. He sinks down, staying perfectly, torturously still while I'm buried deep inside him, and he pushes a finger inside me. I clutch his thighs, craving his movement, gritting my teeth over the pressure mounting inside me.

"Move, T," I snap. "I need you to move."

He does, but not where I need it. He fucks me with his finger, and I swear he's got me hovering on the verge of an iconic explosion.

"One day, Alex, your ass is going to be mine."

I can't take it another second. I yank him down in a demanding kiss, wrestle him to his back, and drive my cock into his ass. I want to bury my entire self beneath his skin. I come up for air, and when I lean down for another kiss, he stops me with a firm hand on my chest.

"I *will* have you," he says fiercely. "Your ass *will* be mine, Alex Wells."

"Shut up and kiss me or I'll flip you over and fuck you from behind." Since our very first time, I've preferred making love to him face to face.

"One day you'll learn that's not a threat. I'd let you fuck me upside down if you wanted to."

"God, I love that filthy mouth."

We kiss and fuck and there's nothing careful or gentle about it. I pound into him with all the love I feel coursing through my veins, all the greed in my heart. Every thrust drives that love deeper, so deep it begins to block out the ugly things—guilt, anger, and the ache of never having said goodbye to my grandmother—until all that's left is goodness and the unlikely emotion that kept me alive for so many years. *Hope.*

I run my hands through his thick hair, kissing his mouth, his cheeks, his chin, and that hard jaw that I love so much. I wrap my hand around his cock, stroking him as we make love. He grabs my biceps, and his shredded torso rises off the bed.

"Kiss me, Alex. Kiss me while we come."

I capture his mouth, and we surrender to the unstoppable force that we've become. His breath becomes mine, and my heart becomes solely, effortlessly, and completely *his.*

Tristan

"WHAT IS IT about a guy in uniform that makes me want to cream in my pants?" I say to Alex as we walk up to the doors of the military pediatric clinic. He's a formidable man, but in his army uniform, he looks even bigger, broader, and more commanding.

Alex looks around nervously, gripping the box of mini sculptures like a shield. "Remind me never to bring you around the guys I fought with."

"Let me correct my statement." I pull open the clinic door and say, "What is it about *you* in uniform that rattles me to my core?"

"Better." A gratified grin lifts his lips. "Maybe it was the good fucking you got a few hours ago." He winks and walks inside the clinic, immediately stepping to the side of the doors to allow a family to pass behind us.

The color drains from his face. "I'm not sure what to say to the kids."

"I'm going to start with *hi*," I say, trying to ease his nerves. I touch his arm, and he bristles.

He leans out of my reach. "You can't do that here." His eyes dart around the waiting room, which is filled with military families, men and women in and out of uniform, children playing, and babies asleep in their parents' arms.

My gut knots up. "Can't...?"

"They allow, but they don't accept," he says harshly. "I told you that."

Knowing this is a tough time for him, I try to let the dismissal roll off my back, but it sticks like sap, making my skin feel too tight and unearthing my painful past, which no longer feels very far away. Alex's eyes move over the room, and I realize just how uncomfortable this visit is for him—and now for me.

The clinic is smaller than most hospitals, but the setup is the same. A large desk sits across from the entrance. Parents hold their children, the shadows of worry in their eyes masked by feigned smiles for the benefit of their offspring. Or, possibly, for themselves.

Alex's eyes shoot to me, and I see a battle ensuing behind them.

I shove my hurt and anger down a notch, telling myself this visit isn't about me. "Are you okay? If this is too much, we can go. Maybe it's too soon."

The muscles in his cleanly shaven jaw jump and he shakes his head. "No. I'm good. And I'm sorry, but I don't need to garner the wrong type of attention."

"Whatever," I say too harshly, but it fucking stings. For a guy who says he's sick of hiding, he sure slipped back into his straight jacket pretty easily.

His eyes shift over the waiting area again, and more specifically, to a little boy who looks to be around four years old sitting on his mother's lap with tears streaming down his cheeks. Alex doesn't look at me, he doesn't reach for me, but his body keels closer, and I realize this line he's drawn is not one he wants, but one that's been ingrained in his mind over eight long years. My ego took a slap, but his took a beating.

"Do you want kids, T?" he asks with a serious tone.

The question takes me completely off guard. "Um, yeah. Sure. I'd like a dog first, but sure, someday." I would like to one day have a family of my own, but given my history with men, I haven't put much hope in the idea.

He nods, eyes narrow as he watches the tearful boy. "Me, too. Let's do this."

He takes a confident step forward, and I see him as the soldier he once was: the leader, pushing past his dislike of hiding his sexuality, pushing past his fear and taking steps to help others. I didn't anticipate the slap on the wrist about my attempted minor PDA, but that's nothing compared to the emotional tumult Alex is dealing with.

I've already made arrangements with the staff, and they greet Alex with all the respect and excitement that a war hero deserves. We're brought into a large room in the back of the clinic that is set up like an enormous living room. Three young children are sitting on a carpet around a pile of building blocks, each constructing their own tower. One of the boys has a prosthetic lower leg. Another has burns along the right side of his face and arm. He has only three fingers and a thumb on his right hand. On the couch, two young boys who appear to be about eight or nine are playing with Game Boys. One of them has a cast from hip to toe. Another pair of boys is sitting on the floor in front of a television set playing Xbox. Three little blond girls with their hair in pigtails and wearing cute matching dresses are playing with a dollhouse in the corner. The youngest one sits on the floor. Her right leg is amputated just above her knee.

"The parents know you are here to meet the children and bring them gifts," the woman who brought us back tells Alex. "When you're ready, I can introduce you, or—"

"It's okay," Alex says confidently. "I don't need to be introduced. May I go talk with the children, or should I speak with the parents first?"

I'm so proud of him right now it's a struggle not to touch

him or whisper something supportive.

"You may do either, Mr. Wells," she says kindly. "Whatever you feel most comfortable with. We appreciate you taking the time to reach out."

Her last words fall on deaf ears, as Alex is already crossing the room toward the kids sitting around the building blocks.

CHAPTER SEVENTEEN

Alex

I LOWER MYSELF to the floor beside the little boy who has burns along the right side of his face and arm. He can't be more than five or six years old, and everything inside me twists into knots. He's a baby, an innocent child, and even though I have no idea how he got the scars, or why he's missing two fingers, I know whatever he went through probably hurt like a son of a bitch.

He blinks up at me with big blue eyes and long dark lashes that sweep over his cheeks. I set the box of sculptures beside me and give him my full attention. I feel myself trying not to look at his scars, and focus on his friendly, curious eyes.

"Hi," he says in a chirpy voice. "Are you a soldier?"

"I was. I got hurt, and I can't fight anymore."

"I got burns." The blue-eyed boy lifts his arm. "It was a long time ago. I don't remember it, but my mom said I cried a lot."

"I cried a lot, too, when I got hurt." I've been trying to figure out what to say to these kids all morning, and now I don't even have to think. The answers come easily.

"Soldiers don't cry," the other little boy says.

"Can I see your boo-boo?" a little girl sitting on the other side of the blue-eyed boy asks.

A chill runs down my spine. The little girl has scarring around her right ear, which is deformed. These children can't hide their scars with a pair of jeans and a standoffish demeanor. Pushing past the discomfort that's been with me since the attack is like trying to swim through sludge.

"Can we see it?" the blue-eyed boy asks.

The boys who were sitting on the couch notice our conversation has turned to show-and-tell and join us on the floor. My heart beats erratically and I search for Tristan. I don't have to search far. He's standing a few feet away, smiling down at me. He is my strength. He is my answer.

"If you tell me your names, I'll show you," I offer to the kids.

"I'm Bobby Evers," the blue-eyed boy says.

And all at once the other kids start shouting their names— Jenny, Michael, Peter, Chrissy. Within minutes the children have formed a circle around me, with curious eyes and eager smiles, like I'm Santa Claus and it's Christmas morning. Their parents watch from the perimeter, and fear comes trickling in again.

"Well, Bobby, Jenny, Michael, Peter, Chrissy—" I rattle off every single name they've shared, until they're giggling. "I'm Alex."

"My uncle's name is Alex," Bobby says. "He's a soldier, but he didn't get hurt. Maybe he's a better soldier than you are."

I can't suppress the laugh that brings. "Maybe he is." I lift my eyes to Tristan, whose arms are crossed, but the smile on his lips and his slight nod are exactly the support I need to push on.

"Mr. Alex?" Mary, a pretty little blond girl with an amputated leg, asks.

"Yes, Mary?"

She lifts the skirt of her dress and points to her leg. There's no sadness in her face, no flush of embarrassment rising on her cheeks. She's simply pointing to her leg. "I got a boo-boo, but the doctors made it all better." Behind her, a woman who I assume is her mother covers her heart with a shaky hand and her eyes go damp.

My throat thickens so badly I have to clear it. "Thank goodness for great doctors," I manage. "My doctors fixed me up, too."

I reach for my pants leg, and a little boy with a cast on his leg asks, "Did you get shot?"

"I did," I say with a modicum of unexpected pride. I'm aware of every eye in the room watching me as I pull up my pants leg, and I distinctly feel Tristan's gaze not on my leg, but on my face. Whatever pride I felt a moment ago has sunk to the pit of my gut, replaced with remorse for having to put space between us while we're here.

"Take your socks and boot off," Bobby demands as he goes up on his knees to get a closer look.

I do as he asks, and Bobby's little eyebrows pull together. "Wow. You're missing part of your leg like I'm missing my fingers."

I let out a breath I didn't realize I was holding. "Yes, I am."

"I was in a car accident," Bobby says. "Were you in a tank? Did it blow up? Or were you in a hole in the ground? Or—"

"Bobby, that's enough," a conservative-looking man who I assume is Bobby's father says.

"That's okay," I reassure him, and go on to explain, in the most child-friendly terms I can, what happened to me.

Two hours later, I've given out all of the sculptures and each of the children has shared their personal stories of what led them to the clinic. Their parents filled in the gaps, explaining about congenital birth defects that led to the amputation of Mary's leg and Michael's premature birth, which caused a stroke, resulting in a weakened leg. They were told he'd never walk, and with the help of a WalkAide, which leverages functional electrical stimulation, he's proven them wrong. I've learned more about confidence and resilience from these children than I ever did in the military.

As Tristan and I walk toward his car at the far end of the parking lot, out of sight from the entrance, I reach for his hand. Despite the fact that I've hurt him, he allows me to take it. *He* is resilience personified, and I hate myself for expecting him to be so damn resilient.

"T." The endearment hangs heavily between us. The guarded look in his eyes slays me, and I know there's nothing I can say that will make my behavior seem acceptable.

Because it isn't. Not by a long shot.

Tristan

"LET'S GET OUT of here." I pull open the car door, and Alex squeezes my hand, but I'm too conflicted to play nice. I climb into the driver's seat, and when he leans on the doorframe, my gut instinct is to tell him it's okay, but I fight it, digging deep to retrieve the balls I was so proud of finding the other night. "Get in."

"Tristan," he says, and it's all I can do to shake my head.

He stalks to the passenger's side and settles in as I start the car, trying to formulate what I want to say. My mind is a combat zone of feeling proud of Alex for following through with something I know was difficult and wanting to beat the shit out of him for dismissing our relationship the way he did.

We drive back to Harborside in silence. Alex keeps looking at me, but I can't meet his gaze. It would be too easy to let him off the hook, which part of me thinks he deserves, because I saw how hard that visit was for him. But the hurt in me runs deep, and even if it's forced deeper by past experiences, I can't ignore it.

When we pass under the arch over the road that reads HAR-BORSIDE, WHERE HEAVEN MEETS EARTH, Alex reaches across the seat and takes my hand.

"I'm sorry, T."

I glance over, and my resolve softens at the remorse swimming in his eyes.

"Goddamn it, Alex." I swerve over to the shoulder and throw the car into park. Too frustrated to sit in a confined space, I push my door open, but he's out of the car before me, and meets me on my side.

"Tristan, I know that was shitty of me."

"*Shitty?* Do you think you could have warned me? Given me the chance to tell you to fuck off before we got there?" I wasn't even thinking about telling him to fuck off, but now that it's out there, I realize how deeply this cut me. I pace beside the car, and can't stop years of anger from tumbling out. "I have never hidden who I am, and I refuse to be shoved to the side because you need to be more of a man."

Alex grabs my arm and spins me around. "Is that what you think that was about? My need to feel like more of a man? How'd you come to that conclusion, Tristan?" He walks forward with every sentence, knocking his chest against mine and forcing me back. "By the way I kiss you? The way I turn into fucking *putty* around you? The way words like 'baby' fly off my tongue after being ripped out of my heart?"

Every word hits me with the impact of a bullet, driving the hurt, anger, and confusion deeper. "So it's okay for you to fuck me here in Harborside, but the minute we pass under that sign, I'm supposed to act like you're my buddy?" I shove him backward, and he stumbles. As if there's an unbreakable connection between us, I reach a hand out to steady him and curse under my breath at my weakness.

He grabs my wrist and tugs me toward the sign. We're both panting in anger, and I want to beat the hell out of someone— only it's *not* Alex. I can see this is killing him as much as it's killing me.

I want to tear apart the military—all of them. For making him feel like he had to hide, for taking parts of him he can never get back, and for leaving broken soldiers for those who love them to put back together. And I can't decide if knowing I'd do it all over again for him and that I'd fight for him to do the right thing for *himself* as much as for us makes me weak or strong.

He drags me past the WELCOME TO HARBORSIDE sign, and as soon as we're on the other side, he crashes his mouth to mine. I fight against the assault, but my body's already his, alive and throbbing with the need to be close despite the anger coursing through my veins.

He tears his mouth away but holds my arms so tight I know he'll leave bruises. "I'll strip down right here and let you take me, Tristan," he seethes. "If you think for a second I'm trying to hide that you're my man, you're wrong. I'm trying to save my fucking sanity." He tugs me hard, and our bodies collide.

The pleading look in his eyes claws at my heart, and I don't fight him this time. We're on the same team, no matter how messed up it is.

"The military drills shit into your head, and I have no idea how long it will take to go away. But that doesn't mean it's fair or right or acceptable to ask you to deal with it. I get that, and I'm sorry. I lived, showered, ate, and fought with my team. Those guys protected me, T. The same way I protected them. We're talking about *life* and *death*, and when I told them I was gay, no matter how much I wanted to pretend I didn't see it, they *changed*. They kept their distance, made jokes about dropping the soap and all that infantile shit I heard growing up. And all I kept thinking was what happens when we're in the field? If they're covering my ass and a straight guy's, would it make a difference? Would they fight harder to cover the straight guy? I wasn't going to take that chance, and I know it's a fucked-up way to live, but it was my *life*. My life, Tristan, not a bad day at work." He pauses, inhaling deeply, and lowers his eyes remorsefully, though his grip on my arm remains tight.

When he lifts his face again, the anger has morphed to deep, gut-wrenching regret. "I'm not asking you to be okay with this. I hate myself for being too weak to step up to the plate and own who I am when I'm on base, but I'm trying. I just…It's not easy. When I see a guy in uniform, my insides freeze and my spine straightens. I'm surprised I don't salute every damn time. But I don't want to be the person who makes you feel less important than you are. I want to be the man you're proud to have by your side. *Every* fucking day."

He releases my arms, but I can't move, because the only place I want to be is wrapped around the man before me. But I also want the impossible: a guarantee that Alex will one day be able to act like he's with me regardless of who is around. Is that unfair of me? Where's the line between enabling someone to hurt me and supporting a lover through his biggest fear?

"I'm sorry," he pleads. "You can push me away, and I'll understand it if you do, but that doesn't mean I'll give up. I'm not going anywhere, T. I told you that. What we have is too good to walk away from. I would give anything to start over."

"Start over, Alex? Where? How far back? You'd still have joined the military. You'd still have gone to war…" My unsaid words play louder than any of the spoken ones—*You'd still be too fucked up to walk onto a military base and admit you're gay.*

All the anger recedes from his face, and his shoulders drop heavily.

I feel sick for acting like such a jerk and admit the truth with a healthy dose of venom. "I'm scared of making a mistake. I understand everything you've just said. I do. Life or death is a hell of a lot different than getting a sneer from someone on the boardwalk. But I don't want to worry about how you'll react if we're out in town and someone you know from the military happens to see us—or someone you don't know, which seems to be just as big a problem."

He grips my shoulders, and I bristle against my inner conflict between wanting him and needing to protect myself. He looks so conflicted, but his feelings for me ride the surface, impossible to ignore. When he touches his forehead to mine, I can barely breathe.

"I don't want half of a life with you either, T." He squeezes my shoulders and stares directly into my eyes with such sincerity my walls come crashing down. "I just need help getting there. A little understanding. A kick in the ass. A fight to the death."

I smile despite all the angst between us, because a fight to the death is exactly how the past few hours have felt.

"And I totally get it if you can't give me those things," he continues. "Because I feel like a dick asking you to. Especially after all you've been through."

His hand slides to the base of my neck, and the sounds of cars driving by compete with the sound of my head telling me he's worth taking the chance.

"I can't be on full alert every time we go someplace new," I say adamantly.

"I know."

"It is not okay for you to treat me like we're not together. Not anywhere, not for any reason."

His hands drop to his sides. "So, this is it? We're just going to be friends from here on out? Can you do that?" he says accusingly, then softens his tone. "I'm not sure I can go cold turkey from you, T."

Feeling like we've been battered in a hurricane, it takes a minute for me to realize he's misinterpreted what I've said.

"I'm not walking away from us. I'm just pissed off. I didn't see that coming."

"You should be pissed, T. I knew what I did back in that clinic was wrong, but I couldn't stop. I couldn't deal with it."

"You have to *try*. If you don't try, we have nothing." I say it much more calmly than I feel. "You can't fuck me over, Alex. If you're going to fall for me, do it like you mean it, because half-assed will never be enough."

"I don't ever want to fuck you over. But this shit is so ingrained in my head. I'm trying, and I'll try harder. I recognized it when it happened. As shitty as that is, it's a start."

I can't disagree. It is shitty, but he's right. It's a start.

"Now you see why I don't want to go to that stupid award

ceremony? The whole system stands for all the wrong shit."

"The whole system doesn't stand for the wrong shit. The military stands for the right things. It's the politics of some of the people in it that are wrong."

He squints like he wants to argue the point, and I try not to think about how we'll navigate a ceremony if we can't even deal with visiting a frigging clinic.

"You fought for our country. That's honorable. You deserve the award, Alex, and you're going to the ceremony."

He clutches my hand. I know we're in the same dark place, facing fears that are bigger than either of us. The question is, are we strong enough together to win this battle?

CHAPTER EIGHTEEN

Tristan

AFTER A RESTLESS night's sleep, I get up early and go for a run, thinking about yesterday. I know Alex wants to get past whatever bullshit the military has pounded into his head, but the thought of feeling like I did at the clinic again makes me nauseous. I run a few miles up the beach to Wyatt's house and find Brandon on the deck drinking coffee. His hair is disheveled and his eyelids are heavy, as if he's been up all night.

"Hey, man," he says as I ascend the steps. "Where's wifey?"

"He's not a runner." It strikes me that I'm doing a different type of running by heading out for my run instead of sticking around to have this conversation with Alex. I sit at the end of the table feeling like a coward.

"And you haven't been running since you two first got together. Trouble in paradise?"

That's an astute assessment for the man who knows nothing about relationships, but then again, this is Brandon. He's not stupid; he's just rebellious.

"A little."

The doors to the deck are open, and I hear Delilah and Ashley come downstairs. When they see me sitting on the deck, their faces light up. They look like beach bunnies with their blond hair and sun-kissed skin, wearing sweatshirts and cutoffs. Delilah has on her favorite black boots, and Ashley is looking at her like she's the most wonderful girl on earth. I know that feeling. My heart is swimming with Alex despite yesterday's events. I was proud of him for going in and talking with the kids and for admitting the truth to me rather than shutting down.

"What are you doing here so early?" Delilah leans down for a hug. "Ew, you're all sweaty."

"I was out for a run."

Ashley tousles my hair. "I'll skip the sweaty hug, but it's good to see you."

They sit across from me and hold hands.

"What are you guys doing here so early?" They each have an apartment a few blocks away, although I'm pretty sure they stay together every night.

"Dee and I are going up to Provincetown to hang out with some friends for the afternoon, and she wanted to grab an easel she has in the attic," Ashley answers. "But we can't get in there until Wyatt's up. Why are you here so early? Brandon said you've practically moved in with Alex."

"He has boyfriend trouble," Brandon says.

I shake my head. "I didn't say that."

Brandon rolls his eyes. "A *little* trouble in paradise, aka boyfriend trouble, which we all know means someone's being emotionally tortured."

I don't even try to deny it, because they've known me too long to think they can't read the emotions written all over my face. Besides, that's how things work around here. We stick our noses into each other's business and talk about everything, which is probably why I ran here in the first place. I needed a reality check.

"Did he cheat or something?" Brandon's jaw clenches.

"No, he'd never do that." As I admit this, I realize how easily the answer came, and how important that answer is. "Alex's loyalty is one of the things I admire most about him."

"It's what you've always wanted." Delilah's tone softens. "So what's going on?"

I tell them about what happened at the clinic, about the total mind trip the military did on him, and about the talk he and I had on the way home. It doesn't feel like a betrayal sharing any of this with them, because I need to know if I'm in too deep to see clearly. I need to know if I'm making a mistake, and I know without a shadow of a doubt that my friends will lay the truth on the line for me, no matter how much it hurts.

"I want to be with him, but I've been down this road before. Being disregarded is my Achilles' heel."

"Dude," Brandon says. "That guy acts like you're married. I don't know what you're talking about."

"He usually does," I admit. I'm careful not to tell them about the award ceremony, because Alex asked me not to, but I give them enough to help me make the right decision. "But he has an event coming up on a military base, and after seeing him yesterday at the clinic on base, I'm not sure he'll be able to act any differently when the time comes."

Delilah and Ashley exchange a knowing glance. I remember how hard it was for them when Delilah wasn't out. Helping them had come easily. It was clear to me that Delilah loved Ashley no matter how hard it was for her to openly accept her sexuality. Why is this so much more difficult? I believe in Alex's feelings for me.

"I think we know a little about this subject," Ashley says.

"Wasn't it you who told me that accepting my sexuality wasn't a race?" Delilah reminds me. "You said it was a slow progression of coming into my true self, and no one could set that pace but me. Tristan, if he's really had that much of a mind trip, then maybe it's as bad as the guilt I had about my parents' beliefs. That's not an easy thing to come out from under. You remember how hard it was for me."

"I still say loud and proud," Brandon quips.

I open my mouth to give Brandon my usual response— *Loud and proud isn't for everyone*—and snap my mouth shut.

"Holy shit," I say more to myself than to them. "I'm a hypocrite."

"So go fix it," Delilah suggests.

"We're not broken. We're just…We're walking on a tightrope. All this shit went down yesterday, and I want to help him through it. But even thinking about what it might be like knots up my stomach."

"I can't believe I'm pushing for anyone to remain in a monogamous relationship, but, Tristan, Alex adores you. The guy looks at you like you're sporting a magical dick. That's what you've always wanted—it's what you *deserve*—and we can all see how you feel about him. I think you're negating the most important thing in this equation."

I draw in a deep breath, preparing for a brash, ridiculous response, and ask, "What's that?"

"You want a guy who will walk over fire for you, but you want your path paved with sand. Man up, dude. So he has an Achilles' heel, too? How often are you on a military base? How often do you *see* military guys?" Brandon leans forward with a piercing stare that tells me for once in his life, he's not fucking around. "Give the guy a break. He needs you. And yes, you might get hurt again, but if he wasn't worth it, you wouldn't have stayed at his place last night."

"I know he's worth it, but the reason I was taking a break was because I put myself in these situations. Don't you think I'm stupid for setting myself up to be hurt? For falling right back into the pattern of being with guys who will hurt me like Ian did?"

"Ian was a dick," Ashley says.

"He treated you horribly," Delilah adds. "Alex loves you, even if he hasn't said it. I see it. We all do."

"You've changed, bro," Brandon says. "You're here. You're talking about it. You're looking at all sides of this situation. With Ian, you refused to acknowledge how badly he treated you. You're not stupid. You're just scared."

Alex

I'M SITTING ON the patio listening to the waves roll in and thinking about the last few weeks. I remember the first night I saw Tristan at the bar and the morning I saw him jogging on the beach. I was drawn to him from the very first second I saw him, and I've only gotten reeled further in with every second we've spent together.

I reach down and rub my throbbing leg, remembering how lovingly he washed it and thinking of the shock I felt the morning I woke up in the hospital almost a year ago. I thought I knew pain. Pain of my injuries, pain of losing my grandmother, pain of all those years pretending to be someone I wasn't. But none of it, even when put together, amounts to one-tenth of how much it hurts knowing I caused Tristan the kind of pain he told me he never wanted to feel again.

I can't sit on my ass hoping this fixes itself. Nothing in life fixes itself.

I push to my feet to head down the beach and look for him, when I see him jogging toward the house. My heart skips as his legs pound out a beat mine no longer can. He accepts that about me. He accepts everything about me. I need to get over this military mind fuck, no matter what it takes.

He jogs up the hill, and I meet him on the steps. My chest constricts, knowing I caused the fatigue I see on his face, and shame clings to me like a second skin.

"I'm sorry," we both say at once.

My voice sounds strangled, which is exactly how I've felt since yesterday.

"Everything we're going through is my fault," I admit. "I don't know how, T, but I'll fix this. I want to fix this."

He doesn't say a word, and I know it's because he can't more than that he doesn't want to.

"T...?"

"Alex," he whispers.

"I'm so sorry." I step closer again, and he takes my hand. I gaze into his eyes and see desire and longing looking back at me. That he wears his heart on his sleeve is just one of the many things I love about him.

"I need you, T."

"Alex," he whispers. "Every time I think about going to the ceremony, or not going to it...Every time I think about how you must have felt at that clinic, I want to kill someone. I don't know how to let it go."

His pain cuts me to my core. "You don't have to let it go.

We need to get through this together, figure it out, take it apart. I know who I *want* to be. I know how I *want* to act. That has to count for something. Can you give me time? Have a little faith? I'm fixable, Tristan. For you, I know I can be. I don't know how or how long it will take, but I *will* fix this."

Emotions well in his eyes, and he leans in so close his breath becomes mine.

"Alex—" He pushes his hands into my hair. "I believe in you. I'm just scared."

His mouth meets mine in a needful kiss, so different from our usual battle for control it takes me a minute to catch up and accept this for what it is. A kiss of mutual desperation. A kiss of hope and uncertainty, laced with determination to cross the tenuous bridge that separates us from our certain future.

When our lips part, his hands remain in my hair. "Take me inside, Alex. I need you. I need us."

We kiss as we make our way inside, but we're not rushing. This isn't the same explosive greed that has carried us so many times before. These kisses are fueled by a deep-seated need to become one, to rebuild our trust and strengthen our foundation. In the bedroom, we strip each other down, and I don't give an ounce of thought to my scars or my leg. My mind is too full with the desire to heal the hurt I've caused Tristan to think about anything else.

Taking my lover's face in my hands, I promise what I truly hope to be true. "I *will* beat this, T." I kiss him again, pouring my soul into the connection.

We lower ourselves to the bed, and as I settle between his legs, we gaze into each other's eyes. All the heat, all the hurt, and our determination to make our relationship stronger, merges into one unbreakable bond.

When our mouths come together again, the kiss is languid and loving, though our hearts hammer to a frenetic beat. Our hips take on a life of their own, grinding and thrusting, and the kiss turns possessive. Needing more of him, I deepen the kiss and shift to the side, taking hold of his eager cock. We both groan with relief as I brush my thumb over the sticky tip. His mouth devours mine, and I swear I feel the shattered pieces of us coming back together.

"Alex," he growls as I clamp my teeth over his neck and suck. "*God*, Alex. Suck me."

I move down the bed, and he clutches my head, thrusting his hips forward and fucking my mouth with the need of a sex-starved prisoner. He pumps fast and angry, banging the back of my throat with his thick, hard cock. I want whatever he'll give me. I cup his balls, tugging gently, and he groans so loud it echoes in my ears, and when it fades, I hear, *mine, mine, mine*. He drags me up by the sides of my head, claiming me in another rough kiss.

"I want you in me, Alex. *Now*. I need you close."

He reaches for the lube, and I take it from his hands.

As I get him ready, his eyes close and he whispers, "I can't think when you touch me."

"Don't think, baby." I align our bodies and push into his tight channel and lock our hands together. His eyes open, and my heart swells with love. "Feel what you do to me, T. Only you, baby."

We kiss as we find our rhythm. Our bodies fit together perfectly. We fall into sync without any awkwardness. I've never felt anything as right as when I'm with Tristan, and I refuse to let the military take this from us.

His fingernails dig into my hands, and when I kiss his neck, his head tips back, giving me better access. I suck and lick, and he tears one hand from mine, reaching for his cock. I rear up, still buried deep inside him, and push his knees back. He's breathtakingly sexy as he works his cock and his body accepts mine over and over, so tight, so willing. The sight takes me right up to the edge of release.

"Finish it, baby," I say roughly. "I want to see you come."

His eyes fly open, and heat blazes between us. He strokes himself harder, I thrust faster, and he reaches for me with his free hand.

"Kiss me," he begs.

He groans into the kiss, and the sensual sound vibrates down my spine. When he comes, his ass clenches around me, and he bites my lower lip. The metallic taste of blood spills over my tongue and I spiral over the edge, holding back the words clawing for release. *Love you, T. Love you so damn much.*

He draws back with a brutally loving look in his gorgeous eyes, and it takes all I have to hold those words back. I know he won't be able to fully accept them until I get my shit under control, but I'm so thankful for his love. I need this connection. I need *him*.

I collapse beside him, kissing him softly, and brush my hand over his handsome face. "I will slay this enemy. For both of us."

CHAPTER NINETEEN

Tristan

THE NEXT MORNING, for the first time since Alex and I began staying at his place, I wake to an empty bed. I'm not surprised, because Alex might not wear his heart on his sleeve like me, but everything he does comes from the heart, and I know he's torn up about what happened at the clinic. All of his life decisions have come from his heart—his desire to make his family proud, his drive to become a man his partner can be proud of, throwing his life on the line time and time again. Even the crappy stuff that happened at the clinic happened because he was protecting *his* heart, and that has to matter, even if it meant hurting mine. His heart is equally important.

I step from the bed and pull on a pair of jeans and the sweatshirt Alex was wearing the first day I saw him on the beach. I zip it up, inhaling his masculine scent lingering in the fabric. I thought when I met the right person everything would be easy. We'd both be swept away. Some guys dream about being football stars or running empires. I dream about having a special man by my side to love and share my life with. If that makes me a pussy, then so be it, but I have always wanted the type of life, and love, my parents have. A love I know will last through the bad times and the good. I'm not a fool. I know relationships take work, but part of me truly thought when I found the right person, everything would simply fall into place. Alex makes me realize how naive I was. Our relationship isn't the easy one I *thought* I needed, but somehow I know in my heart that he's the right man and this is the right relationship for me. Maybe *everything* isn't easy, but loving him sure is.

I gaze out the bedroom window at the sun creeping over the horizon, and somehow I know we'll find our way through this.

When I turn to leave the bedroom, I catch sight of the sculpture his grandmother made of him standing in front of a flag. Alex sees a whole man in that sculpture and someone different when he looks in the mirror. As I go in search of my tormented boyfriend, I wonder if I'll be able to help him see they're both one and the same.

There's a cold breeze coming in through the back door. Alex is sitting on the stone steps with his shoulders hunched against the morning chill. The screen door creaks as I push through it, and Alex turns. A warm smile curves his lips, and my insides melt.

"Was I too loud when I came outside?" he asks as I lower myself to the step beside him.

"You know noise doesn't wake me." I normally sleep like the dead, but I've gotten used to sleeping with Alex, and my brain has formed some kind of Alex Is Missing alarm. "Your absence is what woke me."

His expression warms even more. The way he looks at me confirms everything I feel. It's hard for me to look at him and reconcile the man I see as the uptight guy who dismissed me at the clinic. It's like they're two different people—a hurt and hiding man and a loving, caring boyfriend.

"I'm sorry," he says, and hands me his coffee. "I couldn't sleep."

We stayed up late talking about what it was like hiding his sexuality while he was on active duty, and as I look at him now, strong and brooding, I know the brooding is caused by what he's done to me. I think Delilah is right, and he is falling in love with me. He cares so deeply for those he loves, which is why he carries so much guilt about Arty. He's brooding because he wants to fix it all, and I know I'm right to have faith in him.

"I hate that I'm too weak to just make up my mind and instantly get over the military mind fuck."

"And I hate that I let it hurt me instead of just being supportive and understanding and keeping my mouth shut," I say honestly. "We both have weaknesses, but together we will ride out this storm," I assure him. "I'm not sure I could have done what you did for all those years—being a soldier and pretending to be someone you weren't. That took insurmountable strength. If anyone is capable of overcoming this, it's you."

"You stand up for what you believe in regardless of what it costs you, T. That takes more courage than being too weak to oppose ignorant people."

I take a sip of his coffee and hand it back to him. "That's all new, Alex. Before you, I sat back and took all the crap I was given."

"So why are you willing to fight dragons with me?" He shakes his head and smiles. "Don't answer that. I don't care why. I'm just glad you are."

I laugh softly and rest my head on his shoulder, gazing out over the water. I love being here with him. I love our privacy, our talks, these moments of truth.

"Because I think you're worth it, and what do you mean

you're glad?" I lift my head from its cozy perch. "Wouldn't it be easier if I shut my mouth and took it?"

He scowls. "Do you think I'd want you to do that? No way, T. I want you to be happy and to know with complete certainty how much you mean to me. I want everyone in the whole damn world to know how important you are."

He puts his arm around me and pulls me closer. "I want to walk onto a military base holding your hand, and one day I will. I want to promise you that, but I know better." He looks out over the water.

"I know you're trying."

"I want to show you I'm serious about moving forward in *all* parts of my life. I might be messed up where the military is concerned, but in every other aspect of my life, I'm not only capable of handling anything, I'm focused and driven enough to succeed."

"You don't really think I doubt that, do you?" I smile, and he returns the look, then leans in and kisses me.

"I don't know what you think, but I'm going to prove I'm the right guy for you, even with my giant, glaring faults."

I set the coffee mug down on the step below us and wrap my arms around him. "I like a few of your giant qualities a whole hell of a lot."

"Ditto, dirty boy." He leans in for another kiss.

He tastes like coffee and my badass boyfriend, my favorite flavor any time of day.

"What do you say we hit a few bookstores and just chill until you have to go in to work?"

The smile tugging at my lips gives him his answer.

He pushes to his feet and reaches for my hand, tugging me against him. "Let's take a walk before we go back in."

I notice he's barefoot, and he catches me glancing down.

He gazes down at his scarred foot. "I've got to do this some-time."

I choke up, because the truth is, he doesn't have to do any of this—let others see his foot or his leg, or be with a guy who can't handle the few times in our lives we'll be around service-men or -women.

I squeeze his hand. "You don't have to, but I'm glad you're willing to try."

CHAPTER TWENTY

Alex

WEDNESDAY MORNING I finalize the paperwork, pick up the keys, and bring in a few pieces and hang the sign I made. I still haven't told Tristan about the space, and I'm glad I waited to surprise him. By eight o'clock Thursday night I'm about ready to burst at the seams as I wait at a table outside of the Taproom for Tristan to get off work. The Taproom is busy, and I prepare for Tristan to have to stay late, as he sometimes does. I sit at a table on the pier and review ideas for the website and marketing materials we've been putting together.

Brandon saunters up to the table. "Hey. Mind if I hang with you?"

"Sure." I kick a chair out from the table and he sits down. Brandon and I have gotten to be friends over the last few weeks. He likes to push the envelope, but I can tell he's a good guy at heart.

He nods to my notebook. "What're you working on?"

"I need a website and marketing materials for my furniture business." I spin the notebook around so he can see it.

He scans the page, and his brows knit together. "Who's doing the site?"

"I have no idea yet. I'd like to find someone who can help me with all of it, business cards, promotional materials, the site."

Livi's waitressing today, and she comes over and sets a beer down in front of Brandon. "Your usual." She looks at me and says, "Your boyfriend is in there arguing with Charley over who's hotter—you or Zac Efron."

Brandon laughs, and I can tell he's holding back a smart-ass comment, respecting the line I've drawn.

"What, no comment from the peanut gallery?" Livi asks.

"I like having teeth," Brandon answers.

Livi gives me a curious look, and I shrug. "Well, if it helps, I voted for you." She smiles and leaves to help other customers.

"Thanks," I say to Brandon. There's no need to elaborate.

He sits back and stretches his long legs out, crossing them at the ankles. "For what it's worth, you're about a hundred times hotter than Efron. But if she'd have said one of the Hemsworth boys…"

We both laugh.

"Seriously?" I tease. "I think I'm hotter than Liam."

"Keep dreaming, pretty boy. When do you need the site by?"

"As soon as possible. Maybe three weeks or so."

"Three weeks?" Brandon scoffs and scratches his stomach. "That's a lifetime. I can have this done in a week tops."

"A week?"

"Piece of cake, but I think you're missing a few things on the site. You want ecommerce, don't you? The ability for customers to place custom orders online and pay for them up front? Testimonials? Pictures?"

All great ideas I hadn't thought of. "Yes, sure."

"And I thought Tristan said you make more than furniture."

"I make accessories, too." I take out my phone and show him the pictures of my work.

Brandon begins outlining an infrastructure that baffles my mind. The guy's a design savant, and he does it in about fifteen minutes flat, explaining as he outlines.

"To your customers, the landing page is like the front door. You want to visually engage them. Think of walking into a furniture store. You've got beds to the left, desks to the right, but you also have a mix of things in the entrance. The idea is to catch your customers' interest so that while they're looking at desks and beds, they're also thinking about the other stuff they saw when they walked in. The way you do that with a website is with a banner."

"Sounds good. What do you need from me?"

Brandon sits back again and locks his hands behind his head. "I'll make you a list of what I need. Details mostly, like the company name, address, and a few more specs on the stuff you have here."

"I really appreciate this, but what's it going to cost me?"

"Not much." Brandon looks me in the eye and says, "Unless you fuck over my boy Tristan."

I sense Tristan behind me before I feel his hand on my shoulder.

"Did I hear my name?" Tristan kisses my cheek as he takes the seat beside me.

"Aren't you two cute? Time for me to blow this taco stand and find a couple who wants a third spoke in their wheel." Brandon waggles his brows and pushes to his feet. He guzzles his beer and sets the empty bottle on the table. "Text me your email address and I'll shoot you a list of the things I need to get started."

"Started?" Tristan asks.

"Brandon is going to design my website." Brandon gives me his cell phone number and I zip off a text with my email address.

"Cool. He's really good at graphic design, websites, and all that technical stuff I can't stand." After Brandon leaves, Tristan sighs and says, "What a day."

His dark hair stands up like he's just pushed his hand through it. His Taproom shirt stretches tight across his pecs, and a thrill runs through me thinking about the bite mark hiding beneath it on his left shoulder from earlier this morning.

"My day just got a thousand times better." I pull him into a kiss. "How can I miss you so much after just a few hours?" I greedily take another kiss. "I've got something I want to show you."

He eyes the bulge in my pants with a sly grin. "Now we're talking."

"Come on, before I bend you over the table." I hand him his motorcycle helmet, grab mine and the notebook and eye the table.

"No," he says, and laughs.

We've discreetly stocked every room in the house with lube to avoid having to run back to the bedroom when the mood hits us—which is about as often as we inhale.

"Fine, but I make no promises about the next table we see when we're alone."

Tristan

ALEX PARKS BY Jesse's restaurant, which still doesn't have a name. He reaches for my hand and walks toward the other end of the street.

"Where are we going?"

"There's a place up here I want to check out." He points to the store on the corner.

"This place has been empty for months. It was on my list. Did you ever ask Dave about it?"

"Yeah, but it was under contract by some asshole." He reaches into his pocket and pulls something out. He flashes the crooked smile that first caught my eye and dangles a key from his fingertips.

I feel my eyes bug out. "You *bought* it?"

"Well, lease to purchase. This was the space I saw with Dave after I dropped you at home the first day we went out looking with him. And now it's ours." He points to a large wooden sign above the door with the words ARTSEA DESIGNS burned into it. "I wanted to use my grandmother's name since she pretty much led me to Harborside, and this was the best I could come up with."

"It's perfect." I remember what he said when I asked him if he was taking care of his grandmother's estate and then moving on—*In a sense, coming here is my way of moving on*—and then it hits me that he said *ours* and my thoughts stutter.

"Wait, Alex. *Ours?*"

"You've got the magic touch with people, T, and the vision for how to make this work. I'm just good with my hands. You don't have to commit, but the hours are available if you want to work with me over the winter when you cut your hours at the bar. And there's an awesome spot out back for a rock garden, I mean, if you know anyone who might want to make one."

"A rock garden?" I say in complete and utter shock.

He hands me the keys, and they're attached to a wooden charm I can tell he's made. It's in the same wavy shape as the sign, with ARTSEA DESIGNS etched into one side, and on the other he's burned a capital *A* and used the crossbar to form the top of a *T*. My chest feels full at the sight of it.

God I love this man. I know the emotions I see in his eyes are real, and the love I feel when he touches me is genuine. I've never had that certainty before, and this key ring is silly as hell, but I fucking love it, too.

"You're like a teenage girl writing our names on your notebook," I tease to keep my rising emotions at bay.

"Shut up. That one's yours." He pulls out another set of keys with a matching insignia. "This one's mine."

He backs me up against the door with a devilish grin.

"Want to make fun of me some more?" He presses his lips to my neck, and his tongue snakes along my skin. "Because the punishment will be severe."

Craving his touch after a long day of thinking about him, I play right into his hands. "It's a pretty *girly* thing to do."

With his big body pressed against mine and a serious look in his gorgeous blue eyes, he demands, "Open the door, T."

"I don't want to move."

He presses in tighter, grinding his hips against mine. "Open. The. Door."

"No way," I say, and slide my hands into his back pockets, keeping him right where I want him. I love it when he gets domineering, because no matter how much he tries, he can't do it and mean it. He's got too soft of a heart when it comes to me. He'll love the hell out of me, but he'll never physically hurt me.

"You're going inside. Your punishment awaits." He reaches around me, settling his teeth over my neck and sucking as he unlocks the door.

"Fuck, Alex. That feels good."

He grinds harder, and his hand comes around my waist. "Want to call me a sissy again?"

"More than ever."

He pushes the door open and kisses me as we stumble inside. Keeping me prisoner with one hand, he reaches behind him and locks the door. "Eight hours is a long time to be away from you."

We're on each other like depraved animals, kissing and groping as we stumble through the space. He guides me around a wall, through a doorway, and we're thrown into pitch-darkness. My back hits a piece of furniture, and he cages me in with his arms. My body thrums at the promise the privacy holds.

"Oh, look," he says with a lusty voice. "A table."

He pushes a hand between my legs and masterfully drives me out of my mind. He claims my mouth again, plundering and taking as he works the button on my jeans free and shoves his hand down the front.

"Aren't we…?" I suck in a sharp breath as his fingers wrap around my cock. "Supposed to be…?" He kisses my neck, and my thoughts spin away.

He fists his other hand in my hair, tugging to the point of scintillating pain, and continues stroking me into a panting, rocking, pleading mess.

"I fucking love your body," he says against my mouth.

I'll never get enough of his mouth—on mine, on my dick, on my ass, *everywhere.* "Show me how much."

The corner of his lips lift, and heat flares in his eyes. Without a word, he yanks down my jeans and takes me in his mouth. My eyes roll back in my head as the sheer pleasure of his hot, talented mouth pulls me under its spell. He takes me to the back of his throat, then withdraws, slicking his tongue over the head, sending tides of heat through my veins. I can't resist guiding him, clutching his head and pumping into his heavenly mouth faster, harder, and he takes every second of the invasion, moaning like he can't get enough of me—and I know I can't get enough of him.

He releases my cock and grips the root with his rough hand. His lips are red and swollen, and his eyes are fierce.

"I need to fuck you." His rough voice sends another thrill down my spine.

He rises to his feet and drops his pants. His heavy cock springs free, and my mouth waters. I reach for him, and he spins me around, pushes my hands to the edge of the table, and kicks my legs apart. His rough hands press against my sides as he sinks lower, and his tongue slides down my crack. My head falls between my shoulders.

"I have a serious infatuation with your mouth."

He spreads my ass with strong hands, and then his mouth is on me, his tongue is in me, and I feel like I'm going to explode. I hear the familiar *click* of the top of a tube of lube.

"Where—"

"Pocket," he says, and slicks lubed-up fingers into me. "But don't you worry, babe. I'll keep a stock here, just like at home."

I suck in a sharp breath with the invasion. He works me loose, sliding a third finger in as his other hand strokes my cock.

"I wanted you to come in my mouth," he says, and presses a kiss to my back.

Lust shoots through me. "Fuck me; then I'll come in your mouth."

His fingers leave my body, and for a split second I mourn our broken connection, and then his cock is nestled against my entrance. He hugs me tightly around my middle as he pushes into my body, stretching me with his formidable girth, moving painfully slowly, until he's buried to the root.

"Christ, Alex."

He fists my cock and begins to move. Pleasure spreads through me like wildfire, searing, claiming, branding me as *his*. My eyes won't stay open, my thighs burn, and my body trembles with need. I reach down and still his hand.

"Don't, or I'll come." I want to come in his mouth. I want to give him everything he desires. I want to claim *him* from the inside out, and I want it more with every hour we spend together.

He clutches my hips and pumps harder, faster, until every nerve is buzzing, we're both sweating, and my head is spinning. I cling to the edge of the table with one hand, squeezing the base of my cock with the other, trying desperately to stave off my release. I feel him swell impossibly thicker, and his next thrust brings a roar from my man as he shatters inside me. I feel every throb, every pulse.

"Tristan. Tristan," he grunts out. When the last aftershock ravages through him, he rests his cheek on my back and whispers. "God, Tristan. I love you."

My mind is spinning from the mind-blowing sex, and he turns me in his arms and whispers, "I love you, T."

He presses his hand to my face, his thumb brushes over my

jaw, and I'm aware of everything: the scent of our lovemaking in the air, the feel of our bodies trembling, the slick sweat slipping down my chest, and the adoration in my lover's eyes. He touches his lips to mine, then sinks down to his knees and takes me in his mouth, and—*holy fuck that feels incredible*—obliterates every other thought. I grab his head, guiding him to the speed I need. His voice whispers through my mind like a mantra—*God, Tristan. I love you*—ramping up my pleasure to explosive levels. He loves me. This incredible, sexy, talented, kind, honest, virile man loves me. I force my eyes open, fighting the urge to give in to the soul-searing need to come, and he lifts his gorgeous blue eyes. My breathing quickens at the sight of him loving me with his mouth.

Heat tears down my spine, and my emotions pour from my lungs like liquid fire. "I love you, Alex."

My orgasm consumes me, as erratic as a winter squall. I force my eyes to stay open, watching as he takes every thrust of the hot torrent spilling down his throat. His eyes never leave mine, and when the last of my release pulses through me, he takes me in his arms. His breath carries my scent, his lips are slick and swollen, and his eyes tell me what I already know. When he says, "Tell me again," I don't hesitate.

"I love you, Alex."

He touches his cheek to mine and breathes us in. "God, T. Hearing you say it is a million times better than hoping for it."

I fight with all my might to resist the unfair words vying for release, but years of going out with dickheads has wrecked me the same way the military has wrecked Alex, and they're irrepressible. "Just try not to deny my existence again."

He grips my face, and his eyes turn feral. "Never again, baby. Never again."

His emotions are raw, his intentions pure. I believe that with every ounce of my soul. But the award ceremony looms like a viper ready to strike, and as we kiss, I reluctantly admit to myself that some demons may never be slayed.

CHAPTER TWENTY-ONE

Alex

TRISTAN AND I spend Friday afternoon painting the store. The floor is covered in tarps and the walls are almost done. I'm still buzzing on cloud nine like a goddamn girl because my man said he loves me, and he is taking far too much pleasure in teasing me about it, which means I'm grinning like a lovesick pussy. We've been painting for hours when Tristan heads out to pick up pizza, and Brandon stops by to go over tweaks for the website and marketing materials. He's explaining the changes, but my mind is stuck on Tristan, what it will be like to work together here at the store, and how much our lives have come together over the past few weeks.

"Alex?"

Brandon is shaking his head, and I wonder if I've missed something important while I was zoned out.

"Are you sure you and Tristan have dicks? What is wrong with you? So the guy loves you. Who cares? How does it change anything? *Focus*, dude."

I'm stunned that Brandon knows Tristan has told me that he loves me. "He told you?"

"Tristan's like a girl. He spilled his guts like blood from an open vein."

Why does that make me fall even harder for him? "Careful saying my man is like a girl."

"Right. Sorry." Brandon's hand cruises through his hair, lifting his bangs out of his eyes. For a flash I get a peek at them. They're the eyes of a tortured artist. A look I know all too well.

His hair flops right back into place, the perfect camouflage.

"I get that you two belong together," Brandon says. "I mean, anybody can see that. But I don't get why anyone thinks monogamy is a good thing. There are so many fish waiting to be caught and released."

"Why is that better?"

He shrugs. "I'm just sayin'. I don't get it. Why settle when you can have your pick?"

"What's to get? It feels good to have the connection Tristan and I have. To love someone and be loved back."

"And what happens in a month, or a year, or ten years, when whatever it is that turns you on changes? What about when Tristan loses his hair or gets fat? Or he can't get it up anymore?"

I wonder where these questions are coming from. Especially since he's not nearly as close to me as he is to Tristan and his other friends. And then I realize this might not be the type of conversation he wants to have with someone who knows him that well, and that endears him to me even more.

"That's the thing, Brandon. What I feel for Tristan goes deeper than looks or sex. I mean, he's hot as sin, but he could gain a hundred pounds." I think about my leg. "Anything could happen, but it won't change who he is. I love him for his ability to accept and push, for his strengths *and* his weaknesses. I love him for being able to look past my deficits and see who I really am." I realize how true each of these statements are, and I also realize I'm telling them to the wrong person. I need to let Tristan know how I really feel about him, and I mentally begin trying to figure out how.

"You mean like your leg?"

A sharp pang slices through my chest at the thought of Tristan telling his friends about my injury.

Brandon must read my discomfort, because he says, "Tristan didn't say anything. You limp, dude. You don't wear shorts. Sometimes when you're sitting at the table your pants leg gets caught, and..." His gaze softens.

These are all things I know, and I wonder why I thought I could fool anyone into thinking anything other than the truth. I have sustained a massive injury. It's a cold, hard fact, and as I sit beside Brandon, with the topic hanging between us like a live grenade, I begin to wonder why I've let it rule me for so long.

"Not because of my leg. Not *only* because of my leg," I correct myself. "I've got a lot of baggage."

"Doesn't everyone?"

"I don't know. Probably." I wonder what he's really getting at. "Why *don't* you want those things? A special guy or girl to share your life with?"

Brandon smirks. "Because I don't want to give up either— guys or girls."

"Then we're kind of on the same page. You don't want to give up what makes you happy, and neither do I.

"Brandon, I want to do something special for Tristan, but I need your help." I've been thinking about this for a while, and I wasn't sure the best way to go about it, until now.

"Anything for my boy Tristan."

We discuss the surprise, and then we work through the

details of the brochures and a short while later Tristan and Charley come through the front door. He's carrying a pizza box above his head and Charley's carrying a six-pack of sodas and laughing. Her hair is pinned up in a ponytail, swinging as she grabs for the pizza box, which Tristan lifts out of reach.

"Look who I found wandering around Main Street." Tristan sets the pizza box on the table.

"Finally." She rips open the box and grabs a slice of pizza with two hands, then makes a big show of taking a bite. "Mm. I wasn't wandering around. I was deciding where to eat."

Brandon leans toward me and says, "Wifey's home."

Tristan smacks him upside his head.

"Loser," Brandon says.

"That's 'sexy loser' to you," Tristan corrects him.

Brandon grabs a piece of pizza. "Charley, I thought you were out this week on some shark thing with Dane."

"Dane Braden owns the Brave Foundation, where Charley works part-time. He's one of the leading shark experts," Tristan explains.

"He was going to take me shark tagging, but he had to head back to Florida. There was some kind of emergency at the foundation headquarters." Charley takes another bite of her pizza.

"Well, I'm glad you're going to be here," Tristan says, and leans against the table beside me. "My brother Brody's coming into town Tuesday. I told him we'd meet for lunch at the Taproom. I know he'll want to see Wyatt and Delilah, and anyone else who can make it. Is that cool with you?"

"Absolutely. I look forward to it." Tristan's told me about Brody, who he says is a little like my mother—restless, jumps from job to job, works his schedule around surfing, and has no real interest in settling down.

"Brody's a blast." Brandon snags another piece of pizza and takes a bite.

Tristan leans closer and lowers his voice. "Would you mind having dinner with my parents, too?"

"Serious stuff, going home to meet Mom and Dad," Brandon says.

"Serious is good in my book. Sure, whatever you want, T."

Charley finishes her pizza and reaches for Brandon's can of soda.

"Hey, there are five more right there." Brandon points to the soda cans.

She takes a sip of his and says, "Other people's drinks taste better. And Brody's coming? Hm…"

"No," Tristan says adamantly.

"T, he's your brother."

He raises a brow. "Yeah, and he plays around too much for her. Charley, he's not the right guy for you."

She rolls her eyes. "I'm beginning to believe there is no 'right guy' for me."

Brandon flashes a grin. "I'd be happy to be a stand-in for an hour."

"You know I love you, Brandon," she says. "But if I get that desperate, shoot me."

"You'll come begging eventually," Brandon responds. "Before I forget, some of my buddies are putting together a Battle of the Bands on the beach a week from Wednesday. Can you guys come?"

The event is the same day as the award ceremony. Tristan flashes a supportive glance. I know how much he wants me to attend the ceremony, but staying here and going to the Battle of the Bands sounds a hell of a lot less stressful.

When the hell did I become a no-backbone pussy?

I straighten my spine like the man my grandfather—and I reluctantly admit to myself, the military—groomed me to be. The military has taken enough from me. I fought for our country, lost part of my leg, missed my grandmother's funeral, and denied who I was as a man. All that aside, Tristan is right. The *politics* of the institution might be off-kilter, but the military serves a proud and necessary purpose, and I deserve the medal. Hell, every soldier deserves a frigging medal. But accepting the medal and accepting the mind fuck are two different things. I refuse to let that institution undermine my relationship with Tristan for another minute.

"Tristan and I will be out of town," I say to Brandon. "But we'll be pulling for you."

Tristan

ALEX AND I finish painting the store Saturday, and Sunday we move the furniture in from the storage unit. The late-afternoon light streams through the windows as we move chairs, coffee tables, desks, and the other furniture Alex has made into place. Working together, we create displays that we hope customers can easily envision in their own homes. We add books to the shelves and set up teacups with saucers on a delicate-looking table he's built from narrow and winding pieces of metal and wood. We hang chandeliers he's built from wood and various metals, situate lamps on tabletops, and carefully place candlesticks and other accessories throughout the store. We bought a few decorative throw rugs on the way over, and they give the nooks we've created an eclectic feel that reminds me of Arty and Metty.

When we're done, we walk through each area together, sitting on the chairs and benches, admiring the setup, adjusting angles. Alex's smile reaches all the way up to his eyes as he takes my hand.

"I couldn't have done this without you." He brings me closer, holding me against him. "Do you know how long I've dreamed of this?"

"About as long as I've dreamed of having a relationship like ours?" We're not perfect—no couple is. But I can't imagine loving a man more than I love Alex. "When do you want to have the grand opening?"

"I'm not sure. Brandon said he'll be done with some kind of SEO something or other he's doing in a day or two, and then we have to wait for the brochures and flyers to be ready. And there's my *boyfriend's* schedule to consider."

"Wyatt's prepared to cut back my hours whenever I'm ready to do it."

His eyes widen. "So you're really ready to commit? You're going to do this with me? All the way?"

"Aren't we already doing this *all the way*? I'm no longer sure where you start and I end."

"That's the way it should be." He kisses me with a wide smile on his lips.

"But we should look at what else is going on around town over the next month and see if we want to coordinate with any other events."

"I love that brain of yours."

I laugh. "You love a hell of a lot more than my brain." I lean on one of the tables he's made and cross my arms, watching him take it all in, and I wonder if he's as proud of himself as I am of him.

"Arty is smiling down on you right now."

"You think so?"

"I know so. You're here, in the town she adored, where she wanted you to build your life." I push from the table and go to him again. I can never stay away long. "Where, according to you, she wanted you to find me."

He searches my eyes, and I wonder if he sees what I'm not saying. And as I've come to expect from Alex, who sees so much more than anyone ever has, he touches my cheeks and says, "What is it, T?"

My throat thickens. I don't want to say what I feel, but our relationship is built on honesty. We've walked over painful truths like beds of nails, and each step has made us stronger.

"In a week and a half you're getting the award of a lifetime, and I'm so proud of you I can barely see straight. But every time it comes up, you get a tortured look in your eyes. I don't want to cause that conflict for you, so I don't want you to worry about acting like you're with me or not with me. I want you to relax and be proud of your accomplishment, because whether or not anyone else in the room knows you love me makes no difference. What matters is that you're being honored for something you deserve, and *I* know you love me."

"Tristan, the last thing I want to do is stand up and accept an award and act like you're not the man I love. Saying you'll support me no matter what is more than I ever hoped for, but it's not what either of us wants. I hope you know that."

"I do."

"But we both know there's a damn good chance I'll become instasoldier again, and *Lock down, shut up, and act straight*, will roar through my head like it did for eight long years."

"I know that, and I'm okay with it." As I say this, I know it's true. I really am okay with this concession. I've come a long way, and there's a big difference between making a concession for someone I love and being disregarded out of disrespect.

He frames my face with his hands. His jaw is tight. My attempt at easing his anxiety obviously only made it worse. "But where does that leave me in the eyes of the only man I care about?"

"It leaves you exactly where you should be," I tell him just as adamantly. "Accepting an award you deserve, being a proud soldier and a proud boyfriend, even if only in your heart."

CHAPTER TWENTY-TWO

Tristan

TUESDAY MORNING ALEX receives a phone call from Mr. Hinkley inviting him to speak at the Harborside Gallery Association meeting today at noon, the same time we're supposed to meet Brody for lunch. He paces the living room, rubbing the back of his neck the way he does when he's stressed, and arguing with me about going.

"I'm not going to miss meeting your brother after I've already committed," he insists.

"Brody won't mind. You'll see him tonight at dinner with my parents. The association only meets every two months. This is the perfect time to go and get your name out there before the grand opening."

"Tristan." He glares at me. "It's not about Brody minding; it's about not letting you down."

Alex has been trying so hard to do all the right things, but as much as I love him for it, I can't let him miss this opportunity. After much convincing, my stubborn boyfriend finally agrees, and at noon my friends and I are sitting with Brody and his buddy Colby at a table in the back of the Taproom. Wyatt and Livi are working, which sucks, but at least Brody can still touch base with them. That's the only hardship about working with friends. Someone's always stuck waiting tables or bartending.

"Are you ever going to give your restaurant a name?" Brody asks Jesse. "I mean, come on. Brent and Jesse Steele. How about BJ's? BJ Steele's."

"Sounds like a strip club," Jesse says.

"What about just Steele's?" Colby suggests.

"Steele Rod?" Brandon suggests.

Jesse shakes his head, and the rest of us laugh.

"What's wrong with Steele Rod? It's a surf and turf restaurant," Brandon offers, though we all know what he was really thinking. "Hey, I could have said Cock and Balls."

"Yeah," Brody says. "I'm sure lots of people want to eat at a restaurant called Cock and Balls. Well, except my brother and you, the king of *if they can stand up they can lie down.* Mr. Indiscretion himself."

"And proud of it," Brandon quips.

Livi brings our lunch and sets a beer beside me.

"I didn't order this." I hand it back to her, and she pushes it away, lifting her eyes over my shoulder.

"I did." Alex touches my shoulder, and my body ignites.

"What are you…?" I rise to my feet, equally confused and thrilled that he's here.

He kisses my cheek. "This is what boyfriends do. We show up to meet your family. We care. We *try.* If you want me to leave, I w—"

"Stay, but what about the meeting?"

"I went over, introduced myself, and told them I had a prior commitment but that I'd be happy to meet with them another time. Mr. Hinkley's going to try to schedule something in a week or two."

"You didn't have to do that." *But I'm so glad you did.*

"I'm done doing what I have to do. I wanted to." Alex takes control, as he does so well, and extends a hand to my brother.

"Alex Wells. You must be Brody. I can tell by the mass of dark hair and Brewer eyes."

"Stop flirting with me. I'm straight," Brody teases. "I'm glad you made it after all." He nods to Colby. "This is my buddy Colby."

Colby rises from his seat, and Alex's eyes sweep over his tall, broad frame, taking in the tattoos running down his arm. Both men square their shoulders, and it's like watching Alex at the clinic all over again. A curious flash of recognition passes between them.

Alex shakes Colby's hand more stiffly than he did my brother's. "Colby."

Colby nods. "Alex."

My friends' faces mirror my confusion.

"You two know each other?" Brody asks.

"No," Alex says sharply. "What branch?" he asks Colby.

"Navy," Colby answers, his eyes moving between me and Alex. "You?"

Understanding comes with their rigid exchange, as silence falls around the table. How on earth did they recognize each other as military? It feels as though everyone is holding their breath, but I'm sure it's just me. I'm waiting for Alex to disengage, readying myself for the sting of denial, and I wonder how he's going to dismiss the kiss he just gave me and the comment from Brody.

Alex's eyes remain trained on Colby as he drapes an arm over my shoulder, shocking the hell out of me, and says, "Army."

"Loud and proud," Brandon mumbles with a smirk.

Time stands still. The muscles in Alex's jaw tighten. In my stunned silence, the magnitude of Alex's actions hit me full force, and the walls of the Taproom feel like they're closing in around us. I wanted this so desperately, and now that we're here, standing in the midst of what I am sure is the most powerful moment of my life—and most excruciating for my lover—I realize how selfish I've been. It's all I can do to remember to breathe in what feels like an agonizingly *long* pause as Colby, who has never had an issue with my sexuality, processes the sight before him combined with the knowledge of Alex's military affiliation.

Alex's hand tightens on my shoulder with an alarming amount of pressure. He's not running, he's not dismissing me, and he's certainly not disengaging.

He's not the one who ran away when things got tough. That was me.

He's here and he's not going anywhere, just like he promised.

"Cool," Colby says casually, making me wonder if I've imagined his lengthy consideration. He pulls out the chair beside him and says, "Take a load off. I'll buy you a beer."

No matter how much I'd hoped for it, how much I believed in him, some part of me still worried he'd fail me.

As Alex guides me into the chair beside him, my mind begins to claw its way out of stunned silence, and I realize—*I accept*—that until this very second, I was incapable of truly believing he could give me what I needed. And at the expense of torturing himself, he's given me more than I ever could have hoped for.

CHAPTER TWENTY-THREE

Alex

"I DON'T CARE what changed," Tristan says as we stumble through my living room kissing. I push at his shirt, frantically tugging mine over my head, and work the buttons on our jeans.

"I care." I press my hands to his face, holding his hungry stare. "I woke up, T. Fear has two faces." God, he's so beautiful, so trusting, I'm shaking. "I was an ass for taking so long to see the light and do the right thing. Fear can paralyze or propel, and I've been standing on the wrong side for way too long."

I kiss him hard as we both struggle to get out of our clothes. Our naked bodies slam together with the force of wrestlers battling for dominance as we fall against the bedroom door. Our teeth *clank* as we both *take*. I can't get close enough. I feel like I've been lost at sea and finally found dry land. Like I need him to survive. Tristan claws at my back, rocking against me and bringing us both to near madness. His hands push into my hair, crashing his mouth to mine in another wild kiss. Words aren't strong enough to express what I feel for him. When he moans into my mouth, I grab his ass, seeking his hole and teasing him as he grinds. We stumble to the bed, and I pin him down on his back and push his legs to his chest. He strokes his cock, watching me as I lower my mouth to his ass and slick my tongue from his hole to his sac and back again. He's groaning and stroking and there is nothing hotter than this man giving himself over to me. I love him with my mouth, then lower his legs and lick the length of his eager, swollen cock.

"Alex, I need more."

"So do I, baby. I need more of you."

The words come straight from my heart, and as I roll us over, giving him the advantage, our eyes lock. As understanding dawns on him, his gaze turns to liquid fire. His hands travel down my sides and up my chest like streaks of lightning. He lowers his body to mine, aligning our swollen cocks. His outer thighs rub against the inside of mine, and he traps my hands beside my head. He slicks his tongue over my lips, and the air rushes from my lungs.

"There's no going back from this," he says in a fast, heated breath.

I feel his cock jerk against my stomach, and I want to feel it inside me. "I don't ever want to go back, T. Not now, not ten years from now."

A slow, secretive smile spreads across his face. "You have no idea how many times I've fantasized about fucking you." He kisses my neck, laves his tongue along the ridge of my jaw, and I can't suppress the needy noises slipping from my lungs.

"You're shaking."

"I have a hard cock against my stomach, and I want it in my ass," I say sharply. "I'm shaking because you're so fucking hot I can't stand you torturing me."

That grin spreads wider, and he rolls to the side. His eyes move lazily down my torso, over my cock, and he licks his lips. I feel every second of his piercing gaze like a stroke of heat. He grabs the lube from the nightstand with a wicked glint in his eyes, moving too damn slow.

"Fuck, T." I reach for my cock and he grabs my wrist.

"Hands off." He moves my hands above my head and wraps them around the wooden spokes of the headboard. "My turn."

He settles his sexy body between my legs, sitting back on his heels, and roughly grabs me behind my knees, thrusting my legs apart and up, laying me open for the taking. He licks his lips again, and my cock jumps. When he lowers his mouth to my hole, my eyes roll back in my head. He licks and prods and thrusts his tongue inside me, then brings his fingers into play. When he pushes his finger inside me, I suck in a sharp breath.

"So tight, baby," he says, and works his finger in and out. Releasing one of my legs, he wraps his hand around my cock and lowers his mouth to the crown, circling it with his tongue.

The world careens away as he fucks me with his finger and sucks my cock. I grip the headboard so tightly I fear it'll snap. When my shaft falls from his mouth and his fingers withdraw from my ass, my eyes fly open.

"More," I beg.

"Oh, you're going to get more, baby. You won't be able to sit for a week."

He lubes up his fingers and returns them to my ass, working one in, then two, as he claims my mouth in another earth-shattering kiss. I love the strength and softness of his mouth, the scratch of his whiskers. He nips at my jaw, kisses his way down my chest, and sucks my nipple so hard I nearly lose it. He grazes his teeth over my flesh and my hips piston off the bed.

"More," I demand, and feel him push a third thick finger into my ass, stretching me, loving me as he kisses his way south and takes me into his mouth again.

Need courses through me, desire builds, pressure mounts, and I can't fight it for another second. I grab his head, moving him faster, fucking his mouth as hard as I want him to take me. Heat sears down my spine, gathers in my balls, and I'm powerless to stop the explosion as it shoots from my cock. He doesn't slow, doesn't retreat, as I come down his throat. My neck arches back with the intensity of my release. I'm panting, my head is spinning, and I'm lost in him. When I feel a whoosh of cold air over my cock and feel the weight of my lover come down over me, my brain snaps alive again. He kisses me so thoroughly there's no escaping the taste of come on his lips. He's fucking my mouth, claiming me, possessing me so completely, I get hard again in no time.

He rears up and lubes his cock, stroking it once, twice, and by the third stroke I want to bend him over the bed and pound into him. I fist my hands in the sheets, biding my time, anxious and excited for what's to come. I'm so in love with him I ache for more. I don't just want him to be my first. I want him to be my one and only.

Tristan comes down over me, propping himself up with one arm as he guides his slick heat to my entrance.

"I'll go slow," he assures me.

"I want everything you have to give." I push a hand to the back of his neck and pull him closer, brushing my lips over his. "Take me, T. Make me yours."

Tristan

I'VE FANTASIZED ABOUT this moment so many times I can barely breathe. I have to pause and take in the sight of the man I love, *truly love*, giving himself over to me. All of him laid bare for the taking and that riveting, plump mouth glistening from our kisses. He's *mine*. His strong, rough hands clutch my hips, and his eyes turn volcanic as he pulls me down and his hips rise, his pelvis tilts, angling to accept me. The head of my cock pushes into his tight entrance, and his eyes close.

"Eyes open," I demand, and he obeys. His eyes are so expressive, I don't want to miss a second of seeing what he feels as we come together this way for the first time. I push past the tight rim of muscles and he grits his teeth, groaning with the force it takes to breach his virgin ass. My fear of hurting him is bigger than my need to claim him, and I freeze.

"Too much?"

"Never," he grinds out through clenched teeth, and tugs me into a kiss, forcing his tongue into my mouth.

He's taking control, forcing my brain cells to fail and my body to take over—and it works like a fucking charm. Everything fades except the feel of his hot, wicked mouth loving mine and the exquisite tightness swallowing my cock as I bury myself deep inside my lover. His hands begin driving our lovemaking, guiding our speed, and I allow him to, because that's what we both need.

"Love you, T," he pants out between kisses. "So fucking much."

I'm right there with him, riding the wave of our passion, as heat consumes me from the inside out, annihilating every other experience from my memory, engraving this moment into my mind. There's only the two of us, the feel of our slick, sweaty bodies sliding so perfectly in sync, the sound of our ragged breathing and the strength of his strong hands squeezing my hips.

He pulls back from the kiss, and the current between us changes. His hands travel up my sides and come to rest on my cheeks.

"You've become my whole life, baby," he says in a heady voice, and pulls my mouth toward his again. "Let go for me."

As his lips meet mine, I realize he's giving me the reins, becoming completely, utterly mine, and that amplifies the energy between us. I push my hands under his back and cradle all his power against me, loving him with *my* strength, *my* rhythm. His body conforms to mine in a different way, like a surfer giving in to the strength of the sea. He follows my pace, and it's magical. Blissful. *Intense.*

When I get close, I rear up, push his legs open wider, watching as his body accepts every inch of me. I keep up the pace as I take his cock in my hand, stroking him to the same rhythm.

"Faster," he demands.

I move my hips and my hand faster, unsure which he's asking for and wanting this to be as mind-blowing for him as it is for me. As I near my release, I can't concentrate on both, and he takes over stroking himself. It takes only a few eyefuls of his hand around his cock to send me over the edge. I fall forward, catching myself with one palm as he yanks up his rigid length, spilling his release over his chest.

Panting and sweaty, he rolls us onto our sides. His thigh rides up mine. His hand splays across my back, trapping me against him, the evidence of our love a hot, sticky mess sealing our bodies together, and we kiss like he's going away to war.

When our lips part, he gazes into my eyes and I can see I was wrong.

He's finally left the battlefield behind.

CHAPTER TWENTY-FOUR

Alex

TRISTAN'S PARENTS' HOUSE feels like a home should feel. Family and love fill every room. Their walls are covered with photographs of Tristan and Brody, mapping their lives from birth to sometime recent. Most families display only the happiest of moments. But the photographs on the Brewers' walls include pictures of four- or five-year-old Tristan, red faced and teary eyed, knee deep in the ocean beside Brody, who's beaming and holding Tristan up by his arm. There are pictures of the two boys as toddlers in the bathtub, and preteen Tristan, all knees and elbows, standing with his arm around Brody, both of them holding surfboards. Scattered among the photographs of the children are pictures of their parents—as a couple and with their sons. My favorite of all of the pictures hangs in the living room beside the doors to the deck. It's only a five-by-seven, dwarfed by many larger frames, but it's *perfectly Tristan*. He's lying on the end of a boat with a thoughtful, happy gaze, as if he's finally taking a break after a long day in the hot sun. His arms are crossed beneath his cheek, and a small smile curves his lips.

"He was nine," his father says as he comes to my side. Ralph

Brewer is a conservative man with salt-and-pepper hair, kind eyes, and a broad physique. He's soft spoken, the perfect complement to his wife Elsa's boisterous personality.

"We'd been out on the boat for hours, and the boys spent the afternoon swimming," Ralph explained. "Brody was sitting across from Tris, telling him a story. Tris would listen to Brody's stories night and day. Brody's imagination has always run wild. Their mother will tell you that Tris has lived all of Brody's adventures through the tales he shares. They're two very different men. Tristan has never had a wandering spirit."

"Tristan's a great listener," I say, thinking about earlier, after Tristan and I made love—and that's what it was, so different from fucking. I told him about my visit to my grandmother's grave, and how it opened a door for my future. When I shared that with Tristan, he listened. He didn't try to offer advice or tell me I did the right thing. He knew exactly what I needed.

"I have never met anyone like Tristan," I add as we walk out to the deck, where Tristan and Brody are leaning against the railing looking out at the water. "You've raised a great man."

Ralph nods, looking thoughtfully at his sons. "I'm proud of them both."

We don't interrupt Tristan and Brody's conversation. Instead, his father takes me on more trips down memory lane. He tells me stories about Tristan and Brody when they were younger, playing ball on the beach, sneaking the car out at night when they thought their parents were asleep, and how on Christmas, Brody would drag Tristan downstairs at four o'clock in the morning.

"Brody still calls him at four in the morning on Christmas, so be ready for that," he warns.

"I think I can handle that."

Their lives are weaved of memories and rituals. Thanksgiving dinners around the same table where we just finished eating, birthdays celebrated as a family with colorful cakes and silly cards. Being here makes me want to reassure Tristan's family that I'll do right by him, and doing right by him means stepping out from behind the walls of my past. It was wrong of me to ask Tristan not to talk about my injury or the award with the people he loves most. He's such an open, loving person, and I don't ever want that to change because of me. He's my safe harbor, my dirty desire, and everything in between. Most importantly, I know with my whole heart he's my future, and if I have a chance in hell of making a man like Tristan happy, I need to be as forthright and open as he is in *all* aspects of my life.

"Tristan's life has been markedly different from mine," I admit with no small amount of discomfort.

Ralph reaches for his wife's hand as she joins us on the deck. "That's probably why you two are so good together," he says, and kisses his wife's cheek. "This pretty lady grew up in a family of nine siblings, and I was an only child. Her family owned a hundred-acre farm in Illinois, they made their own clothes and grew their own food, while I grew up right here in Harborside, with a mother who worked full-time and didn't even own a sewing needle."

"I thought he was stodgy, and he thought I was free-spirited trouble." Elsa touches his cheek. "He was right about me. I don't like to follow *all* the rules."

"Which is why the boys were allowed to sneak out with the car," Ralph says with a lift of his brows. I see Tristan's face in his expression.

"But we followed them." Elsa touches my shoulder and

smiles. Tristan definitely has her warm smile. "They got to rebel and we got to keep them safe without them knowing."

Tristan turns, and there's an instant gravitational pull in his direction. Brody swats Tristan's arm, saying something I can't hear, and Tristan blushes a blue streak. My heart tumbles in my chest. I want to be his naughty rebellion *and* his knight in shining armor.

"We know better than anyone that everyone dances to a different beat. All that matters is that you love each other enough to work through your differences and create one sustainable, happy life without either of you missing out on what matters most."

"And that is?" I ask.

They exchange a look as Tristan comes to my side and takes my hand.

"Only you two can decide what matters most," his mother answers.

Tristan is looking at me like I've hung the moon, and guilt tightens like a noose around my neck. If anything, I'm the storm that keeps the moon at bay. I have a big hurdle to jump over before I'm the man Tristan deserves, but with each passing day I get a little closer. Being the man Tristan deserves has become my bigger purpose.

I squeeze his hand and take another step toward redemption. "Did Tristan tell you we're going to Washington, DC, in two weeks?"

His parents give him a curious look, and disbelief washes over Tristan's face.

A sense of pride courses through me as I take what is probably a baby step but feels like a giant leap of faith. "I was injured in the line of duty and received a military discharge. I'm receiving the Silver Star at Walter Reed National Military Medical Center."

Their eyes widen in surprise. Tristan's fill with what I hope is relief, pride, or full-on happiness—and I wonder what the hell took me so long.

CHAPTER TWENTY-FIVE

Tristan

"ALEX," I HOLLER as I come through the kitchen door Monday night after work. I set the box I'm carrying down on the table and hear him come in through the back door.

"T? I thought I saw your headlights."

He comes into the kitchen wearing a pair of cargo shorts and a black hoodie, and I swallow my voice. It's the first time I've seen him wear shorts, and he looks hot as hell.

"What's that look on your face?"

Surprise? Pride? How do I answer? It's been almost a week since we had lunch with Brody and dinner with my parents, and I still have moments of shock over his openly owning his military career *and* sexuality to Colby, as well as his unexpected admission to my parents. It's a little overwhelming to see him take so many steps all at once, and seeing him wearing shorts, even though we're alone in the house, feels like another really big step. I'm not sure if I should mention it. Maybe it's more supportive to take it in stride?

His hands circle my waist and his blue eyes heat up. "Spit it out, T, before you burst."

"You're wearing shorts," comes rushing out, revealing the

awe I feel. "You look *amazing*. Now that I know what you look like in shorts, there's no going back. You're going to be wearing them all summer, every summer."

"You're just excited because it means you get to buy more clothes."

I smile as he kisses me. "Well, there is that fun tidbit." I step back and eye him up. "Damn, Alex. I'm glad we're alone tonight." I take his hand and drag him toward the living room. "I bet those shorts will look even better on the floor."

He tugs me back to him, eyeing the box on the table. "What's in the box?"

"The guy from Quick Print came by the Taproom to drop off the brochures we ordered." The website is up and running, the store is stocked and organized, and the planning for the grand opening is taking shape. We're hoping to open the last week of October, and I'll cut my hours back at the Taproom two weeks before to help Alex with last-minute details.

"Come on." I pull him toward the living room again, and he removes something from his pocket.

"I'm not going anywhere with you unless you put this on." He dangles a black eye mask between his fingers and thumb.

"You're into kink and decided to withhold that info until now?" I grab the blindfold and run my fingers over the silky material. "What else should I know?"

He takes it from my hands and slips it over my head and into place over my eyes.

"Dude," I say with a laugh. "Not that I'm complaining, but there's nothing I wouldn't do with you without the blindfold."

His lips press against my neck, and my whole body shudders. He nips at the base of my neck, then slicks his tongue over my skin. The blindfold definitely brings this to a whole new enticing level.

"I've never been into kink," he says in a rough voice beside my ear. "But seeing you blindfolded turns me on."

"Then why are we standing here?" I reach for him, and my hand finds his waist. I follow the curve of his body and cup his balls. In the next breath he's hard against my palm. "Bedroom."

"Damn it." He grips my wrist and pulls my hand away. "We can't. Not yet."

What? He never denies me.

He gives me a chaste kiss, and I grab his head before he can pull too far away and kiss him again. He overpowers me, clutching my hands as I hold his face, and *holy hell he feels so good* as he presses his body against mine. I stumble backward and slam against the wall with an *oomph.*

"Love kissing you," he says as his hands move through my hair, down my arms, and he clutches my ass.

I arch toward him, giving him better access to anything he wants. I want his strong, rough hands all over me. I can't see a damn thing, but I can smell him, feel him, and taste him. I push his shirt up, struggling to get it off, but he's resisting.

"T," he pants out. "We can't do this. Not now."

At first I think it's a game, like he's teasing me about the first time we kissed, right here against this wall, and I keep trying to push his shirt up his body.

"T," he says sternly.

I tear the blindfold off. "What the he—" My words are silenced by the tortured look in his eyes. "What's wrong?"

"What's *wrong* is your idiot boyfriend thought it would be a good idea to plan a big surprise for you, but if we go out there like this, we'll be known as the *boner boys.* I don't know what made me think I could blindfold you and not want to feast on every inch of your body."

We both laugh.

"A surprise?" I look around, but we're still alone, and it's dark outside. "Why would you plan something for me?"

"Why?" He runs his hand down my shirt and takes a step away, sending ripples of heat down the length of my body. "Because I love you, and you've supported me and been here for me, and you're willing to put up with my military bullshit, and I want to give you everything."

"Alex…" I reach for his hand.

"The problem is, I also want to *give* you *everything*." He eyes the bulge in my pants, and we both laugh again. "All your friends are outside waiting, and we don't have time for cold showers."

"First of all, thank you." I kiss him softly. "Second of all, I'll proudly be the boy to your boner."

He smiles and shakes his head.

"And third of all, my friends saw you in shorts?"

"I'm trying, T. I also told them about the award, and the trip next week, and I apologized to them for asking you to keep those things from them. I want transparency in all aspects of our lives. I was wrong to ask you not to talk about my injury or my award. I want you to be proud of me, not feel like you have to worry about what you say around your friends."

"I *am* proud of you, Alex."

"I know you are, but I need to do better by you. I needed to overcome my feelings of being less of a man, and I need to overcome the biggest hurdle of all…"

He doesn't need to say the *military mind fuck*. We both know what we're facing. I love this man so much more than I ever thought possible, and I know that next week when I'm watching him accept his award, it won't feel wrong to act like his proud friend rather than his lover, because he has truly become my very best friend.

I put on the blindfold again and he takes my hand. "Let's go get surprised."

"We are definitely going to put this to good use later."

Alex

I GAZE UP at the starry sky and remember far too many nights when the sky was illuminated by the evils of war. It seems like a lifetime ago when I carried weapons like schoolchildren carry pencils. I look down at my hands, rough and calloused from woodworking instead of war, and it's hard to believe how much my life has changed over the past year. Tristan stands at the water's edge with our friends. Everyone helped me get this party ready for Tristan. I know how important they are to him and how important they've become to me, and when I thought about surprising Tristan, I knew it would be selfish of me not to include the people who loved him. They helped me put up six twelve-foot wooden poles and string lights over tables I rented from a local party store. We brought grills down to the beach, and everyone pitched in to help make a fabulous dinner. Cassidy has been taking pictures all night. I've never had a photo album, and with cell phones, I'm not sure anyone does anymore. But it's something I feel like I missed out on when I was growing up—collecting memories in a book that will be around forever. I look forward to having that with Tristan.

As I take in my boyfriend and all my new friends, my feelings toward my injuries and scars morph into something different. It's a horrible thought to be thankful for an injury, but mine led me to Tristan. How can I not be thankful for that?

Tristan hands me a sparkler. "Time to light up my life, big guy."

Brandon and Brent begin singing "You Light Up My Life" while they play their guitars. Tristan and I both laugh, but inside, I'm loving every second of their impromptu serenade.

We light our sparklers, and Charley, Livi, Cassidy, and Wyatt join us, lighting their own sparklers.

"Write your name!" Cassidy calls out.

"Hell no," Wyatt says as he swats Cassidy's butt. "I'll write *your* name."

Jesse, Brooke, Delilah, and Ashley were sitting on a blanket by the bonfire roasting marshmallows. Now they're heading down to the water's edge to join us.

"Does it bother you that we're as ridiculous as twelve-year-olds?" Tristan asks as we spell out *I love you* with our sparklers.

"No, because I never had this at twelve. I never had this at fifteen, or twenty-five." My thoughts turn to my mother, who called yesterday to say she'd met a man, an artist, and they were on their way to his ranch in Colorado. She's going to miss my award ceremony, which came as no surprise. I never understood why my mother uprooted us so often, but I think I finally understand. She's spent her life searching for what I've finally found. Maybe this time she'll get lucky.

I take Tristan's hand, unable to remember ever feeling happier than this very second. "Are you ready to see your surprise?"

His eyes widen. "There's more?"

"You didn't think your man would do things half-assed did you?" Brandon asks. He and Brent play their guitars as we all walk in a group toward the house.

"I want an Alex," Charley says in a loud whisper.

"You find the guy and we'll share him," Brandon answers.

Charley slaps his arm and they both laugh.

"We're going inside? But the party's out here." Tristan hikes a thumb over his shoulder.

"We're coming back down." Wyatt did me a huge favor by asking Tristan to come into work early today to do inventory. I spent all day working on this surprise, and as we reach the bottom of the stairs, I withdraw the blindfold for the second—but definitely not the last—time this evening.

"Again?" Tristan complains. "Okay, but I'm pretty sure no one else wants to see what we have planned."

Everyone laughs and begins to whisper.

"Don't worry, T," I say as I guide him up the steps. "What I have planned for this blindfold requires no audience."

"Now we're talking," Brandon says. "Remember, I'm available for threesomes."

"Shut up and play," Wyatt reminds him.

When we reach the back of the house, Delilah stands ready to flip on the porch light, and everyone quiets. I turn Tristan so he's facing the water and remove the blindfold. He blinks a few times in confusion. When he tries to turn around, I hold him in place.

"T, you said when you figured out where you wanted to settle down, you wanted rock gardens of your own. I think it's time we make this official and move you into the house." I turn him around, and Delilah flips on the lights, illuminating the rock garden I spent all day creating.

"Metty and your mother helped me choose the plants, to ensure they'd thrive in our yard."

Tristan's eyes widen as he takes in the river of rocks that

flow into a sea of colorful flowers and leafy plants. I built a knee-high wall on the far side and inlaid a wooden sign that says ALPHA AND TANGO, connected at the *A*'s. Beside the garden is a newly tilled plot waiting for Tristan's creation.

His eyes glass over and he tugs me against him, holding me so tight I can't breathe.

"Is that a yes?" Brooke asks.

"Yes, it's *yes*!" Tristan pulls back and searches my eyes. "You made me a rock garden. You freaking made me an *amazing* rock garden."

The look on his face is worth the dull ache in my leg from spending so much time on my knees. "Mine will pale in comparison to yours, but you said to fall for you like I mean it. I mean it, T, and I'll do everything within my power to give you everything you ever want."

He yanks me into another hug. "I love you, Alex. I hope you know I would have moved in even if you didn't make me an exceptionally awesome rock garden."

He's so serious my throat clogs with emotion. "Because of my listening skills and giant cock?"

"Ha! Now I *really* want an Alex," Charley says with a loud laugh, which makes everyone crack up.

"Yeah, something like that," Tristan says, and claims me in a scorching-hot kiss.

I love this man from the surface of my skin to the marrow in my bones, and as we kiss beneath the stars, with our friends whistling and hollering around us, I feel drunk with it.

When our mouths finally part, I keep him against me. "I can't imagine ever wanting to leave this place, T. I know things will change, that years will pass. We'll all get older and our priorities will change, but you and your friends are proof that what I spent my whole life wishing for is attainable."

Tristan presses a kiss to my lips. Then another. He kisses me a third time, and I wonder if everyone will notice if we slip inside for a quickie.

"Get that look off your face," Tristan whispers. Then, a little louder, he says, "Our relationship should prove that to you."

And it does. Over and over again.

CHAPTER TWENTY-SIX

Tristan

I'M NOT SURE who's more nervous the morning of Alex's award ceremony, him or me. He's pacing the hotel room like a caged animal, and I'm powerless to offer any relief. Last night we watched a couple of Silver Star award ceremonies on YouTube so we would know what to expect. Even in the privacy of the hotel room, Alex sat up straighter as he watched, his breathing shallowed and his expression stoic. His hands fisted so tight his knuckles blanched, and it took him a solid twenty minutes to relax again.

I can't change what he feels, which I know is a mix of anger, nerves, and embarrassment—because he's a prideful man and he's worried that not being able to overcome what he feels will make him less of a man for me. As I watch him pacing in his dress blues—beneath which his chest bears a new tattoo that reads TANGO and ALPHA connected at the *A*'s—looking more handsome than any man on the planet has the right to, I do the one thing I can to try to make today a little easier for him.

I reach for his hand, and he pauses from wearing a path in the carpet and lifts his troubled eyes.

"Would it make things easier for you if I waited here? You

don't need the added pressure of me sitting in the audience, and I promise you I won't be upset over it if you'd rather I did."

He clenches his jaw and takes both my hands firmly in his. "Do you really think I'd hurt you like that after all we've been through?"

"This isn't about me, Alex."

He rubs the back of his neck and grimaces. I move behind him and massage his knotted muscles.

"I'm not the same person I was when we met." It's an honest explanation, and he deserves to hear it. "I was hurt, and my priority was to have enough respect for myself that I'd never accept being treated poorly again. I wasn't sure I'd ever get there."

I turn him to face me. His blue eyes are so full of love I feel myself falling for him all over again, and when I see a hint of the crooked smile I adore, I know there's nothing I wouldn't do for him. This is my path, paved with fire and ice, and I'm ready to walk it to eternity.

"You helped me through that, Alex. You helped me become stronger and realize there are too many shades of right and wrong to try to draw lines between them. Two men can do the exact same thing for different reasons, making one wrong—and the other *clearly* right."

"T." No words follow, but his loving expression hides nothing.

"Staying in this room will hurt—you're right about that—but it won't hurt nearly as much as knowing that my presence caused you undue pressure. I have unwavering faith in us. We *will* overcome this. If not now, then next year, or in ten years. We've got nothing but time, Alex. What matters is that you stand up on that stage and accept that award as the proud, deserving man you have always been."

"That's not good enough, T. Not by a long shot." His eyes narrow and his chest rises as he inhales a deep breath. "I want you in the auditorium with me."

Alex

MILITARY BASES ARE worlds unto themselves, with rules, standards, expectations, levels of authority, and clearly decorated uniforms to display them, and I swear the air changes when we drive through the gates. My body draws upward, my shoulders square, and my neurons go on high alert. This is not a reaction to my being gay in a military setting. These adjustments are merely part of being a soldier. Or rather, of having been a soldier. We're trained to be aware of our surroundings at all times. We are positioned to be members of an elite team. I have lived up to that honor, and without Tristan I might not have realized that as fully as I do.

I'm glad he's with me as we walk through a sea of uniformed men and women. When we reach the auditorium, he smiles supportively, but he's careful not to touch me. He's respecting the boundaries I set up that day we went to the clinic, and as much as I love him for it, I am pissed at myself. Tristan is the kind of strong, selfless man who deserves to be respected, protected, and put on a fucking pedestal. I'm acutely aware of people milling about, men and women holding hands, soldiers filing into the auditorium to attend the ceremony. But I'm even more aware of how gut-wrenchingly wrong it is for Tristan to accept this distance between us.

The woman who coordinated the event approaches in uniform. Her hair is secured in a prim bun, her face is void of makeup, and when she smiles, it's a tight, cordial smile. A soldier's smile. "Sir, they're ready to go over the details of the ceremony with you."

"Thank you." I wait for her to give us some privacy, but she stands by like a dutiful soldier. Instinct brings my hand to Tristan's back. "I guess I need to go, but I'm glad you're here."

A silent *Do you realize you're touching me?* passes between us. I press my hand more firmly to his back in response.

"You'll do great, *Alpha*," he says with an appreciative, loving smile that I'm sure anyone watching can read as nothing less than what it is.

"See you in there, *Tango*."

I have the urge to make sure he gets settled in his seat before I walk away, which is ridiculously overprotective of my six-two lover. But that's what love is, worrying about the person you care most about at all times, whether they can handle battles alone or not. I want to be there for him. I want to be his anchor as he's been mine.

I force myself to follow the woman to the room behind the auditorium. My heart thumps so hard against my chest you'd think I was heading out to the field to fight instead of facing one of the biggest honors I'll ever receive.

The commander explains that they are presenting two Silver Stars today, one to me and one to the man standing beside me. He looks about my age and wears the tough and eager mask of a proud soldier. I saw him kissing his wife earlier.

My mind tumbles back to Tristan. When we first met, I told him about the nightmares of war, and he graciously accepted that some nightmares continue well past the tour of duty. I'd imagine this man's wife did the same thing. We're no different, this man and I. Two men who fought alongside hundreds of others. But we're the chosen ones. The men who have been hand selected as going above and beyond the call of duty. On the battlefield, I still don't believe there's an *above and beyond*. We were there to save lives. We were doing what we were supposed to do. But on the home front, there's definitely a difference between those who go through the motions and those who go above and beyond the call of duty. Tristan is a supreme example of the latter.

When the commander mentions there will be time at the end to bring our significant others up onstage for photographs, my initial reaction is to bite my tongue and let the opportunity go.

Tristan's voice whispers through my mind. *I think the part that you lost left you a stronger man, but until you feel that way, those ghosts you're wrestling with will never leave.* We were talking about my injured leg, but I now realize my injury isn't what made me feel like less of a man. Not standing up for who I really am was what made me feel like I'd lost a piece of myself in that war.

I'm done biting my tongue.

I SEE TRISTAN sitting a few rows back beside an elderly gentleman. Every time our eyes meet, he smiles, and even when I have to shift my attention to the general as he presents my Silver Star, I feel Tristan's supportive and proud gaze. The ceremony is short and meaningful. The general reiterates what we've done to earn the award. He talks about the war and pays homage to those we've lost. He speaks of the importance of soldiers like us and the meaning of valor. I catch sight of the other soldier's wife wiping tears from her eyes, and I know my grandmother would have been proud to sit in this auditorium beside Tristan. She'd probably have held his hands and shed tears, too.

We're each given a chance to say a few words. The other recipient speaks first, and he says all the appropriate things— thanking his team, the military, the country, and of course, his wife, which causes fresh tears to fall down her cheeks.

The crowd applauds as he takes his seat and I step up to the podium. My rehearsed speech feels contrived. I look out at the expectant faces, seeking the only man I want to see, and I swear the space between us nearly ignites. I'm surprised there isn't a thread of smoke setting off the fire detectors. I was trained to protect, to put team members first, and never to accept defeat. Tristan *is* my team member, and I will *never* accept defeat where he's concerned.

I draw in a breath and blow it out slowly to steady my nerves, and I don't recite my speech. I say what comes to mind.

"It's an honor to be the recipient of this distinguished award, and it was an honor to fight among so many brave men for so long. Every soldier is a hero, and the families of those who are at war are fighting the good fight right alongside them." I pause, surprised at the steadiness of my voice. "They may not be on the battlefield, but they're enduring their own struggles holding down the home front. When their significant other returns home, they fight a different type of battle. Rebuilding lives that are forever changed, dealing with PTSD, missing or injured limbs, head injuries, or a multitude of other conflicts and difficulties. I was lucky I made it out alive. I know and appreciate that. I would not be standing here today if it were not for talented medics, helicopter pilots, doctors, nurses, physical therapists, and I'm sure a hundred other people in various positions. I will be forever indebted to all those who helped save my life and my leg. But I wouldn't be standing here *in this auditorium* if it weren't for one very special man."

The crowd turns to see who I'm focusing on, and a sea of emotions cross Tristan's face. Even from this distance, I know his eyes are damp. My throat thickens with emotion—but there is no fear. That's how I know I'm ready to go above and beyond my call of duty.

Tristan

DON'T FUCKING CRY. The man beside me must see how hard it is to hold back, because he shoves a tissue into my hand and nods curtly. I can't thank him. I can't take my eyes off of Alex standing proudly at the podium and saying things I never thought he'd be able to say.

"My boyfriend, Tristan Brewer, has shown me what a true hero looks like. Thank you, T. I love you."

Damn it. Tears escape down my cheeks, and when the audience applauds, heads turning to take us both in, I give up trying to hide my emotions. Tears flow like a river, and I feel like my heart is going to explode out of my chest.

The ceremony comes to an emotional end, and the man beside me leans in and says, "You must be very proud of him."

"Yes, sir. Very proud," is all I can manage, but really, what's left to say? Alex Wells has blown me away.

The audience rises for a final round of applause, and as the other soldier leaves the stage and returns with his wife for the photos, Alex descends the stairs, those piercing baby blues set on me. When he reaches the row I'm sitting in, he holds out a hand.

"You have to get your picture taken," I say quietly.

He grips my hand tightly. "*We* have to get our picture taken."

I can't even form a response as he leads me toward the stage.

We stand side by side, his arm circling my back, and as the photographer gets ready to snap the picture, Alex says, "I told you I'm the man you deserve."

In that moment I'm certain of two things. Alex Wells is more of a man than I ever dreamed, and when we see these photographs, I'm going to be smiling like a lovesick fool in every single one of them.

EPILOGUE

Alex

I CAN HARDLY believe how many people show up for the grand opening of Artsea Designs. Tristan did an incredible job of spreading the word, and Brandon produced such an awesome website, we had orders piling up before the doors even opened.

"I have to show you something." Tristan takes my hand and weaves through the crowd, pointing out customers marveling at the furniture and accessories I've made. "You did this," he says. "Everyone loves your work. Arty would be so proud of you. *I'm* proud of you."

"*We* did it, T. Both of us." Nothing compares to working with and living with Tristan. I wake up with the man I adore and spend hours building our future together. Granted, many days we get more make-out time in than actual work done, but hey, what more could a man ask for?

As we walk to the back of the store, my mother comes into view. She's gazing up at her new boyfriend, Craig Miller, the artist from Colorado she met the week of my award ceremony. She looks happier than I've ever seen her. Craig leans down and kisses her.

Tristan licks the shell of my ear, which he knows drives me

insane, and whispers, "She's been with him longer than a month. Think he might be around for Christmas in June?"

Now I'm thinking about Tristan's tongue, of course, but I'm also touched that he remembered that story about my mother's strange Christmas tree habits, and I manage, "I sure hope so."

It's crazy how the right person can change your whole world. When I walked into the Taproom that very first night, hoping to meet Tristan, I never imagined falling madly, deeply in love with him. And now I can't imagine my life without him.

We walk out the back doors to the slate patio, and the sight of the elaborate rock garden Tristan designed and we created together still thrills me. Tristan's rock gardens far outshine mine. The one he made at the house is the most incredible garden I've ever seen, and I know, like his mother, he'll spend years making them even more interesting. I can't wait until we have years together and I can look back and say, *Remember when?* to the man I love.

I'm looking forward to spending our first Thanksgiving and Christmas together and starting our own family traditions, which is something I've never had.

Tristan squeezes my hand and nods at Charley, sitting with Brandon and Brooke on the bench I made. Brandon stretches and puts an arm around both of the girls, pulling them against him. He says something and both Brooke and Charley slap him in the chest and get up laughing.

Some things never change.

Tristan and I move off to the side to allow his parents to pass by. His mother touches each of us on the shoulder and mouths, *Love you*, as she and his father join another couple. It's a great feeling to be included in a family as stable and loving as the Brewers.

I slide my hand into Tristan's back pocket and he comes willingly against me.

"I'm going to say something sappy, so just go with it, okay?"

He smirks. "You don't do sappy. That's my job."

"You're rubbing off on me."

"You want me to rub you off? Here?" He rocks his hips against mine and I let out a low groan.

"Damn, T. You freaking own me." I hold him tighter. "As I recall, you like to have your hands on wood."

He laughs. "Totally not sappy, alpha boy."

"Right, sorry." I give him a chaste kiss.

"Hurry up. Brandon's watching us like he wants to jump in the middle."

"In his dreams." I shake my head at Brandon, who rolls his eyes.

Tristan grabs my chin and draws my eyes back to his. "Focus. If I stand pressed against you any longer, I'm going to drag that fine ass of yours into the office and fuck you until you can't remember your name."

I blink.

I blink again.

And then I take his hand and head directly for the office.

"Alex," he whispers loudly as we move through the crowd. "You can't leave your own grand opening."

"Who's leaving? We'll be in the office." I give him a nudge through the office door, closing and locking it behind us, and cage him against the wall with the force of my body as I capture his mouth—and his complaints—in a ravenous kiss.

"God I love you," he says as he gasps a breath.

I push my hands into his hair, holding him exactly where I

want him, and claim him in another punishingly hot kiss. He surrenders to my will, his leg inching up my hip, and we frantically tear each other's pants open, wrestling for dominance. *Some things never change.* I grab him by the collar and slam him against the other wall, and in seconds he overpowers me—

Or so he thinks…

As his lips descend toward mine, I whisper, "You've helped me become the best man I could ever hope to be, Tristan. I adore you."

He draws back with a serious look in his dark, sexy eyes. "Don't think for a second that *sappy* will stop me from giving you exactly what you deserve."

I can't suppress my smile. "That's what I'm counting on."

Ready for more Harborside Nights?

Sign up for Melissa's NEWSLETTER
to be notified of future releases.
www.MelissaFoster.com/Newsletter

**Please enjoy this sneak peek of TRU BLUE,
Melissa's sexy new standalone romance**

He wore the skin of a killer, and bore the heart of a lover…

*There's nothing Truman Gritt won't do to protect his family—
Including spending years in jail for a crime he didn't commit.
When he's finally released, the life he knew is turned upside down
by his mother's overdose, and Truman steps in to raise the children
she's left behind. Truman's hard, he's secretive, and he's trying to
save a brother who's even more broken than he is. He's never needed
help in his life, and when beautiful Gemma Wright tries to step in,
he's less than accepting. But Gemma has a way of slithering into
people's lives and eventually she pierces through his ironclad heart.
When Truman's dark past collides with his future, his loyalties will
be tested, and he'll be faced with his toughest decision yet.*

TRUMAN GRITT LOCKED the door to Whiskey Automotive and stepped into the stormy September night. Sheets of rain blurred his vision, instantly drenching his jeans and T-shirt. A slow smile crept across his face as he tipped his chin up, soaking in the shower of *freedom.* He made his way around the dark building and climbed the wooden stairs to the deck outside his apartment. He could have used the interior door, but after being behind bars for six long years, Truman took advantage of the small pleasures he'd missed out on, like determining his own schedule, deciding when to eat and drink, and standing in the fucking rain if he wanted to. He leaned on the rough wooden railing, ignoring the splinters of wood piercing his tattooed forearms, squinted against the wetness, and scanned the cars in the junkyard they used for parts—and he used to rid himself of frustrations. He rested his leather boot on the metal box where he kept his painting supplies. Truman didn't have much—his old extended-cab truck, which his friend Bear Whiskey had held on to for him while he was in prison, this apartment, and a solid job, both of which were compliments of the Whiskey family. The only family he had anymore.

Emotions he didn't want to deal with burned in his gut, causing his chest to constrict. He turned to go inside, hoping to outrun thoughts of his own fucked-up family, whom he'd tried—*and failed*—to save. His cell phone rang with his brother's ringtone, "A Beautiful Lie" by 30 Seconds to Mars.

"Fuck," he muttered, debating letting the call go to voicemail, but six months of silence from his brother was a long time. Rain pelleted his back as he pressed his palm to the door to steady himself. The ringing stopped, and he blew out a breath he hadn't realized he'd trapped inside. The phone rang again, and he froze.

He'd just freed himself from the dredges of hell that he'd been thrown into in an effort to *save* his brother. He didn't need to get wrapped up in whatever mess the drug-addicted fool had gotten himself into. The call went to voicemail, and Truman eyed the metal box containing his painting supplies. Breathing like he'd been in a fight, he wished he could paint the frustration out of his head. When the phone rang for the third time in as many minutes, the third time since he was released from prison six months ago, he reluctantly answered.

"Quincy." He hated the way his brother's name came out sounding like the enemy. Quincy had been just a kid when Truman went to prison. Heavy breathing filled the airwaves. The hairs on Truman's forearms and neck stood on end. He knew fear when he heard it. He could practically taste it as he ground his teeth together.

"I need you," his brother's tortured voice implored.

Need me? Truman had hunted down his brother after he was released from prison, and when he'd finally found him, Quincy was so high on crack he was nearly incoherent—but it didn't take much for *fuck off* to come through loud and clear. What Quincy needed was rehab, but Truman knew from his tone that wasn't the point of the call.

Before he could respond, his brother croaked out, "It's Mom. She's really bad."

Fuck. He hadn't had a mother since she turned her back on him more than six years ago, and he wasn't about to throw away the stability he'd finally found for the woman who'd sent him to prison and never looked back.

He scrubbed a hand down his rain-soaked face. "Take her to the hospital."

"No cops. No hospitals. *Please*, man."

A painful, high-pitched wail sounded through the phone.

"What have you done?" Truman growled, the pit of his stomach plummeting as memories of another dark night years earlier came rushing in. He paced the deck as thunder rumbled overhead like a warning. "Where are you?"

Quincy rattled off the address of a seedy area about thirty minutes outside of Peaceful Harbor, and then the line went dead.

Truman's thumb hovered over the cell phone screen. Three little numbers—*9-1-1*—would extricate him from whatever mess Quincy and their mother had gotten into. Images of his mother spewing lies that would send him away and of Quincy, a frightened boy of thirteen, looking devastated and childlike despite his near six-foot stature, assailed him.

Push the buttons.

Push the fucking buttons.

He remembered Quincy's wide blue eyes screaming silent apologies as Truman's sentence was revealed. It was those pleading eyes he saw now, fucked up or not, that had him trudging through the rain to his truck and driving over the bridge, leaving Peaceful Harbor and his safe, stable world behind.

THE STENCH OF urine and human waste filled the dark alley—not only *waste* as in feces, but *waste* as in drug dealers, whores, and other deviants. Mud and graffiti streaked cracked and mangled concrete. Somewhere above, shouts rang out. Truman had tunnel vision as he moved swiftly between the tall buildings in the downpour. A dog barked in the distance, followed by the unmistakable yelp of a wounded animal. Truman rolled his broad shoulders forward, his hands fisted by his sides as memories hammered him, but it was the incessant torturous wailing coming from behind the concrete walls that had him breathing harder, readying for a fight. It sounded like someone—or something—was suffering inside the building, and despite his loathing for the woman who had brought him into the world, he wouldn't wish that on her—or wish the wrath he'd bring down on whoever was doing it on anyone else.

The rusty green metal door brought the sounds of prison bars locking to the forefront of his mind, stopping him cold. He drew in a few deep breaths, pushing them out fast and hard as memories assailed him. The wailing intensified, and he forced himself to plow through the door. The rancid, pungent scents of garbage and drugs filled the smoky room, competing with the terrified cries. In the space of a few heart-pounding seconds, Truman took in the scene. He barely recognized the nearly toothless, rail-thin woman lying lifeless on the concrete floor, staring blankly up at the ceiling. Angry track marks like viper bites covered pin-thin arms. In the corner, a toddler sat on a dirty, torn mattress, wearing filthy clothes and sobbing. Her dark hair was tangled and matted, her skin covered in grit and dirt. Her cheeks were bright red, eyes swollen from crying. Beside her a baby lay on its back, its frail arms extended toward the ceiling, shaking as it cried so hard it went silent between wails. His eyes landed on Quincy, huddled beside the woman on the floor. Tears streaked his unshaven, sunken cheeks. Those big blue eyes Truman remembered were haunted and scared, their once vibrant color now deadened, bloodshot with the sheen of a soul-stealing high. His tattooed arms revealed the demons that had swooped in after Truman was incarcerated for the crime his brother had committed, preying on the one person he had wanted to protect. He hadn't been able to protect anyone from behind bars.

"She's…" Quincy's voice was nearly indiscernible. "Dead," he choked out.

Truman's heart slammed against his ribs. His mind reeled back to another stormy night, when he'd walked into his mother's house and found his brother with a bloody knife in his hands—and a dead man sprawled across their mother's half-naked body. He swallowed the bile rising in his throat, pain and anger warring for dominance. He crouched and checked for a pulse, first on her wrist, then on her neck. The pit of his stomach lurched. His mind reeled as he looked past his brother to the children on the mattress.

"Those your kids?" he ground out.

Quincy shook his head. "Mom's."

Truman stumbled backward, feeling cut open, flayed, and left to bleed. His siblings? Living like this?

"What the hell, Quincy?" He crossed the room and picked up the baby, holding its trembling body as it screamed. With his heart in his throat, he crouched beside the toddler and reached for her, too. She wrapped shaky arms around his neck and clung with all her tiny might. They were both featherlight. He hadn't held a baby since Quincy was born, when Truman was nine.

"I've been out for six months," he seethed. "You didn't think to tell me that Mom had more kids? That she was fucking up their lives, too? I could have helped."

Quincy scoffed. "You told me..." He coughed, wheezing like he was on his last lung. "To fuck off."

Truman glared at his brother, sure he was breathing fire. "I pulled you out of a fucking crack house the week I got out of prison and tried to get you help. I *destroyed* my life trying to protect you, you idiot. *You* told *me* to fuck off and then went underground. You never mentioned that I have a sister and—" He looked at the baby, having no idea if it was a boy or a girl. A thin spray of reddish hair covered its tiny head.

"Brother. Kennedy and Lincoln. Kennedy's, I don't know, two, three maybe? And Lincoln's...Lincoln's the boy."

Their fucking mother and her presidential names. She once told him that it was important to have an unforgettable name, since they'd have forgettable lives. Talk about self-fulfilling prophecies.

Rising to his feet, teeth gritted, his rain-drenched clothes now covered in urine from their saturated diapers, Truman didn't even try to mask his repulsion. "These are *babies*, you asshole. You couldn't clean up your act to take care of them?"

Quincy turned sullenly back to their mother, shoving Truman's disgust for his brother's pathetic life deeper. The baby's shrieks quieted as the toddler patted him. Kennedy blinked big, wet, brown eyes up at Truman, and in that instant, he knew what he had to do.

"Where's their stuff?" Truman looked around the filthy room. He spotted a few diapers peeking out from beneath a ratty blanket and picked them up.

"They were born on the streets. They don't even have birth certificates."

"Are you shitting me?" *How the fuck did they survive?* Truman grabbed the tattered blanket that smelled like death and wrapped it around the babies, heading for the door.

Quincy unfolded his thin body and rose to his feet, meeting his six-three brother eye to eye. "You can't leave me here with *her*."

"You made your choice long ago, little brother," Truman said in a lethal tone. "I begged you to get clean." He shifted his gaze to the woman on the floor, unable to think of her as his mother. "She fucked up my life, and she clearly fucked up yours, but I'll be damned if I'll let her fuck up *theirs*. The Gritt nightmare stops here and now."

He pulled the blanket over the children's heads to shield them from the rain and opened the door. Cold, wet air crashed over his arms.

"What am I supposed to do?" Quincy pleaded.

Truman took one last look around the room, guilt and anger consuming him. On some level, he'd always known it would come to this, though he'd hoped he was wrong. "Your mother's lying dead on the floor. You let your sister and brother live in squalor, and you're wondering what you should do? *Get. Clean.*"

Quincy turned away.

"And have her cremated." He juggled the babies and dug out his wallet, throwing a wad of cash on the floor, then took a step out the door. Hesitating, he turned back again, pissed with himself for not being strong enough to simply walk away and never look back. "When you're ready to get clean, you know where to find me. Until then, I don't want you anywhere near these kids."

—End of Sneak Peek—
To continue reading, buy **TRU BLUE**

Everything's naughtier after dark...

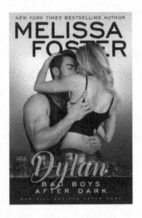

He's a savior, a knight in shining armor, and his mighty talented sword has no trouble bringing damsels in distress to their knees. She's a gorgeous cutthroat sports agent who looks like sex on legs, fucks like she's passion personified, and wouldn't let a man help her if she was hanging onto a ledge and he was her only hope. One night and too much tequila might change their lives forever. The question is, will either one survive?

WITH HER PHONE pressed to her ear, Tiffany Winters ducked out of the rain and into the Kiss, an eclectic Manhattan bar, to return calls and take care of a mountain of text messages that had piled up during her dinner meeting. She listened to her client's wife explain why she didn't want her husband traveling too often to endorse a hotel chain Tiffany was planning on pitching him to next week. Her client had already nixed any mention of his family in the advertisements, and reducing his travel would make it an even harder sell.

"I hear your concern, Allison," she said as she sat on a barstool. "If you and Matt decide this isn't the right thing for your family, we'll turn our efforts in another direction." As a sports agent, dealing with significant others was part of the job, a part Tiffany enjoyed and other agents rued. Sure, some wives assumed their husband's success granted them the power to be overly demanding. Ass kissing *was* part of the game. Sometimes she wished she could give the meeker wives lessons in how to be tough. Teach them to have balls as big as their husbands' and come right out and say what they meant instead of beating around the bush with bullshit hypotheticals. She reminded herself often that not every woman grew up in a testosterone-laden house with two competitive older brothers and a father who won the Heisman in college and went on to play pro sports—a house where mincing words didn't cut the mustard.

"You missed the wedding."

The deep male voice drew Tiffany's attention from her phone call to the fine specimen of a man standing behind the bar. He looked like he'd just stepped off a Hot Guys in Suits Pinterest page. His tie hung loosely around the collar of his white dress shirt, which was open three buttons deep, revealing a smattering of dark chest hair, a rarity nowadays, when so many men manscaped every inch of their bodies. Tiffany preferred a man to look like a man, which included hair in all the right places. His sleeves were rolled up to his elbows, exposing heavily corded forearms, and his jacket hung casually from two fingers over his left shoulder. Her fingers itched to send the last few buttons—and that jacket—flying to the floor. The guy's chiseled jaw and dark eyes were movie-star classic, and his dark hair was thick enough to hang on to. She'd had a long, hard day, and he looked like he could provide a long, *hard*, pleasure-filled night.

Perfect.

Holding his gaze, she spoke into the phone as he laid his jacket across the bar, giving her the impression he wasn't the bartender, but rather a guest who'd happened to wander back there. "Allison, I'll see what else I can come up with and get back to you. Right. Okay, hon. Thank you." After ending the call, she responded to the stud behind the bar. "Wedding? Who gets married at a bar?"

"My brother, for one." He nodded across the room to a group of men and women who were holding their glasses up in a toast.

She zeroed in on one she recognized as her tall, dark colleague. "Mick Bad is *married?*" The high-powered attorney was a workaholic like her, and he'd been unattached two months earlier, when they'd worked together on a deal for one of her clients. She'd never understand couples who claimed to fall in love practically overnight. Love was a crutch for weak people who needed someone else to lean on. Except Mick Bad had never needed anyone to lean on. She wondered if his new bride was pregnant.

"The one and only." Hot guy's eyes took a long, luxurious stroll down her body, lingered on her breasts, then roamed north, hovering around her mouth, before finally meeting her gaze. He flashed a wolfish grin full of sinful promises.

"Dylan Bad at your service."

Pushing thoughts of her newly married colleague's expedient nuptials aside, she focused on his very available brother. *A definite player*, which was fine with her. She had no time—or interest—in anything but a quick hookup, and the six-two or - three stud had already shot to the top of tonight's fantasy list.

"What's your pleasure?" he asked with more than a hint of innuendo.

You. Naked, with your head buried between my legs, to start.

"Surprise me." She watched him turn to prepare her drink and checked out the way his dark slacks hugged his perfect ass. It had been a long time since she'd found a man *this* attractive. But Mick Bad's brother? That spelled trouble.

A minute later he slid two drinks across the bar. A cocky smile spread across his handsome face. "One *Leg Spreader* and one *All Night Long*." He dragged out each seduction-laden word.

"A little overly confident, aren't you?" She had no qualms about taking what she wanted—in a boardroom or a bedroom, and Dylan's confidence was a definite turn-on.

He leaned across the bar, and the temperature around them spiked. "I was going to add a *Blow Job*, but I wasn't sure how much you could handle."

She held his challenging gaze. "I think the question is, can you keep up?"

"Dylan!" a guy called from across the room.

Dylan held up a finger in the guy's direction, his eyes never leaving Tiffany's. He leaned in so close she could smell alcohol on his breath—and God help her, she wanted to suck the taste off his tongue.

"Mark my words, gorgeous, you'll be leaving here with me tonight."

Heat streaked down her spine. "Cocky. I like that. Tell Mick I said congratulations." She dropped her eyes as if she weren't hanging on the very thought of devouring him, but couldn't resist stealing another peek at the tempting beefcake as he walked away. Okay, maybe *several* long glimpses, of which he caught two or three and returned with an I-can't-wait-to-fuck-you grin that had her insides igniting.

She answered another call and a few text messages, and a short while later, Dylan's voice spilled like warm cognac over her shoulder.

"You know what they say about wedding hookups?"

She lifted her gaze as he sat on the stool beside her. "What *do* they say?"

"They say they can't happen if you don't put your phone away." Dylan boldly placed his hand on her thigh. Long, strong fingers pressed into her flesh, sending rivers of desire to the apex of her thighs.

She wondered how big other parts of his anatomy were, and couldn't help stealing a quick glance. Oh yeah, he was packing major heat. A whiff of his spicy, masculine scent brought all her best parts pulsing to life. His scent alone probably brought more women to their knees than the Pope, but coupled with the sinful promises in his dark eyes, the guy was lethal.

"I don't put my phone down for just anyone," she answered, still holding his gaze. His hungry eyes dropped to her mouth, lingering there long enough to make her salivate. "Are you as good in the bedroom as you are behind the bar?"

"I'll let you be the judge of that." He leaned closer, placing his mouth beside her ear. "I'll even let you hold your phone until you're sure I'm worth it."

Now, that was a plan she could get on board with, except for one minor worry. "You're my colleague's brother. I'm not sure you're the *smartest* choice for me tonight."

He flashed a wicked grin that she was sure opened many bedroom doors. "A gentleman never tells."

"You might just be the perfect man." Her phone vibrated again. She glanced at it, noting a follow-up email from Allison, and the time. It was nearly midnight. Dylan's hand traveled further up her thigh, his fingertips sneaking beneath her skirt. He was brazen, and she liked that in a man.

He eyed her phone with a smirk and pressed his large hand to her cheek. His thumb moved over her lower lip and hooked behind her front teeth. Her entire body electrified as he delved deeper, brushing the tip over her tongue.

"When I get done with you, you will have forgotten what that thing in your hand is."

He was smooth, practiced, and knew exactly what he was doing. *Thank God.* She had so little time for sex, she couldn't afford to waste it with a guy who needed to be shown. Sliding her purse over her shoulder and still clutching her phone, she turned to step off the stool. His hand traveled even higher up her leg, a fingertip away from brushing over her sex, and she felt herself go damp. Her pulse accelerated with the urge to slide forward on her barstool and let him feel what he was doing to her, but she wasn't ready to give him the upper hand.

She casually moved his hand and rose to her feet.

He spoke in a greedy voice directly into her ear. "We're going to have to change your name." He swung his jacket over his shoulder and guided her toward the door.

"You're far too hot for *Winters*." He pushed the door open and lowered his mouth to her neck, grazing his teeth along the base—the absolute *most* sensitive spot on her entire body—and sending shivers down her spine. "From now on, you're my *Summers*."

As her body flamed and her insides melted, her mind struggled to figure out how he knew her name *and* to deny what he'd just said. She was no *man's* anything. She turned to tell him just that, and he backed her up against the brick wall. A cool breeze sailed over her skin as he grabbed her wrists and pinned them beside her head, trapping her between the wall and his hard body. He claimed her mouth with fierce domination. The way he ate at her mouth and his hips gyrated against hers with no care about being out in public should have had her fighting harder to regain the upper hand. But the harder she fought to reclaim her rational thoughts, the more she craved him. Every part of her tingled and burned for more. Her nipples tightened to painful peaks, her sex throbbed, and her knees weakened. She couldn't remember the last time she'd encountered someone so potently male, if ever, and she fucking loved it. Shocked at her own hungry response to his ravishment, she gave in to the unfamiliar thrills racing through her and returned his efforts with reckless abandon. But the more she gave, the softer the kisses became, until his lips were brushing lightly over hers, taunting her. He pulled back with every crane of her neck as she sought more. Still restraining her arms, he put space between their bodies. Cool air *whooshed* between them, causing her nipples to prickle even more painfully with the need to be touched.

"Oh, yes," he said with a territorial look in his eyes. "You're my *Summers*, all right."

As blood began to flow to her brain again, the realization of her loss of control was staggering. She lifted her chin and wrenched her hands free. Holding his challenging, and so-fucking-hot, gaze, she grabbed hold of his loosened tie and tugged him in for another scorching kiss. When she felt his muscles relax, she spun him against the wall with a *thud*, grinning at the shock registering in his gorgeous eyes.

"I'm no man's *anything*. But you can be *my* stress relief for the next hour." She dragged her hand down his impressively broad chest and over his taut abs, still clutching her phone, and cupped the formidable bulge in his trousers.

"That is, *if* you can keep it up that long."

—End of Sneak Peek—

To continue reading, buy

BAD BOYS AFTER DARK: DYLAN

MORE BOOKS BY MELISSA

LOVE IN BLOOM SERIES

SNOW SISTERS
Sisters in Love
Sisters in Bloom
Sisters in White

THE BRADENS at Weston
Lovers at Heart
Destined for Love
Friendship on Fire
Sea of Love
Bursting with Love
Hearts at Play

THE BRADENS at Trusty
Taken by Love
Fated for Love
Romancing My Love
Flirting with Love
Dreaming of Love
Crashing into Love

THE BRADENS at Peaceful Harbor
Healed by Love
Surrender My Love
River of Love
Crushing on Love
Whisper of Love
Thrill of Love

THE BRADEN NOVELLAS
Promise My Love
Our New Love
Daring Her Love
Story of Love

THE REMINGTONS
Game of Love
Stroke of Love
Flames of Love
Slope of Love
Read, Write, Love
Touched by Love

SEASIDE SUMMERS
Seaside Dreams
Seaside Hearts
Seaside Sunsets
Seaside Secrets
Seaside Nights
Seaside Embrace
Seaside Lovers
Seaside Whispers

The RYDERS
Seized by Love
Claimed by Love
Chased by Love
Rescued by Love
Thrill of Love

BILLIONAIRES AFTER DARK SERIES

WILD BOYS AFTER DARK
Logan
Heath
Jackson
Cooper

BAD BOYS AFTER DARK
Mick
Dylan
Carson
Brett

SEXY STANDALONE ROMANCE
Tru Blue

HARBORSIDE NIGHTS SERIES
Includes characters from the Love in Bloom series
Catching Cassidy
Discovering Delilah
Tempting Tristan
Chasing Charley
Breaking Brandon
Embracing Evan
Reaching Rusty
Loving Livi

More Books by Melissa
Chasing Amanda (mystery/suspense)
Come Back to Me (mystery/suspense)
Have No Shame (historical fiction/romance)
Love, Lies & Mystery (3-book bundle)
Megan's Way (literary fiction)
Traces of Kara (psychological thriller)
Where Petals Fall (suspense)

CONNECT WITH MELISSA

TWITTER
www.twitter.com/Melissa_Foster

FACEBOOK
www.facebook.com/MelissaFosterAuthor

WEBSITE
www.melissafoster.com

FAN CLUB
www.facebook.com/groups/melissafosterfans

ACKNOWLEDGMENTS

Thank you and big hugs to all my fans and readers for sharing my books with your friends, chatting with me on social media, and sending me emails. You inspire me on a daily basis, and I can't imagine writing without our interactions. Some of you have even had characters named after you, which is always so much fun for me. Thank you for sharing yourselves with me. And a special thank-you to Alexis Bruce for our fun chats about our alpha boys and to Alex Ong for answering ongoing questions. You're a saint.

If you don't yet follow me on Facebook, please do! We have such fun chatting about our lovable heroes and sassy heroines, and I always try to keep fans abreast of what's going on in our fictional boyfriends' worlds.

www.Facebook.com/MelissaFosterAuthor

Remember to sign up for my newsletter to keep up to date with new releases and special promotions and events and to receive an exclusive short story about Jack Remington and Savannah Braden that was written just for my newsletter fans.

www.MelissaFoster.com/Newsletter

For a family tree, publication schedules, series checklists, and more, please visit the special Reader Goodies page that I've set up for you!

www.MelissaFoster.com/Reader-Goodies

As always, heaps of gratitude to my amazing team of editors and proofreaders: Kristen Weber, Penina Lopez, Jenna Bagnini, Juliette Hill, Marlene Engel, Lynn Mullan, and Justinn Harrison.

Melissa Foster is a *New York Times* and *USA Today* bestselling and award-winning author. Her books have been recommended by *USA Today's* book blog, *Hagerstown* magazine, *The Patriot*, and several other print venues. She is the founder of the World Literary Café and Fostering Success. Melissa also hosts Aspiring Authors contests for children and has painted and donated several murals to the Hospital for Sick Children in Washington, DC.

Visit Melissa on her website or chat with her on social media. Melissa enjoys discussing her books with book clubs and reader groups and welcomes an invitation to your event.

Melissa's books are available through most online retailers in paperback, digital, and audio formats.
www.MelissaFoster.com